Death in the Halls of Eternal Life

By some trick of acoustics, the circumscribing boards vibrated strongly to the chords that Mr Amos, up in the loft, was conjuring from the organ.

A frayed drugget stretched from the door to the hole in the paving; a hole roughly oblong, and of a depth varying between two-and-a-half and five feet.

All this Jurnet both saw and did not see. Just as he both heard, and did not hear, the Professor's rasping "My God!" He went down on his knees by the hole in the cathedral floor, his Sunday-trousered legs pressed into the dust. He knelt and he looked. He had no need to touch what lay there, half in and half out of the hole that housed the tomb of Little St Ulf. He had seen death often enough to recognize it for what it was.

Even when he had not seen it for 840 years.

Also by S. T. Haymon

DEATH AND THE PREGNANT VIRGIN
DEATH OF A GOD
A VERY PARTICULAR MURDER

RITUAL MURDER

S. T. HAYMON

BANTAM BOOKS
NEW YORK • TORONTO • LONDON • SYDNEY • AUCKLAND

This is a work of fiction. All the characters and events portrayed in this book are fictional, and any resemblance to real people or incidents is purely coincidental.

This edition contains the complete text of the original hardcover edition.
NOT ONE WORD HAS BEEN OMITTED.

RITUAL MURDER

A Bantam Crime Line Book / published by arrangement with St. Martin's Press

PRINTING HISTORY
St. Martin's edition published 1982
Bantam edition / October 1991

PRINTED IN THE UNITED STATES OF AMERICA

RAD   0 9 8 7 6 5 4 3 2 1

Anyone who has read *Death and the Pregnant Virgin*, or who knows Norfolk, will recognize that Norwich is the starting point for my city of Angleby. But only the starting point. The city and its inhabitants are the figments of my imagination; and no reference is made to any living person.

S.T.H.

RITUAL MURDER

1

Pretending it was more convenient, Detective-Inspector Benjamin Jurnet parked his car in a side street and came into the Close by an alley few even of the locals knew, unless they were the churchy kind, at home in the purlieus of the cathedral. He did not care to admit, even to himself, that the FitzAlain Gate, the main gateway with its high pointed arch and its niches full of maimed statuary, casualties of time, daunted him.

For that matter he did not care to admit that he found the entire cathedral precinct not much less daunting than its ceremonial entrance. Why it should be so was hard to say. The lovely old houses sunned themselves like cats in the spring warmth: you could almost hear them purr. Mists of blossom veiled the shining flints, the mellow brick.

Beautiful. But definitely not Ben Jurnet.

Never mind: the Superintendent had to have his little joke. It was one of the perks of power. Jurnet had seen it coming before ever a word was uttered: the barely perceptible tremor at the side of the mouth, the eyes widening in a predatory joy. If they hadn't disliked each other, the two of them, just that little bit, they could never have worked so well together.

The Superintendent explained, "Getting in touch was the Bishop's idea, but the Dean's the one you'll be dealing with. Dr Carver."

"Oh ah."

"Not that, so far as I can see, there's a blind thing we can do, except make the right noises—"

"And what might they be, sir?"

"Now, Ben—" the Superintendent was smiling un-
ashamedly—"don't be bolshie. One touch of that Latin
charm and they'll be feeding out of your hand—"

The road ahead, leading to the Upper Close, was
empty save for two pigeons, decorous in grey-blue,
processing with ecclesiastical gravity. A woman in a
cardigan and a flowered apron was polishing the brass
plate at the side of a nobly pilastered door. In the
Upper Close, two of England's least memorable mil-
itary commanders, Old Boys of the Cathedral School
which filled the north side of the wide quadrangle,
turned their bird-spattered backs on each other at either side of a central lawn. Between them, and shocking as a Coke tin on the manicured grass, a redheaded
young man in jeans and T-shirt lay fast asleep.

Jurnet grinned with pleasure at the sight, and went
into the cathedral.

Dr Carver, the Dean, awaited him at their rendez-
vous, the bookstall, where a poorly favoured woman
of indeterminate years, unnerved by the proximity of
the great, was rearranging the postcards and the illustrated guides with a good deal of unnecessary fuss.

"Detective-Inspector Jurnet, sir."

"Ah, yes!"

If there was any element of surprise in the encounter, it was all on the cleric's side. Jurnet found exactly
what he had expected. Even discounting the long
black coat with its ample skirts, there was no mistak-
ing the stigmata of high ecclesiastical office: the air of
cheerful authority, the courtesy that masked, ever so
courteously, the merest suggestion of threat. The Dean,
on the other hand, might well have been unprepared for
the tall, lean man with the dark, Mediterranean looks
that, back at Headquarters and strictly out of earshot,
had earned him the nickname of Valentino.

The two shook hands and the Dean said straight-
away, in tones which told the detective all he needed
to know of the delicacy of diocesan relationships, "The
Bishop takes the view that we have a duty to let the
police know what has occurred. Others—among

whom, to be frank, I number myself—would prefer to treat what happened on Saturday as a purely domestic matter: one for which, particularly considering that any hope of apprehending the culprit, or culprits, seems doubtful in the extreme, we have no right to trespass on valuable police time. However—"

He sucked in his lips with a slight smacking sound which said more than words; turned without further ado and walked away, not looking back, rightly confident the detective would follow. Broad and purposeful, the Dean nevertheless looked strangely diminished beneath the vaulted roof, a matchstick of a man against the thick-girthed pillars of the nave.

All that bloody stone! thought Jurnet, following as expected. Even the roof was stone, high enough for angels but heavy on the spirits as last week's suet pud. Any angels up there, Jurnet reckoned—and in a brief suspicious glance upwards almost fancied he glimpsed some, tucked away among the exuberant nonsense of the vaulting—would be hanging upside down by their feet in bunches, like bats, too torpid with cold to spread their wings and fly.

The Dean led the way down the nave to the north transept and a wrought-iron screen where a man in the long grey gown of a verger stiffened respectfully at their coming, and opened a door for the two to pass through.

"Ah, Harbridge!" the Dean greeted him. "There you are!" And to Jurnet, "Mr Harbridge had to have four stitches. Turn round, Harbridge, so the Inspector can take a look."

" 'Tweren't nothing," said Harbridge, turning obediently. He was a man in his fifties, on the short side, but with a look of wiry strength that had Jurnet guessing he had not exactly turned the other cheek to his assailant.

The detective commented, "You should've called us in, soon as they started making trouble. We'd have handled it discreetly."

"I'm sure you would." The Dean inclined his head in acknowledgment of constabulary tact. "Though I imagine that on Saturday the police were sufficiently occupied in the immediate vicinity of Yarrow Road, without having any further call on their resources. Besides—" looking at Jurnet with eyes of a candour that contradicted the clerical opportunist the detective had put him down for—"we were so tickled to see them, don't you know? Visiting football fans don't usually include a tour of the cathedral in their programme. It was certainly something to encourage rather than turn thumbs down on."

"Taking a risk, all the same."

"My dear fellow, what else are we in business for? Whilst I appreciate your concern, Inspector, you really mustn't confuse Angleby Cathedral with a branch of Marks and Spencer. This is not a supermarket where everyone who comes through the door is a potential shoplifter. On the contrary, all who enter here are offered, to take away with them freely and without obligation, that most precious of all treasures, life everlasting." The Dean smiled. "But I embarrass you. Now that sex has become as platitudinous as old boots, religion—have you noticed?—is the one subject left that can still bring a blush to the cheek, even that of a policeman. The Bishop would be sorry to know I made you feel uncomfortable. Let me show you what His Grace particularly wanted you to see."

St Lieven's chapel, on the further side of the wrought-iron screen, was an unassuming space occupied by a number of rush-bottomed chairs, an equal number of embroidered kneelers, and a simple oak table by way of altar. Cromwell's men who, 300 years earlier, had knocked most of the stained-glass out of the cathedral windows, had thereby rendered unnervingly explicit the details of a painting on the altar which had inexplicably escaped their attentions, a medieval representation of St Lieven in his bishop's robes, holding in a pair of pincers what at first sight appeared to be a raw frankfurter and, at second, his tongue.

"Very fine, isn't it?" The Dean followed the direction of Jurnet's revolted gaze. "Now take a look at our more recent masterpiece."

Between the two round-arched windows of the chapel, a sheet of brown paper had been cellotaped to the wall. Harbridge reached up to remove it, taking, so it seemed to the detective, a long time over the job.

The Dean asked, "Well? What do you think of it?"

Jurnet's first impulse was to laugh, a purely nervous reaction. He did not feel in the least like laughing.

On the other hand, he did not feel shocked either, which was what was clearly expected of him. He looked away from what was revealed beneath the paper to the faces of the two men, both servants of the cathedral, bound to it by bonds of love and usage. He saw that they were sorely aggrieved by what they saw, and because he was, on the whole, a compassionate man, and one given a bit too easily to anger, caught something of their pain and their outrage.

The two commingled and flared up inside him, quite agreeably. It was the first warmth he had felt since stepping out of the spring sunshine.

"Shameful!" he exclaimed, in all sincerity.

On the chapel wall, in tall red capitals that seemed to have burnt themselves into the stone, were two words, brief and to the point: SOD GOD.

2

In the FitzAlain chapel opening off the ambulatory, the walls were plastered: and here the blasphemy, inscribed as before between the windows, seemed to have abated some of its outrageous irreverence. The plaster had absorbed some of the paint, feathering the edges of the letters, and, by softening the medium, tempering in some degree the import of the message.

"Any more?"

Dr Carver shook his head, then qualified the negative. "None we've come upon, at any rate. Harbridge is going to take another look round."

"I'd'a seen it, if it was there to be seen," Harbridge asserted. He looked with hostility at the detective, the stranger to whom the cathedral's shame had been published. "Now you've had an eyeful, can I get a bucket of whitewash an' cover it over?"

"Just put the paper back for the moment." Whilst Jurnet had not the slightest idea what, in practical terms, he could do, he had an inbuilt resistance to making away with evidence. To the pair of them he offered the only comfort he could think of, "At least, whoever did it was a Christian. I mean, you wouldn't bother, would you, with sodding a God you didn't believe in?"

Harbridge looked unappeased, but the Dean's face lightened.

"That is a very perceptive remark, Inspector. I must remember to tell the Bishop."

"Not much help in finding out who did it."

Turning away from the wall, Jurnet took a look at the painted tomb which was the most prominent object in the small chapel, and where Bishop FitzAlain, resplendent in mitre and cope, slept benignly, palm to palm in prayer, as he had already slept for 400 years, confident of a sweet awakening.

What a place! the detective thought. Even the ruddy beds were stone.

Still nursing his resentment, Harbridge announced darkly, "They always bring along their own booze, tha's the trouble."

Letting the implied compliment to Angleby ale pass without comment, Jurnet pointed out, "Whoever wrote that on the wall was sober as a judge. Someone who'd practised, got the hang of it. Anyone can make a scrawl with an aerosol—but properly formed letters in a straight line and all of a size, with no dribbles—"

The Dean observed pleasantly, "Next you'll be telling us they offer a course in it at the Polytechnic." He finished, "If it's any use to you, the aerosol's in a bag behind the bookstall."

"Where did you find it?"

"Propped against the Bishop's chest. Someone having his little joke, I dare say."

"I'll pick it up on the way out—though, if someone left it behind, ten to one he gave it a good wipe first." Jurnet hesitated, then took the plunge. "Doesn't the Cathedral School hold its morning assemblies in the cathedral?"

"The seniors. In the nave. But you can't imagine—"

"And the choir, now." Jurnet pressed on, leaving no doubt that his imagination was capable of more than the Dean gave it credit for. "The choirboys, surely, must be in and out of the place all the time. How many of them are there? The kids, I mean."

"Twenty-four," said the Dean, looking shaken. "But I really must protest! So far as those children are concerned, Inspector, an abiding love for this House of God is part of the very fabric of their lives. To suggest that one of them could actually be responsible for this abomination—!"

" *'Could be'* is exactly what I meant, sir. Not *'is'*. All I'm doing is point out the existence of another whole class of persons beside the football fans who *could* be responsible. Could equally well be some nutter or some menopausal lady with a sexual problem— you'd be surprised what some of them get up to these days—"

"You mean," the Dean did not attempt to hide his relief, "the field's so wide there's really nothing the police can do except make soothing noises—"

Which was so exactly what the Superintendent had maintained earlier that Jurnet could not repress a smile as he returned, "If you'll let me have that aerosol, sir, I'll be on my way."

As Jurnet and the Dean retraced their steps towards the nave, they paused to let a little procession pass.

Jurnet counted twelve pairs of boys, graded as to
height and looking like angelic imps in their scarlet
cassocks. At sight of Dr Carver their expressions became, if possible, even more otherworldly—a detachment which did not rid Jurnet of the sensation that
twelve pairs of bright young eyes had nevertheless
contrived to give the Dean's companion an instant,
comprehensive once-over. For himself, the red cassocks, so vivid against the grey stone, made a greater
impression than the faces topping them. Only two
stayed with him: a pair about twelve years old, by the
look of them. One of these was pale, with a prominent
forehead and pale, bulging eyes. His partner by contrast looked all the more robust, a rosy-cheeked boy
with dark curly hair and an air of cheerful impu-
dence.

In charge of the choristers was a roly-poly little man
who shepherded them towards the choir with an im-
patient tenderness that Jurnet, for one, found oddly
endearing. A vexed click of teeth at his side conveyed
the information that Dr Carver did not share this feeling.

"Good morning, Mr Amos!" the Dean said sharply.

The little man swung round and beamed, unaware
he was not loved.

"Dean! I didn't see you. Good morning! Lovely
day!" with a jolly waggle of buttock he passed out of
sight, following his charges into the wooden lacework
of the choir.

From the aisle, through an arch giving on to the
choir, Jurnet had a glimpse of the little crocodile di-
viding to right and left as the boys filed into the front
stalls on either side of the central gang-way. They
seemed to know the drill and to be quite unawed by
their surroundings. The detective watched as the rosy-
cheeked boy took a wad of gum out of his mouth and
nonchalantly parked it somewhere out of sight beneath his misericord.

Jurnet glanced sideways at the Dean, hoping, for
Mr Amos's sake, that the action had not been noticed.
The Dean's attention, as it happened, was fixed on

a screened-off area ahead of them. A kind of roofless room made of boards some seven feet high, painted grey to blend in with the prevailing colour, occupied a fair amount of space on the north side of the organ loft, and protruded well into the north aisle. From within this enclosure came small noises not easy to identify but enough to convey that the space was not unoccupied.

Jurnet had not noticed that one of the boards was, in fact, a door, until it opened and a girl came out.

She wore dusty jeans, a stained T-shirt and a kerchief that completely covered her hair; and she seemed not absolutely ecstatic at finding herself face to face with the Dean.

"Ah—Miss Aste! Hard at it, as usual?"

"I was just popping out for a smoke, actually."

"Haven't I persuaded you to give it up yet?" The Dean's voice had taken on a playful note which Jurnet uncharitably guessed he reserved for nubile females, especially those shaped the way Miss Aste was shaped. That he made no move to introduce his companion occasioned Jurnet no surprise. As a policeman he was used to being treated, even by the most law-abiding citizens, as an un-person, in whose company it was vaguely shaming to be seen. As a man he was used, as well, to the look the girl directed at him. He had lived too long with his looks not to know they attracted women. And long enough to know that, more often than not, as the women came to know him better, the attraction dissolved into a resentful disappointment that he was not the man he appeared to be. Not much use looking like a Sheikh of Araby all set to fling a girl across your saddle bow and gallop off with her into the sunset, when what you actually had in mind was a three-bedroomed semi with built-in mortgage. Even Miriam, at times, turned from him in sudden exasperation, as if he had promised more than he intended to perform.

The Dean, head cocked to one side, inquired winsomely, "Do I hear the Professor?"

The girl shook her head.

"Only Mosh. I think he said something about looking in this afternoon. Mosh'll know."

She hesitated a moment, then, rebuffed by the professional blankness which Jurnet had pulled down over his face like a steel shutter, she turned abruptly and walked quickly towards the West Door.

Dr Carver gazed after her with a smile not entirely accounted for by the swing of her neat little behind.

He spoke and all was revealed. "Lord Sydringham's daughter. Delightful child." He pulled open the door in the hoarding and projected the upper part of his body inside. "Is Professor Pargeter expected?"

The answer, if there was one, was lost, to Jurnet at least. The detective had a glimpse of a wooden table, a jumble of implements, and a young man with an Afro hair-do powdered with dust sitting with his feet dangling in a hole in the paving, smoking. At that moment a joyful reverberation rolled through the enormous building like the incoming tide. Mr Amos had found his way to the organ loft.

Immediately young voices sweet to the point of paining were lifted up in praise. Jurnet watched the anger reddening the Dean's neck, and the way, just short of insolence, the young man, without getting up, stubbed out his cigarette on an ancient tombstone set into the floor.

The thunderous surge from the organ loft gave way to wanton ripples, among which the boys' voices played like sunlight glinting off water. The Dean, straightening his body, stepped back inside the aisle, shutting the door with a violence that shook the whole makeshift structure.

"I cannot for the life of me understand," he exclaimed, adjusting his coat with little, irritated gestures, "why he has to bring the boys into the cathedral to rehearse. You would hardly think we possess a Song School where such caterwaulings can take place in decent obscurity!"

Jurnet observed, with careful offhandedness, "I thought it sounded all right, myself." Changing the subject, "What are they digging up in there, then?"

"Smoking in the cathedral, did you see that?" Two annoyances at once evidently stretched the Dean's Christian charity to its limits. "I warned Professor Pargeter, but he insisted. His star student, he said, and specializing in the city's medieval Jewry." He looked sharply at Jurnet as if a thought had just that minute occurred to him. "Natural enough," he continued, his voice, with some effort, recovering its affable calm, "for one by name Moses Epperstein. But not here, in the Cathedral of the Transfiguration. And certainly not excavating the tomb of Little St Ulf."

3

The cathedral was filling up: knots of tourists moving diffidently, unsure of the correct posture in a stately home belonging to God of all people, and tending to congregate round the bookstall where money could be spent, something they were familiar with. Miss Hanks, rushed off her feet, dropped a handful of change when the Dean appeared unexpectedly at her side of the counter to reclaim the aerosol.

He did not help to retrieve the scattered money, and Jurnet, waiting a little apart, noted that neither Miss Hanks nor the crowding customers expected him to. Of such is the Kingdom of Heaven. Amply rewarded by his smile, they genuflected with a will, pouncing on the coins with little cries of alleluia. It was the nearest thing to worship the detective had seen so far.

"Bit off your patch, Inspector," commented a voice at his back.

Jurnet looked over his shoulder, then swivelled round. "I could say the same of you."

He eyed the burly figure in front of him. Joe Fisher looked as though he spent a lot on his clothes, every penny of it wasted. The brute flesh and muscle would not be denied. He was kitted out in suede car-coat and expensive cords, and Jurnet had a mind to run him in for indecent exposure.

He wondered fleetingly what kind of look the man would rate from that delightful child, the daughter of Lord Sydringham.

"Hoping to flog a few bits of the True Cross that fell off the back of a lorry?" he asked coarsely.

Joe Fisher looked hurt.

"No need to go on like that, Mr Jurnet. Just 'cause I'm under an obligation to you don't give you the right to chuck insults about like they was confetti!"

"You're not under any obligation to me. Get Millie and young Willie a proper roof over their heads and I'll call you Lord Fisher T. Fish if it'll make you feel better. You've got more on your bloody back this minute than that beat-up trailer of yours is worth lock, stock, and barrel." Jurnet looked at the trendy gear with a wearied distaste. "You know they're out to get an order to tow you off that scrap-heap?"

"Never! Millie likes it there! So does the kid, down by the river."

"Millie doesn't know any better. And as for Willie and the river—"

"All right! So you pulled him out when he could'a drowned! How many times I got to say ta?"

"No times. Just get them moved, that's all. Before they take young Willie into care."

"They never would! It'd break Millie's heart."

"That's what I mean."

The Dean, the crowd at the bookstall parting to let him through like the Red Sea for the Israelites, arrived smiling at Jurnet's side, proffering the bag containing the aerosol. The smile vanished as Joe Fisher moved a step forward and took hold of a handful of sacramental skirt.

"You, mate! Where they keep Little St Ulf, then?"

On the steps that led up to the West Door, Jurnet turned and looked back down the length of the cathedral.

Impressive, he gave you that: but not his cup of tea. Not for a boy brought up to Chapel twice on Sunday and Sunday School in between. Not for Miriam's lover—Miriam's husband if ever the Children of Israel opened their close-packed ranks and let him in. Mr Amos was still playing the organ, but the magic had gone out of it. A musical belly-ache.

The choristers had stopped singing. Had the kid with the cheeky face retrieved his gum from under the seat? The thought made Jurnet feel friendlier. Friendlier to the Dean, friendlier to the God who inhabited the Godforsaken hole. Poor bastard, could be He had no choice. Had His name down for a council house and was still waiting.

The Dean had shaken hands in a professionally cordial farewell.

"I'm sure, Inspector, we can leave the matter in your capable hands." Meaning nothing would be done and a good thing too.

"We'll do our best, sir." Meaning ditto.

Feeling bloody-minded at the other's ready collusion in his own inadequacy, Jurnet added, "Please don't have the writing removed till I give the word."

"Oh dear! Is that really necessary?"

"It would be best not to."

"If you say so."

The Dean sighed, turned to go. Over his shoulder he asked negligently, "It *was* Inspector Jurnet, wasn't it? J-U-R-N-E-T?"

"J-U-R-N-E-T."

On the steps that led up to the West Door Jurnet grinned to himself. Trust the Dean to know his local history if anybody did!

The detective moved gratefully towards the open air. The great central door that, banded with iron, looked made to keep out besieging armies rather than afford ingress to worshippers, was shut. Following the sign, Jurnet made for the modest exit in the north aisle.

He was almost there when some letters cut into a wall plaque in the shadowed corner where aisle and door met caught his eye. It was not the first time he had noticed how alert that eye was to pick out the name Miriam.

Miriam my wyf,
Joy of my lyf,
Heav'n so swete,
Without her was not complete.
God I must not dispraies,
Who has sadden'd my daies.
Wyf, forget not me,
With whom thou once didst sport right merrily.

Miriam,
    Wyf to Robert Coslane,
        Saddler of this citie.
            An. Dom. 1537.

Jurnet's first impulse was to reach into his pocket for his notebook. Then, he decided, no. Born and bred in Angleby and never once set foot in the cathedral: this she had to see.

" 'Miriam my wyf, joy of my lyf,' " he repeated softly, and went out, into the spring.

How delightful the air felt after the chill inside! Jurnet stood for a moment, face uplifted to the sun, eyes closed.

When he opened them he saw that the young man he had left asleep on the grass was awake, sitting up, and listening with every appearance of disgruntlement to what Elizabeth Aste, on her knees at his side, was saying.

The girl's pose of prayer was apt, thought Jurnet, for she seemed to be imploring a favor or, perhaps, begging forgiveness. Apt but surprising. He would not have taken her, with that upper-crust self-assurance she wore like a second skin, for someone either to beg or plead.

But then, if he were to believe those slushy novels Miriam left lying about the flat, not even those whose blood ran blue as the Oxford and Cambridge Boat Race were impervious to the pangs of love.

Now, across the width of lawn, he could see that the girl was crying, or pretending to; a performance which seemed to irritate the young man beyond endurance. He jumped to his feet, picked up the windcheater he had been using as a pillow, and strolled away towards the FitzAlain Gate, the garment slung over one shoulder, hips moving in a little swagger that had Jurnet muttering, "Cocky bastard!"

The girl ran after him, grasped his free arm. Whereupon the young man pulled himself free and hit her hard across the face.

Jurnet, used as he was to covering space without waste of time when the occasion called for it, was nevertheless surprised to find the young man on the same spot towards which he had projected himself before the flailing arm had well found its target. Red hair bright in the sunlight, the man turned on the detective a look of no more than bored incuriosity. There was no apprehension of danger, no remorse for an unthinking act. A cool customer.

Elizabeth Aste had her hands to her face, covering mouth and nose.

Jurnet said, "I'm a police officer. What's going on here?"

The girl dropped her hands. Out of her bruised and bleeding mouth emerged, but still in the accents of Roedean, "Piss off and mind your own bloody business!"

At the mouth of the alley which led through to where he had left his car, Jurnet hesitated, then passed it by, choosing instead to continue along the narrow way which led down to the river. This was the part of the Close where he felt least uncomfortable. Here, the houses were smaller, and a bit ramshackle. A congenial seediness hung about the area, mingling at nightfall with the mists that rose off the river. Jurnet had a theory, for which he had no evidence at all, that this was where the Dean and Chapter exiled sinners and those who were found to be doctrinally impure.

Trust a copper to feel at home in such company!

Where the houses ended the water meadows began, playing-fields where Cathedrans charged about in blue-and-red shorts merging almost imperceptibly with grazings whose resident cows played in black-and-white. Jurnet stepped briskly down to the little staithe where centuries ago the stones that made up the cathedral had arrived from distant Normandy, and turned aside on to a path which bordered the river. The cabin cruisers moored alongside the further bank still had a closed-up, winter look.

A quarter of a mile on, the path ended abruptly in a tangle of bramble and barbed-wire that Jurnet, who had been that way before, had little trouble in nego-tiating. On the further side lay a dreary complex of vandalized Nissen huts and one-storied brick buildings which, in the war, had served some purpose long since forgotten. It was, in fact, because no one could be found willing to admit responsibility for the mess, and so for the cost of clearing it up, that year by year more sheets of corrugated-iron dissolved into rust, thistles and cow parsley and rose-bay willow-herb cracked ever wider the crevasses in the concrete standings, and generations of pigeons from the Close bore away un-molested the asbestos felting of the roofs to line their nests.

Every spring since the war the *Angleby Argus* had printed letters protesting against the eyesore down by the river; to which, every spring, the Town Clerk re-plied, referring the problem to Whitehall, where, the forms observed, it lay decently buried until spring once more set the civic sap rising.

The sole beneficiary of this bureaucratic cock-up—with the doubtful exception of the pigeons, ignorant as they were of the perils of asbestosis—was Joe Fisher. The car bodies and disembowelled refrigerators heaped high on parts of the site were not funeral piles left behind by its aboriginal inhabitants, whoever they might have been. They were part of Joe's stock-in-trade, for scrap-metal dealing was one of the many ways in which he made his dubious livelihood.

The trailer jacked up on old railway sleepers was not part of the scrap metal, although, by the look of it, it could well have been.

As Jurnet came through the hedge he heard a shrill "Coo-ee!" There was a brief silence, and then a high, sweet voice, smudged at the edges but full of suppressed glee, called out, "I see yer! I see yer!"

Jurnet stood still as a slight figure in a torn, ankle-length dress of flowered cotton backed into the space between two of the huts.

"Willie! You c'n come out, then! I see yer!"

Jurnet moved out of the shadow of the hedge into full sunlight, where the girl—or was it a woman?—could see him clearly should she happen to look his way. The last thing he wanted to do was frighten Millie Fisher.

He had forgotten that nothing frightened Millie Fisher. She turned and caught sight of him: stared unafraid with the beautiful grey eyes that seemed the eyes of a blind person until such time as the slow brain had made sense of the image conveyed to it. Then they came alive, sparkled with pleasure.

"Mr Ben!" She rushed towards him, turning her head to shout as she came, "Willie! It's Mr Ben!"

Not much taller than a child, she threw her arms round the detective's hips, crowing with delight. "Did yer come to see me, Mr Ben? Did yer?"

"I came to see you."

A small boy appeared from behind a water tank. Millie sped towards him over the broken concrete.

"Mr Ben's come to see me, Willie! What yer think o' that, then."

The boy, who was about seven years old and as fair as Millie was dark, smiled at her kindly. Paternally.

"I spec' he's come to see both of us." He nodded at Jurnet as to an equal, and turned back to his mother. "An' it's no good your sayin' you c'n see me when yer can't see me. *I* know when you c'n see me an' when yer can't."

"Yes, Willie," she said meekly. Then her face, so soft and pretty and unfinished, brightened. "I did *almos'* see yer, though! I'd'a seen yer in a minute, wouldn't I?"

"Were yer goin' t' look back o' the tank, then?"

The light faded. "I don't know, Willie—"

The boy relented; smiled Millie's smile, thought Jurnet, who, unnoticed, had drawn nearer. Millie Fisher's smile. In Joe Fisher's face.

"I spec' you were. You always do, sooner or later."

Jurnet clinched the matter.

"She was just going to, when I came along and interrupted."

Millie's smile burst out in all its glory. The detective, taking avoiding action before she could be on him again, like an over-demonstrative puppy, swung the boy, yelling with delight, up in his arms. Somewhere on the way up Willie shed his years and his cares, arriving on Jurnet's shoulders a laughing child.

"How's the big boy, then?"

"Mr Ben! Mr Ben!"

Inside, the trailer was dirtier, even, than Jurnet remembered it. He touched a wall and grimaced. The whole place was coated with the fallout of God knew what nauseous fry-ups.

None the less, when Millie, bursting with pride in her role of hostess, invited him to take a seat, he complied unhesitatingly, with a ceremoniousness fully equal to the queenly gesture with which she indicated the filthy bench. Grandly, out of some uncharted hoard of memory, she inquired, "Will yer take tea?" But before Jurnet could answer Willie interposed angrily, "Joe took the gas bit, din' he? Don't be daft!" There were tears in his eyes as he explained to the guest in the house, "He won't let *her* light the ring, an' he won't let *me*! He takes the bit with him every bleeding time he goes out. I c'd make tea, an' beans, an' everything, if *he'd* let me."

Jurnet, secretly glad of Joe Fisher's foresight, said placatingly, "That bottled gas is tricky stuff. Dead scared of it myself." Carefully casual, he added, "Dad in dinnertime, then, to fix you both up something hot?"

The boy looked down and made no answer. Millie sat back and said comfortably, scratching her armpit through a convenient hole, "Joe'll be back. Joe." The monosyllable seemed to please her so much she said it again, for its sheer music. "Joe."

"Once you're at school," Jurnet told Willie, "they'll give you a hot dinner every day."

"Wi' bangers?"

"Twice or three times a week, I shouldn't wonder."

The child considered the paradisiacal prospect.

"Nah," he said at last.

"How's that? Don't you want to learn to read and write?"

Willie lifted his head and looked Jurnet full in the face.

"Who'd be wi' Ma?"

Jurnet smiled into the fair little face, at once so young and so old. The only thought that came into his head—if thought was the right word for it—was the one that, earlier that morning, he had read twice over, proclaimed in capitals on the cathedral walls.

SOD GOD. Sod the God that for His own sodding reasons had made things the way they were.

The thought was cathartic. Having got it out of his system, Jurnet recognized the irrelevance of peevish abuse. Millie's boy, despite being Millie's boy, was quick as a whip. And as to Millie herself, who did the detective know happier than this twenty-two-year-old woman with the mental age of an eight-year-old child?

Certainly Millie's own luck, in a world teeming with agencies panting to get their well-meaning paws on those in her condition, had verged on the miraculous. The offspring of an alcoholic mother and an incestuous father, she had, lacking the brains to know better, taken the drunkenness for jollity and the incest for a natural demonstration of paternal love. Joe Fisher had got her pregnant below the age of consent, but because he had married her on her sixteenth birthday there had seemed no point in sending to prison the one man prepared to look after the backward girl.

And look after her he had, in his own way. Even the succession of social workers who had threaded their eager way between the scrapheaps had, baffled by a radiance unchronicled in the text-books, given up trying to make Millie clean and miserable.

Against all the odds, she had turned out a wonderful mother. Willie, fed on chips and God alone knew what else once her milk dried up, grew straight-limbed and intelligent.

What would happen to the two of them when the truant officer came looking for young Willie, as sooner or later he must: when, the ins and outs of the ownership of that bit of riverside slum finally sorted out, men came with a Court order and a tractor to drag the trailer out on to the road?

Millie smiled at Jurnet across a table covered with oilcloth whereon means innumerable had inscribed their autobiographies. If she had not been a mental defective he would have said she had read his thoughts. As it was, he guessed that, seeing him preoccupied, she had merely, out of the riches of her own overflowing cornucopia, proffered her unfailing panacea.

"Joe'll see to it."

4

Jurnet dropped Miriam off at night school and drove on to the synagogue. She had said not to pick her up on his way back: she fancied sleeping at home for a change.

"I need to use my sewing machine. And I promised Mum I'd pop up to London for a week or two. She reminded me on the phone it's three months since she last saw me. Besides, I feel like being virginal for a bit." Which was daft talk if ever he heard it, after all they had done together.

She had promised to marry him if he became a Jew: a mere formality, it had seemed, to one who found no more difficulty in disbelieving in one God than in three. A parting with a bit of skin that had never served any useful purpose anyway. Remembering the welcome accorded at his Chapel to those who asked to be received into the brotherhood, he had expected his conversion to take a matter of weeks. But here was Miriam into Book-Binding, having worked her way through Macramé, the Golden Years of Hollywood, and the Economic Consequences of the Black Death. What was going to happen when she ran out of courses?

Parking in the synagogue forecourt, Jurnet saw that the lights were out in the Rabbi's flat above the synagogue hall: but, from below, the slam of table-tennis balls told where the action was. The blood-curdling howl that accompanied this sporting tympani like something serial out of Webern emanated, Jurnet knew, from Taleh the Alsatian, whose name, the Hebrew for "lamb", reflecting the gentle nature housed in the fearsome exterior, was a secret closely guarded by the Angleby Jewish community. Since the Rabbi had brought himself to give house-room to a creature unhallowed and unclean, there had been no more swastikas scrawled on the walls of the little building in the quiet suburban street, no deaths to Christ-killers, no invitations to improbable copulations.

Jurnet came into the synagogue hall in the middle of a rally that neither his entrance nor Taleh's welcome did anything to interrupt. It was absurd that Rabbi Leo Schnellman played table-tennis at all, let alone played it to near-international standards. The man was fat, his legs too short for his body, his arms, beneath the rolled-up shirt sleeves, flabby and varicose. Jurnet, waiting for the game to finish, noted the sweat stains that darkened the armpits, the belt straining to contain the jouncing paunch, the glistening bald head to which a tiny *yarmulke* clung like a desperate limpet.

He also noted the face of the Rabbi's opponent, the young man he had last seen smoking, his feet through the cathedral floor.

The Rabbi must have noted it too, for suddenly, without any apparent diminution in the strength of his game, the luck began to go against him. It was very cleverly done, a losing by stealth that took more skill than winning. From 13–17 the younger man improved his position until the score was 19–16 in his favour; then went on to take the game with two strokes which the Rabbi, with exquisite misjudgment, just failed to reach.

Moses Epperstein put his bat down and said, with complacent disapproval, "The trouble with you, Rabbi, is, you don't play to win."

"Oh, yes, I do," said the Rabbi. "Only not the game." He wiped his face with a crumpled handkerchief. "Ben!" he exclaimed warmly. Then: "You two know each other? Mosh Epperstein. Detective-Inspector Benjamin Jurnet."

"Jesus!" said Mosh Epperstein. "The fuzz!"

"The fuzz," said Jurnet, catching up with a bit of unfinished business that had bothered him all day, off and on, "that was with the Dean when he caught you smoking. Care to tell me what brand?"

"Go and screw yourself."

Ignoring the injunction, and with a demure sideways glance at the Rabbi, Jurnet observed, "I'm surprised, Leo, that after being half-stoned on pot this morning, this fellow had the wind to take a game off you."

Epperstein exclaimed, "Prove it! And I'll take a game off you too, any time you say!"

"No more Ping-Pong," said Leo Schnellman, reducing the game and the tension at one go. "Ben's not here to play games. It's the beer he's after. Come on upstairs. I've got half a dozen cans on ice."

"So you've been in the cathedral?" Leo Schnellman leaned back in his Louis Seize armchair, making it cry out in protest. Louis Seize-Who, thought Jurnet, making for the leather pouffe, a souvenir of Israel, which he considered the only seat in the room to be relied on. The flat's furnishings were a memorial to the taste of the Rabbi's dead wife, and, as such, sacrosanct. Epperstein, similarly distrustful, stretched out his gangling length in front of the electric fire, Taleh arranging herself alongside; her muzzle, across the young man's legs, perilously close to the red-hot bars.

"What did you think of it?" the Rabbi persisted.

"Big," replied Jurnet, in a voice that implied "not much".

"It is, isn't it? But then Gentiles, unlike the Jews, haven't had the destruction of two Temples to make them wonder whether the Almighty is really all that comfortable in large structures."

"All that stone. It might as well be the Castle."

"But that's exactly what it is—a fortress, to take heaven by assault, not supplication." The Rabbi drank some beer, wiped the foam from his lips. "Though perhaps one should call it a ship, rather—a great stone ship. Did you know that the word 'nave' comes from the Latin *navis*, a ship?"

"I wouldn't give you tuppence for it," declared Jurnet.

"Funny that, with a name like yours," commented Epperstein from the hearthrug.

Jurnet said resignedly, "Oh, that! Everyone picks on that, sooner or later. Couldn't expect *you* to miss it—just up your alley. Jurnet of Angleby, the Rothschild of the Middle Ages—loans to build cathedrals, launch crusades, arranged on favourable terms. My old man, umpteen generations removed. Maybe. Could be just a coincidence, to say nothing of Edward I booting the Jews out of England anyway."

Rabbi Schnellman said with severity, "To say nothing of your not being a Jew either."

Jurnet, seething with unexpected fury, got up to go.

"Sit down, Ben," said the Rabbi, smiling up at him without apology. "And take that look off your face. You aren't a Jew yet and you'd better not forget it—just a chap who's ready to make a few formalized gestures because that's the only way he can get a nice Jewish girl to make an honest man of him. Not good enough! His prepuce is only the first sacrifice a Jew makes to his God."

"What's the second?" Jurnet sat down again.

"The rest of him."

"You don't ask much."

"Not me," said the Rabbi. "I don't make the rules."

Mosh Epperstein grinned at Jurnet with the first sign of friendliness he had shown. "You must be out of your tiny mind."

Leo Schnellman got up and replenished the beer glasses. He put down a saucer and poured a little for Taleh, who lapped it up with the air of a connoisseur.

"That's because you haven't seen Miriam," he remarked. "What we have to do is convince the man there's more to Judaism than a pretty face."

"Anyone called Jurnet ought to know that in his bones. Anyone in Angleby, for that matter, who knows the first thing about what happened here."

"Little St Ulf, you mean?" Jurnet asked. The other nodded. "For that matter—" getting his own back— "I must say I was a bit surprised to find a chap called Epperstein helping to dig *him* up, of all people. Let sleeping lies lie, I should've thought."

"Trust a copper to go for a cover-up!" Epperstein pushed Taleh's head off his legs and stood up, tall and so thin as to appear, almost, two-dimensional. "It's people like you get history a bad name."

"Look," Jurnet said, reasonably, "it was—how many years ago? Five hundred? Six? There has to come a time to close the books once and for all. I don't know the details—"

"Eight hundred and forty." It was the Rabbi who

interrupted, an unaccustomed heaviness in his voice. "And it's high time you did."

5

"Oddly enough," Mosh Epperstein began, speaking as if he had been there, "it was a moment when, for once, the Jews and the Gentiles of Angleby were getting on like a house on fire. Sure, the Jews went on living in Cobblegate right under the Castle walls so that, in an emergency, they could get themselves inside the gates and under the Sheriff's protection before it came to anything, but it was years since they'd had any cause to worry. Most of the bad feeling against the Jews, when you came down to it, wasn't religious at all, but because they were the tax-collectors and the money-lenders, not exactly popular professions in any age; but as there'd been a series of good harvests and trade was flourishing, people were able to pay their taxes and the interest on loans without too much hassle."

"If it got them such a bad name," Jurnet asked, "why didn't they go in for some other line of business?"

"Not a hope. All the other jobs were organized into guilds. Christian closed shops. A little butchering and baking strictly for themselves, some dealing in second-hand clothes, and apart from usury that was it."

"And medicine," Leo Schnellman put in. "Don't forget about Haim HaLevi."

"How could I? One of my main characters. There was this doctor, Haim HaLevi, who had a tremendous reputation locally. Gentiles, actually, weren't allowed to consult Jewish doctors, but everyone knew Haim had cured the Bishop of Angleby himself when his own doctor'd given him up for dead, so no one took the ban seriously."

"Except the Gentile doctors of the city," the Rabbi reminded him.

"That's right! *They* were livid about the competition, and they complained to the Sheriff—only, as Haim had just got *him* over a nasty case of piles, they didn't get much sympathy in that quarter either.

"That's how things stood the Easter it all happened. It was one of those years with Easter and Passover falling at the same time; and as a result there was a run on flour for holiday baking. Wastel flour, the finest white, something people in those days only tasted on high days and holidays, was what was wanted, and there simply wasn't enough of the stuff to go round.

"One of the people who ran out was a pastrycook called Godefric. So he sent his son Ulf, who was twelve years old and learning the business, with a wheelbarrow and some money to go and get some more from a guy named Josce Morel, who baked the *matzoth* for the Angleby Jews.

"And that was it. Ulf was seen going into Josce Morel's house, and he was never seen alive again."

"Hang on!" the Rabbi exclaimed. "You're giving Ben the wrong impression. You haven't made it clear that all we have to go on are monkish chronicles, set down by men blinded by prejudice, and written years after the events they purport to describe—"

"I'm just telling the story, for Christ's sake! I didn't say swallow it hook, line, and sinker. Whether or not Ulf *was* seen going into Josce Morel's house, people came forward who swore they'd seen him doing it— that's the important thing. Two days later, the burnt-out remains of the wheelbarrow were found on Crows Hill, back of the Leper Hospital, and the day after that the kid's body was found in a disused claypit nearby."

Jurnet commented, "Knocked off for the money, most likely, and the killer got rid of the body best way he could."

"Thank you, Sherlock Holmes!" Mosh Epperstein bowed his head in ironic acknowledgment. "What makes you think we're looking for a logical explanation? Don't they teach you Epperstein's Law down at the nick—that human readiness to accept an explanation for anything increases in direct proportion to its intrinsic implausibility?"

Jurnet laughed, unoffended.

"You're young to be a cynic."

"Mosh?" Leo Schnellman cried. "A starry-eyed romantic who never stops being amazed that human beings don't behave like angels." His mood darkening: "Though the way they found Ulf—or the way the story goes that they found him—you can't blame the ordinary folk of Angleby for believing what they believed."

"Emasculated, and with the blood drained out of his veins." The archaelogy student's lips twisted in a kind of horrified amusement. "And just in case that wasn't enough, nineteenth-century embroiderers on the old story added their own delicate touch. In addition to all the rest, they said, the murdered child had a *magen doved,* a Star of David, cut into his chest and stomach—though, however else the kid was found, it couldn't have been like that, because it was only in the nineteenth century that the Star of David became accepted as a Jewish symbol at all. Still, *ex post facto* proof's better than none, as I'm sure they say down at the nick. With a signature like that, it *had* to be the Jews."

Leo Schnellman looked upset again.

"I can't bear to hear it said, Mosh, even in irony." Again he turned his attention to Jurnet. "From the perspective of time it's easy to look back and say look, that's where it all started—the first accusation of ritual murder, the first time anyone dreamed up the charming notion that the Passover festival is incomplete without the blood of a Christian child mixed into the matzo dumplings. By now we've got used to its utter preposterousness. But think how it must have seemed to the Jews of twelfth-century Angleby, confronted with it for the first time."

"They couldn't take it in," said Epperstein. "They didn't even run for cover to the Castle. Twenty-nine of them were killed the night the boy's body was discovered, and that was only the beginning. They arrested Josce Morel and his wife Chera, who both denied ever seeing the boy, let alone killing him, but they strung them up in iron cages from the city wall just the same. His and Hers. Chera was a tough old bird. They say she took six days to die." After a moment he said, "And of course there was Haim Ha-Levi."

Jurnet asked, "How did he come into it?"

"Some of the city doctors were called in to testify. They gave it as their expert opinion that Ulf's blood had been drained off with such skill, it could only have been done by a trained medical practitioner."

"The bastards!"

"Effective way, though, to get rid of the opposition. Except that it wasn't as easy as all that. Haim had friends in high places. The Sheriff, for one, wasn't keen to lose the only pill-pusher who didn't make him feel worse than he'd been feeling already. So what he did was say that since the Jews were, legally speaking, the King's chattels, the King himself would have to try the case. Haim HaLevi's trial would have to be held over till the next time the King came to Angleby on one of his royal progresses, which could be years away. In the meantime, for security purposes, he moved Haim into the Castle, where he treated him very well, on the principle that it pays to be nice to your doctor."

"Do you know what he did?" asked the Rabbi, with a touching pride. "Haim HaLevi, while he was waiting? He planted a herb garden in the Castle grounds, the first one to be recorded in England; and it became so famous, doctors from all over Europe travelled to Angleby just to get cuttings of his plants, and learn from him their curative properties. And he wrote a treatise on herbal remedies—in Aramaic first, and then he made his own translation into Latin—that was still in use as late as the seventeenth century. You know that famous essay of Francis Bacon's which begins, 'God Almighty first planted a garden. And indeed it is the purest of human pleasures'? Word for word, it's a literal translation of Haim HaLevi!" Leo Schnellman chuckled. "Bacon!"

Jurnet observed, "I bet the Angleby doctors weren't best pleased."

"What do you think?" The archaeology student shrugged. "It turned out to be nearly five years before the King came to Angleby—and during that time something very peculiar began to happen."

"Take note, Ben," admonished the Rabbi, leaning back in his chair. "How to be a saint in ten easy lessons."

"Lesson one," said Mosh Epperstein. "The grave. Godefric buried his son outside his parish church, St Luke's Parmenter-gate. A month later he came into the churchyard to find the raw hump of earth ablaze with flowers like something out of Constance Spry."

"Not very convincing."

"To Godefric it was. He hared it to the cathedral and told the monks, who told the Prior, who told the Bishop. The upshot was that they dug the boy up and reburied him in the cathedral Chapter House."

"Sounds a bit simple-minded to me," said Jurnet. "Even for those days."

"Not at all. It was a consummate stroke of public relations. Martyrs were big business in medieval England. The monks were on to a good thing and they knew it. Especially with a child. Especially with a child who could work miracles."

Leo Schnellman burst out laughing.

"Children and animals! The infallible English combination!" To Jurnet, "They kept a cat in the Chapter House to catch rats. Pretty fierce rats they must have been too, because one of them, just about that time, bit one of the cat's paws off. After that, the cat's fate was sealed, as not being up to the job any longer, and one of the monks went into the Chapter House with a sack, intending to catch it and take it down to the river for drowning.

"The poor old moggy, probably guessing what was in store for it, ran off as fast as it could, its disability permitting, and as it ran it happened that it ran across Ulf's new grave. Instantly, it stopped limping, and, with all four paws back in their proper place, promptly caught another rat and laid it at the astounded monk's feet. There's a miracle for you!"

"Hard on the rat," Jurnet remarked.

"But that's the essence of a miracle! Somebody always suffers. Who knows, when the trumpets sounded, and the walls of Jericho came tumbling down, how many innocent bystanders were buried under the rubble? Even in the utmost revelation of His power, the Almighty reminds us that unmitigated good is not of this world."

Epperstein took over again. "There was this woman who'd heard about the cat, and she had a sick pig. She had a sick child too, as it happened, but that was by the way. Her capital was tied up in the pig, so it was to pray for that, not her child, that she went to Ulf's grave. It was a ruddy great sow, too big for her to fetch with her, but she *was* carrying the sick child in her arms.

"Well, what happened was that the child suddenly got better, though the mother hadn't so much as mentioned its name in her prayers, and when she got home again she not only found the pig in the pink, but the proud mum of twenty-four piglets. That's why pictures of Little St Ulf always show him surrounded with little piggies. A really kosher saint."

"The miracles multiplied—" Leo Schnellman took up the narrative. "Everything from epilepsy to wooden leg, cured while you wait. Pilgrims came pouring in and their money with them, and after a while it was decided to use some of the profits to provide the little saint—for he'd become St Ulf by then: in those days saints didn't have to pass exams before getting their haloes, the way they do today—with a shrine inside the cathedral itself. And there he remained, until the Reformation swept away all such objects of veneration—"

Jurnet cut in, "And until our friend here took it into his head to go digging him up again."

"For Christ's sake!" the student broke in. "The floor fell in! You didn't expect them to put it back without trying to find out what it was all about?"

"What they do in the cathedral's their business. What I can't understand is how a Mosh Epperstein comes to get into the act."

"Pargeter asked me." Then, stung at being put in a posture of defence, "What the hell business is it of yours anyway?"

"Shut up, Mosh!" The Rabbi's smile belied his words. "I'm working hard to make it his business." To Jurnet, "But Mosh is right, Ben. People with as much past to carry around with them as the Jews can't afford to be afraid of it. Anything that clarifies what actually happened has to be OK."

"Me," said Jurnet, "I've got my hands full trying to clarify the present. Like, for instance, why, in the cathedral this morning, I ran into a wide boy name of Joe Fisher. Far as I know he hasn't got a sick sow back home, so what d'you reckon *he* was up to, asking the way to Little St Ulf?"

"You've obviously got an idea," the archaeological student said coldly.

"Call it a glimmering. Ever heard of the English Men?"

Leo Schnellman leaned forward in his chair, suddenly alert.

"What are they up to, Ben, this time?"

"Don't know as they're up to anything. Except I know Fisher hangs out with them, and something like this is right up their alley."

"How did he get to know?" Mosh Epperstein demanded. "Only thing in the papers so far was about it probably being the pit where they cast the cathedral bells. That's what we thought it was ourselves, at first." He flushed, and muttered, more to himself than the others, "Stan Brent."

"And who's Stan Brent when he's at home?"

The young man flushed again. Following a sudden intuition, Jurnet asked, "Lady Aste's fancy man, you mean?"

"Liz isn't a Lady."

"You can say that again."

"Look here, you! Not a Ladyship's, what I meant." Very, very young.

For the first time that evening, Jurnet felt compassion. The man was a lover, like himself. Not the poor bugger's fault there was, however unjustly, something faintly risible in the thought of anyone named Moses Epperstein making it with the daughter of Lord Sydringham.

"What does this Stan character do for a living?" Jurnet asked, with a friendliness of tone that obviously took the other by surprise.

"Mugs old ladies, I shouldn't wonder. Says he dropped out of the University. Doubt it. All he can do to write his name."

"That's proof?" The detective queried, determinedly jovial. "And is he digging up Little St Ulf along with the rest of you?"

"Him? Pargeter's already warned him off more than once. He keeps hanging about, on the chance, I shouldn't be surprised, we'll turn up something worth nicking. Several of the old chroniclers seem to think a lot of the pilgrims' offerings of gold and silver and precious stones were actually buried in the kid's tomb. Myself, I can't see the monks putting all that lovely lolly out of circulation, but that's what they say. You can even read it in the booklet about Little St Ulf they sell at the cathedral bookstall. For all I know, Stan Brent may have got wind of the possibility, and is living in hopes of making a killing."

"In the meantime putting the bite on Miss Aste?"

"He doesn't have to," Epperstein returned bitterly. "She has it all hanging out for him." He looked about the room in a lost kind of way, and Leo Schnellman said gently, "You left your jacket under the Ping-Pong table."

"Ah! Well. Thanks for the game, then. I'll have to give you your revenge."

"You won't!" the Rabbi declared robustly. "Not till I see you here on *Shabbat*. It's time to balance the books a little."

"I'll try."

"Do that. I have a particularly brilliant sermon planned."

"For next Saturday, you mean?"

"For every Saturday. All my sermons are the same sermon. Only the words differ. All of them demonstrations that, despite appearances to the contrary, the universe makes sense."

After the study period was over, and Jurnet and the Rabbi sat over cups of tea, Jurnet remembered. "You never said what happened to the doctor, Haim Ha-Levi."

"Oh, the King came to Angleby, eventually. Not a bad man, in the context of his time. What he did was remind the citizens yet again that, as a Jew, the man was royal property. He warned them that if anyone touched so much as a hair of his head, he'd punish the whole city collectively."

"That was something, at least."

"Nothing at all. Three months later, a mob broke into Haim HaLevi's home—he'd gone back to his house in Cobblegate on the strength of the King's promise—castrated him, broke his arms and legs, and hung him upside down on a cross. Next day, by which time he may or may not have been dead, they took his body down, dismembered it, and threw the pieces down a well. His last words were said to be, 'Water my plants.'"

Suddenly it did not seem like something that had happened 840 years ago.

"And did the King carry out his threat?" Jurnet asked at last.

"You must be joking. Kings have more important things to think about. It was, after all, just another Jew."

6

On his way home Jurnet made a detour so as to pass the Institute. It was shut up for the night, as he had known it would be; no Miriam on the steps waiting to be picked up, the only light an illuminated notice-board advertising a forthcoming course in obedience-training for dogs. He made a mental note to tell Taleh.

Another detour took him to the Close, knowing that the gates, which had once been shut promptly at sunset, would be open however late the hour. Not long before, there had been a fire in the early hours in one of the houses near the river, and the fire engine, arriving at Bridge Gate, had been kept waiting. The chain at the gate rang a bell in the lodge where one of the vergers lived, and the verger, who had been under the weather, had taken some tablets without knowing they were sedative. By the time the clanging had awakened him, and the gate been opened for the engine to pass through, a child had died in the burning house.

Since that night the cathedral precinct was no longer a little world which shut itself off from the city when darkness fell. With its dim lighting and shadowy byways it had become, indeed, a favorite place of resort for courting couples.

Jurnet found a parking space in the Upper Close, and sat in the car feeling envious of the activity he pictured was going on all round him in the vehicles that edged the central lawn. He wished he smoked, or that he had a cassette player in the car. Anything to put off the moment of going home.

Home! That was a laugh. In the flat, he knew, there would be nothing to remind him of Miriam's presence. Always when she left him, even for a night, she took with her all her possessions, down to the last hairpin. Not so much an absence as a desertion. It was almost as if she wished to convince him that she had never existed rosy in his bed, repaying passion with passion, other than as the figment of his overheated imagination.

A car started up somewhere ahead. Then another, and another. In the one immediately in front of him, two heads rose into view through the back window; a dishevelled man got hurriedly out of the back and into the driving seat. In a moment the car moved off, following the others back to the FitzAlain Gate.

Jurnet waited until the man with the lighted torch who had been working his way along the line of vehicles reached him. Then he wound down the window, and said, "Evening, Mr Harbridge. Can't win 'em all, can we?"

"You, Inspector! What you doing here, this late?"

Ignoring the question, Jurnet observed, "I don't have to ask the same of you. Do this every night, do you?"

"No. Mr Quest's off tonight."

"Don't think I know Mr Quest."

"Head verger. His daughter's been took sick in Northampton."

"Oh ah. Keep you at it pretty late, don't they, the Dean and Chapter?"

"I'm not complaining."

"Good for you. What I don't get, though," Jurnet went on evenly, "is why you don't stand at the gate and stop 'em coming in in the first place." No explanation was forthcoming, and the detective finished, "Not half the fun, of course, of catching them actually at it."

Even in the dark Jurnet could see the red that overspread the man's face. Then the anger faded and Harbridge laughed. A straightforward laugh, uncomplicated.

"Bit of a misunderstanding, sir. I'm not one of those. Been on the gate since nightfall, and just nipped back home for a sip of something hot. This lot's what built up while I was gone. Usually me and one of the other vergers does it turn and turn about, see, but wi' Mr Quest called away unexpected—"

"Seems I owe you an apology."

"That's all right. You couldn't be expected to know."

"Sorry just the same."

"Know, I mean, what it means to be part of this." A sweep of the torch indicated the dark bulk of the cathedral. "Even a very humble part, unimportant."

"It's big all right," Jurnet said inadequately.

"It's perfect! Not another cathedral to touch it! At Salisbury they put a few extra feet on the spire—" the verger's tone made it plain that he regarded the addition as un-Christian one-upmanship—"but that don't mean anything—"

"Can't see the point of a spire myself." Jurnet meant it as a joke.

"For me," Harbridge declared simply, "it's the holiest part of the whole building. Holier than the High Altar, even. A finger pointing to Heaven. When I was a lad at school they taught us that parallel lines meet in infinity, meaning, I suppose, never. The way I look at it, that there spire—" turning for a brief, confirmatory glance—"is parallel lines meeting in the here an' now, and the point where they meet is God."

The verger smiled at the other's embarrassment.

"If you don't mind me saying, sir, you don't strike me as a religious man."

Jurnet said, "I don't mind your saying it, at all."

Only to find that he did, a little.

As he slowed down at the gate, a boy and a girl, closely intertwined, came through on the narrow footpath. They were none of his business either, and Jurnet could not have explained why he wound down the car window and called across, "Good evening!"

The pair came apart and stared at him, at first blankly, then in hostile recognition. The girl's face, in the light of the lantern that hung from the centre of the arch, was puffy and discoloured. Into the boy's, as Jurnet watched, came that blend of calculation and artlessness with which, as a police officer, he was only too familiar. They were the ones who really had you worried. The sinners without a sense of sin.

Detaching himself from the girl, the boy stepped into the road towards the car. Jurnet suddenly did not want to hear what he had to say. He set the car in motion, out of the Close, into the sleeping city. In the driving mirror he could see the two together again, in the middle of the carriageway. As if he guessed himself under observation, the boy put his arms round the girl and pressed his body impudently to hers.

Jurnet drove home to his empty flat.

7

When the bells began to chime for Sung Eucharist, Jurnet abandoned hope of Miriam's coming and came into the cathedral. He deliberately kept his eyes away from the inscription in the corner. He knew it by heart anyway.

The people filing into the cathedral out of the pale sunshine were of two clearly differentiated kinds. Most were sightseers, in jeans and anoraks, with cameras dangling from their shoulders. The rest were dressed in Sunday best, the older women—who formed a majority—hatted and gloved and carrying prayer books. Where the first category drifted along the nave with the uncertain air common to all transients through sacred buildings, these others made purposefully for the transepts where rows of chairs had been set out facing the altar positioned under the tower, at the crossing of the arms of the great cross which was the building itself.

The bells stopped. The choristers filed into the choir-stalls, white surplices over scarlet cassocks. On the nave side of the altar rails the onlookers strained forward like visitors to the Zoo waiting for the animals to be fed. What a bonus to see the mechanism working, as it might be a National Trust watermill with the wheel actually going round!

When the first organ notes zoomed into the air, they looked pleased; but the arrival of the officiating clergy, ceremonially robed and preceded by a golden cross brandished aloft like a banner, clearly disturbed some among them. A small man, dwarfed by a towering backpack, expressed noisy disapproval upon discovering that the service, being located bang in the middle of the floor space, frustrated, for its duration, a total perambulation of the cathedral; an obstruction, he appeared to think, on a par with a farmer putting a bull into a field for the purpose of blocking a footpath, and as deserving of censure.

The choir began to sing, something splendid and celebratory but not, Jurnet thought, as soaring as the song he had heard in rehearsal. He craned his neck and saw that the Gentlemen of the Choir, the adult singers, six a side in the second row of the stalls and robust of figure and voice, were hard at it, underpinning the boyish trebles and holding them earthbound. Hard to tell at that distance, but the detective had the impression that the child choristers were one short of their full complement.

Jurnet could not see the Dean anywhere, and wondered whether, like the producer of any other theatrical piece, he was hovering somewhere in the wings, overseeing exits and entrances, biting his nails when someone missed a cue.

Not likely, he decided, after a while. In this performance all the actors were word-perfect. The spectacle proceeded with a magnificent self-confidence that left him, as one brought up to the hesitancies of lay preachers, awed and, against his will, envious.

But then, it was a production that had been running for a long time.

Suddenly uncomfortable at the thought that he, a Jew-to-be, might be deemed to be participating in a

Christian rite, Jurnet retreated down the nave, reassured by the thought that it was hardly the place to run into any of Rabbi Schnellman's flock.

He had forgotten about Mosh Epperstein.

In track suit and plimsolls the archaeology student came loping down the aisle, away from the boarded enclosure. It was not a pace at which people customarily moved through houses of worship, and several of the sightseers looked at him curiously. It was a haste that jarred with the stately swell of the music, the invocation rolling down from the altar, *"In the Name of the Father, and of the Son, and of the Holy Spirit—"*

Looking pale and ill, Epperstein broke into a run; and Jurnet, whose thought it was that the student had been back to the excavation to recover some cannabis cached there—either that, or the fellow was stoned already—set off in pursuit.

Just the same, such was the chemistry of the place, the detective could not bring himself actually to sprint after his quarry. When, at last, hurrying as best he could without giving the appearance of haste, he achieved the Close, Epperstein was nowhere to be seen. Stan Brent was lying on his side on the lawn chewing a blade of grass, and to all appearances in no way incommoded by a scramble of children playing some game in which his prostrate body served some essential purpose, boundary or goal.

Giving up the chase, the detective turned to go back into the cathedral.

The young man called over, "How much is it worth to say which way he went?"

Jurnet gave no sign of having heard; but his face felt hot as he made his way back through the little door into the north aisle.

"Bloody shit!" he muttered.

From the distant transept, some devotional Everest scaled at last, the entire building resounded with a triumphal *"Amen!"*

Elizabeth Aste came towards him along the north aisle, prim and wanton by turn as she crossed the bands of sun and shadow in her transparent muslin shift.

The girl's face, he saw, was almost back to normal. The swelling had gone down. The purple bruise on the cheekbone she could easily have masked with make-up had she wanted to.

She was looking enormously pleased with herself. So pleased as to be willing to include even an interfering copper in her general satisfaction with the world.

"Good morning, Police Officer!" Barely suppressed laughter bubbled in her voice. "If you really are one, that is."

"I really am. Detective-Inspector Jurnet."

"Detective-Inspector—how grand! What on earth are you doing here on a Sunday?"

"It seems quite a popular day for being in a church," Jurnet observed mildly. "I'm not on duty, if that's what you mean."

"How stupid of me! I suppose I always assume policemen never stop being policemanly. You're late for the service."

"So I hear. How about you? Are *you* working? Don't tell me they keep your nose to the grindstone seven days a week?" He hazarded experimentally, "I just passed young Epperstein in a hell of a hurry—"

"Epperstein?" she repeated vaguely, as if she were trying to put a face to the name. "I came by to pick up some slides." She smiled as if she had said something amusing.

Jurnet said, "I'm glad I ran into you. I've been hoping for a guided tour of Little St Ulf's grave."

"I'm only the photographer. Besides, there's nothing much to see so far, except a hole in the floor. You don't need a guide for that."

"That only makes the interpretation all the more important. Anyway, I couldn't get in on my own, could I? Surely you keep it locked up?"

"In case somebody steals the hole? Even if we did,

anyone who wanted to get in would only have to lean on the boards. They'd go down like a pack of cards."

"Just the same," Jurnet said, "I'd have thought . . . To keep out the nosey parkers, if nothing else—"

"There's a notice up, didn't you see? 'Private', in capital letters. Nobody in a church ever opens a door marked 'Private'. Scared stiff what they might find on the other side."

"Just the same," Jurnet said again. "There ought at least be a token padlock and chain. Some kid that can't read could fall down the hole and break his neck."

"Then they could make him a saint like Little St Ulf couldn't they?" Looking past him, "Here's Professor Pargeter. Take it up with him."

"My dear child!" Professor Pargeter cried, at the same time waving to a group of sightseers who had recognized him from the telly. In the few steps that separated him from the pair standing in the aisle he signed his name on a hymn book, the official guide to the cathedral, and a copy of *Penthouse*. "Working on Sunday!" he called across. "This is indeed conduct beyond the call of." Taking in the girl's costume, "Unless the Dean's signed you up for a re-run of the Temptations of St Anthony."

"You *are* awful! I just popped in for some slides."

"Better pop out before the Bishop sees you, unless you want to be exorcized bell, book, and candle."

"It sounds like fun."

"Get along with you, hussy! Besides—" the voice shedding some of its jollity—"I saw the egregious Brent outside. And it doesn't do—does it?—to keep him waiting."

"Don't be horrid, Pargy," she pouted. "I can't think why you always have it in so for Stan."

"I can't think either, unless it's because he's amoral, sadistic, and forty years younger than I am." His eyes, blue as the girl's, narrowed. He put out a finger that did not quite touch her bruised cheek. "He hasn't been knocking you about again?"

The girl positively bloomed. Waiting, as usual, for

his existence to be recognized, Jurnet could see the nipples lifting the thin muslin.

"You *are* silly! Anyone would think you were my father!" Tilting her face so that the bruise was even more visible, she kissed the Professor on the cheek. "I'll have those pictures you wanted ready in the morning." Then, "Oh—this is a police officer. Chief Constable or something. He's investigating who killed Little St Ulf and he wants you to show him the dig."

When she had gone, the two men took stock of each other. Here Jurnet had the advantage, being moderately fond of "Past Imperfect," the programme which had made Professor Pargeter a TV personality and archaeology the biggest thing in spectator sports since all-in wrestling. The man stood up surprisingly well to being viewed in three dimensions. Large and tweedy, he looked powerful but unfrightening, whilst the arrogant cock to the handsome features was more than counterbalanced by a moustache that looked as if it had been stuck on for a joke.

As for the Professor, he said, "I was in the Judaean Hills couple of years ago. Place called Tel Ari. Kind of Mini-Masada where some Israelites held out against the Romans. Full of bodies looking just like you."

Jurnet asked, startled, "How could you tell? Skeletons, weren't they?"

"Well? What d'you suppose you are, under that biodegradable flesh you're got up in? Chief Constable, Liz said. Some kind of joke?"

"Detective-Inspector actually. Detective-Inspector Jurnet."

"What did I tell you?" said the Professor, with no particular surprise. "No need to ask what's *your* interest in Little St Ulf."

"I'm not Jewish, if that's what you mean."

"And I'm not a chap that makes fancy patterns in wet plaster for a living. It's not where you're going, it's where you've been that counts."

The two walked towards the excavation, the Professor stopping several times to sign autographs and shake hands. The buzz of recognition grew, accompanied by a marked movement of people towards the north aisle.

Harbridge and another verger hurried up, clucking annoyance. The Professor, a finger to his lips, complained charmingly to his admirers, "You lovely people are going to get me slung out on my ear, do you know that?"

He shushed their laughter and made an amusing gesture of shooing them away; and although they did not go, they followed him no further, but stood watching his retreating back, chattering excitedly. Harbridge snapped, "Quiet, please! A service is in progress!"

"Try to give it a miss on Sundays as a rule," the Professor remarked to Jurnet. "Only I've been away all week, filming on Hadrian's Wall. Thought I'd take a quiet look to see what the others have been up to while my back was turned."

"Mr Epperstein was here too, earlier."

"Was he, now? And Liz makes two. The helots are more conscientious than I'd given them credit for. Beginning to wonder why I hurried back."

"Hadrian's Wall sounds interesting."

"A ruin, Inspector. That's the beauty of it." Pargeter looked about the cathedral with a jaundiced eye. "Henry VIII must have been out of his mind to leave a place like this standing. Just think what a ruin it would have made! To say nothing of posing enough problems to keep me and my fellow-practitioners off the bread-line till Doomsday. Instead of which, this otherwise delightful city is lumbered with this dreadful Waterloo Station of a place where the stationmaster can't even be certain the trains are running, let alone from what platform."

Arrived at the wooden hoarding, he paused before the door marked "Private".

"Only let myself in for this bit of nonsense because of the Dean. Flossie Carver. We were Cathedrans together. Hated each other's guts." Professor Pargeter gave his moustache a twist that, had it indeed been attached to his upper lip by spirit gum, would have had it off without a doubt. "Ties like that mean something."

Jurnet seized his opportunity.

"Padlock on the door'd be a good thing, don't you think? Kids might get in—hurt themselves."

"Serve the little buggers right!" The Professor pulled the door open. A broom clattered to the ground.

Within the enclosure the air was gritty; a different kind of air from that which filled the rest of the cathedral. A battered table piled with files and boxes, a couple of three-legged stools, sieves and trowels, a bundle of graduated poles, some folded sacks and one bulging with lumps of masonry, were all covered with a grey dust that seemed adhesive, the deposit of some stranded sea.

By some trick of acoustics, the circumscribing boards vibrated strongly to the chords that Mr Amos, up in the loft, was conjuring from the organ; yet the notes themselves arrived debilitated, as if the music had vaulted across the fenced-off space, leaving a bubble below, a vacuum.

A frayed drugget stretched from the door to the hole in the paving; a hole roughly oblong, and of a depth varying between two-and-a-half and five feet.

All this Jurnet both saw and did not see. Just as he both heard, and did not hear, the Professor's rasping "My God!" He went down on his knees by the hole in the cathedral floor, his Sunday-trousered legs pressed into the dust. He knelt and he looked. He had no need to touch what lay there, half in and half out of the hole that housed the tomb of Little St Ulf. He had seen death often enough to recognize it for what it was.

Even when he had not seen it for 840 years.

8

The photographs were appalling. The photographs were worse than the real thing.

The real thing, true, was a boy, horribly murdered, horrifically mutilated. But sooner or later this real thing would be taken out of the mortuary drawer where it now lay tagged and dated like meat in a well-organized home freezer, packed into a coffin and lowered into the busy darkness of the grave, there to return, ashes to ashes, dust to dust, in decent privacy. Give it a few years, plus worms that knew nothing about working union hours, and it would look like any other kid's skeleton: sad, OK, but socially acceptable.

Time was powerless to abate the horror of the photographs. In them the murdered child was abominable forever. The colour might fade a little from the tie buried deep in the skinny neck, the raw wound where there had once been a penis bleach silently in the official folder. But that livid Star of David hacked from throat to navel— Jurnet put the prints down abruptly.

The Superintendent looked up from his chair, across the width of the desk.

"For the moment, let's put aside the tempting overtones, shall we?" He reached over, picked up the topmost photograph, and studied it as coolly as if it were a holiday snap. "The thing is, are we looking at what it appears to be, or at a common or garden sex crime artfully dressed up to look like something else?"

"If it *is* a sex crime, it's certainly not a common or garden one."

"True. The test will be, what comes next."

"Sir?"

"We've released nothing as to the nature of the boy's injuries. But the killer knows, and if the inflection of those particular wounds was his prime motive—if, in short, he killed the boy simply to make it look like Little St Ulf all over again—he won't be able to wait to see it spread all over the media." The Superintendent considered what he had just said, and found it wanting. "Not conclusive. He still might want to raise the biggest stink possible, to make sure we don't latch on to his simple, uncomplicated homicide."

Jurnet said, "Either way, the kid's common or garden dead, that's for sure."

"Now, Ben," the other chided. "You're letting yourself get involved again. How many times do I have to remind you that detachment's the first requisite for a good copper? Not that there aren't days—" the hand holding the photograph had grown tense and white-knuckled—"when I find myself wondering whether the good Lord didn't dangle those quaint appendages on the male torso simply for the fun of seeing them crushed, burnt, stamped on, electric-shocked, cut off, or otherwise put in painful jeopardy."

Jurnet said, "I'll remember what you said about being detached, sir."

For a moment the Superintendent's face stiffened with annoyance. Then he laughed, unaffectedly.

"It's these bloody pictures." He returned to the pile the one he had been looking at. "The corpse as ritual object, eh? T. S. Eliot knew what he was doing all right. Stage a murder in a cathedral, it becomes transmuted into an art form. I doubt they'd ever have thought twice about Becket if he'd been struck down in some Canterbury back alley."

Jurnet forced himself to look at the photograph the Superintendent had discarded.

A common or garden kid, done to death in a sick and barbarous way. Thin arms, knock knees, pot belly showing through the unbuttoned shirt. Could never have been a Little Lord Fauntleroy at the best of times, but presentable enough, as Jurnet remembered him, in scarlet cassock and white ruff, paired with the kid with the chewing gum, filing into the stalls for choir practice.

Aloud he said, "Don't know about Canterbury. Reckon one Little St Ulf's enough for Angleby."

"More than!" the other agreed readily. "Medieval superstition was bad enough in the Middle Ages, let alone today. Unless, maybe, it's that nowadays we simply make superstition respectable by calling it art. Both, after all, have their roots in the same need to propitiate the dark and unknowable forces in the Universe."

"Too deep for me, sir."

The Superintendent's face reddened with an irritation instantly suppressed.

"Me too, Ben. Words to cocoon the nastiness. Let's stick to the knowables, eh? Arthur Cossey, aged twelve years and nine months, murdered in the cathedral between the hours of 6.45 and 8.15 a.m. It seems that the climate of the cathedral poses special problems, and Dr Colton can't be more specific. So—what have we got so far on Arthur Cossey?"

Mrs Sandra Cossey's front doorstep, as white and welcoming as a new tombstone, should have prepared Jurnet and Sergeant Ellers for what to expect inside Number 7, Bishop Row. When Mrs Cossey opened the door, the sight of the apron she wore evoked for Jurnet an instant picture of a woman in cardigan and apron busy with her Brasso in the Close.

The recollection had point. For Sandra Cossey, polishing was evidently more than a means to a living: it was a way of life. Everything in the little parlour that could be polished—and a significant proportion of the furnishings appeared to serve no other purpose—flashed and twinkled with the deadly jollity of a set of false teeth. Jurnet could not remember ever being in a house so repellently clean.

The woman had made no undue outcry when she had first heard that her only son was dead. Jurnet had not thought less of her for it. Grieving was a creative activity for which you either had, or hadn't, a gift.

By now, he saw, she had made some attempt to devise a proper role for herself; taken the rollers out of her hair, and put on a black skirt and jumper. From time to time she dabbed at her eyes—pale and bulging like her dead child's—with a white handkerchief carefully folded to show the drawn-threadwork in one corner. Only her slippers—pink and fluffy with a sequinned heart on the instep—troubled the detective a little, like a clue that did not fit in with the rest of the evidence.

The shame-faced pride that every now and again lit up her face was something else he was familiar with. The reporters would have been round, her name in the papers and on telly, the neighbours in and out of the place, as if she had suddenly done something remarkable. Few could resist the blandishments of fame, however dire the occasion.

He was glad she had not yet been told the full extent of her son's injuries.

"Tell us about Arthur," he prompted gently. "We need to know what kind of boy he was."

The woman looked up sharply.

"He weren't never in any trouble, if that's what you mean."

Jurnet smiled reassurance.

"If he had been, I wouldn't be asking. We'd have heard of it. Kind of thing I mean, for instance—he had a good voice, didn't he? Must have, to be a Song Scholar. Things like that, general. They all go to make up a picture."

"He did have a lovely voice." Her own was thin and complaining. "Artistic as well. Like his Pa."

Jurnet said respectfully, "I heard about Mr Cossey. Terrible thing that was." He did not add that he knew Arthur Cossey's father had been pissed to the eyebrows when, five years previously, he had fallen from some scaffolding during repairs to the cathedral tower. "From what I hear, Mr Cossey was one of the most gifted masons they'd ever had working on the fabric."

"He carved me there—did they tell you that? Left-hand side as you face the altar, under a sort of arch."

"Quite an honour! Terrible for you, though. Two tragedies, both in the same place. And a cathedral!"

Mrs Cossey became quite animated.

"Someone I know—" her pasty face coloured slightly—"went and paced it out. Hundred and five feet, he made it, give or take a few inches, from where Vince landed to where Arthur—" She twisted her handkerchief. "You wouldn't think God'd let things like that happen, not in a cathedral."

"Not for us to question," said Jurnet, who made his living doing just that. "And so you've had to bring Arthur up all on your own."

"I've got my pension. And they've been very good, in the Close. I work for several people there. A very nice class of people—but then, it's only what you'd expect, isn't it?"

Jurnet, who had long ceased to expect anything of anybody, ignored the question, and asked, "And Arthur?"

"He was a very quiet boy, Arthur was. Anybody'll tell you."

"Had a lot of little friends, did he?"

"Friends?" She repeated the word as if unsure of its meaning. Then, "Artistic, like I said. Spent all his time up in his room drawing. Made me stop calling it his room. His studio."

"What about weekends? Did he spend his weekends in his studio too?"

"What with choir practice Saturday mornings and the services on Sunday, I didn't see all that much of him weekends." As if suddenly afraid her answers might reflect on her maternal solicitude, "There was always a meal waiting, if his lordship chose to come in and eat it."

"D'you know what he did weekends between times, when he *was* out? When he wasn't at the cathedral, I mean."

"Mucking about, I suppose. What do kids do? Nothing bad, though. He always came back neat and tidy as he went."

"Last Sunday, did he leave home wearing what he usually wore?"

"They always have to wear their blazers, even if it isn't a school day—" She broke off and looked at Jurnet. "You saw him, didn't you? After?" The detective nodded. "You must know what he was wearing."

"He—he didn't have his blazer on."

"It weren't more than three weeks old!" The thought made her cry a little. "He won't be able to flog it anyway, whoever did it. That'd be a real give-away!"

"I only wish he would. We'd have him quicker than you could say Jack Robinson. You saw the lad go out with it on, then. What time would that have been?"

Mrs Cossey coloured a little.

"I never actually saw him go through the door. I have a bit of a lie-in Sundays. Arthur always was an early riser. Used to be out first thing on his paper round." As if rebutting unspoken criticism, "I always set the table and leave the sugar crispies out the night before. The milk's in the fridge. He'd only got to take it out."

"And did he, on Sunday? Take any breakfast?"

"I don't know about the milk. I didn't think to look, not expecting—" She took thought and said, "The crispies. Even if he didn't have them at the table, he never went out without filling up his pockets. He'd rather eat sugar crispies than sweets any day. Two packets a week he cost me. I used to say to him, 'You'll ruin me or your teeth with your sugar crispies, you will. Arthur Cossey, and I don't know which'll be the first to go!' "

"And what did he say to that?"

Mrs Cossey looked startled.

"I don't know as he said anything. He was a quiet one, was Arthur."

Things went better, upstairs, once Sergeant Ellers had suggested that he and his superior officer take their shoes off to avoid messing up her beautiful floors. The woman did not appreciate the effort it took the little

Welshman, who was sensitive about his lack of inches, to make the suggestion; but she grew measurably more forthcoming as the detectives, stocking-footed on the landing, slid across the glassy linoleum to the door of Arthur's studio.

The room, judging from the type of dwelling, was the largest in the house. Despite appearances, there must be love here, Jurnet thought, heartened by the possibility, to give up the best bedroom for a child's hobby. Either that, or quiet Arthur Cossey had a knack of getting his own way.

Even so, the room was none too large for its contents. A clothes cupboard, a proper draughtsman's table, another stacked with paints and sketch books, canvases, brushes in jars, plastic trays filled with pencils and erasers, pastels and crayons, took up one wall; a chest of drawers and a divan bed the best part of another. A substantial easel, not a child's toy, stood in the middle of the floor.

"Understand now why he called it a studio." Jurnet looked about him. "All this stuff must have cost you a bomb."

"He had his paper round."

"Shouldn't think it could cover all this."

Mrs Cossey looked about her vaguely.

"Arthur always had something or other on."

"Oh ah." Then, "Where'd the youngster keep his finished work? In the chest of drawers?"

The woman looked alarmed. "Arthur never liked me pulling his things about. You must have found the key in his trousers. A key ring with a Donald Duck on it—"

"We'll have to check up on that," Jurnet said smoothly. It was no time to let on that the boy's trousers were as unaccounted for as his blazer. He brought forward the only chair in the room. "Just you sit yourself down while Sergeant Ellers and I take a look. We won't damage anything."

"No need." Ellers, who had been bending over the chest of drawers, straightened up, his chubby face flushed. "They're not locked, any of 'em."

"Not locked!" Mrs Cossey sat down and looked at Jurnet. It was the first time she had looked at him directly. "Anyway, what's all this got to do with finding out who killed him?"

"Blow all, most likely," the detective readily admitted. "But a room like this—so professional. I'm curious to see just how good he was."

"People that kill little boys, it don't make any difference what kind of boys they are."

"I expect you're right," said Jurnet. "Except that, while we're looking for the fellow that did it, we try to pile up as many random facts as we can in the hope that, somewhere in the pile—maybe when we're least expecting it—one of 'em will suddenly poke itself out, like a needle out of a haystack, give us a ruddy great prick where we'll feel it most, and that'll be it—the clue that leads us to the murderer."

"You won't find anything sticking out here," Mrs Cossey insisted, the very idea of a fact, or anything else, out of place in her dusted and polished home clearly outside belief.

"Only one with paintings." Ellers had levered out one of the drawers. He brought it over to the table.

Considering the promise of the room, Arthur Cossey's artistic efforts were a disappointment: highly coloured views of the cathedral and the castle, all the well-known sights of Angleby, exactly as depicted wherever postcards were on sale in the city; executed with a technical assurance astonishing in a twelve-year-old, but with such utter lack of insight as to make their very facility a visual yawn.

Jurnet took up the last picture of the pile. It was a drawing, copied, at a guess, from a book published in the second half of the nineteenth century. The figures, dressed though they were in medieval costume, had an invincibly Victorian look about them.

It was one of the most ambitious exercises Arthur Cossey had attempted. In a nave where every pillar and rib and boss was filled in with painstaking detail, a press of people knelt round a stone altar, upon which stood a boy clothed in a white robe left open to the waist, which was as far, probably, as the proprieties of the original illustrator's day would allow. The boy, whose head was encircled by a halo, had his right hand raised in blessing.

Almost entirely in black and white, the drawing had two points of colour, the more arresting for the surrounding monochrome. They were the halo, glossy with meticulously applied gold leaf, and a Star of David inscribed in fluorescent red upon the exposed chest. The title, LITTLE ST ULF, was lettered in neatly at the foot of the drawing.

Or would have been, had not some other hand crossed it out with a bold stroke; and substituted, with a bravura that was livelier than anything else on the paper, LITTLE ST ARTHUR.

9

Leaving the car outside Bridge Gate, Jurnet came into the Close, Ellers prancing alongside, happy to be back in his shoes and taller by the height of his heels. The detective knew of old that when the little Welshman was excited he rose up on the balls of his feet, a kind of human hydrofoiling; and here he was, at it again, tiptoeing over the cobbles in a way that, to anyone who did not know Rosie Ellers, highly sexed and to all appearances highly satisfied with her husband's performance, might well have raised doubts it were safer not to voice to Sergeant Ellers's face.

Instead, Jurnet asked, "Going to let me into the secret, or do I have to squeeze it out of you like Pepsodent?"

The Welshman laughed and opened his palm in which lay a small, transparent, polythene bag, at first glance empty.

Peering closer, Jurnet saw that the bag contained a sliver of celluloid, or, perhaps, perspex.

"Found it in the one with the pictures in it. Whoever it was that'd been so busy getting the drawers open never noticed a bit'd broken off." He looked at his superior officer. "Who d'you reckon'd want to get into a kid's chest of drawers, and what did he, or she, expect to find?"

"More than one of young Arthur's masterpieces, that's for sure. And not 'she'. Mrs Cossey doesn't strike me as one to know the uses of a bit of plastic in the wrong hands. The kid could've had some money stashed away there. He sounds a real little wheeler-dealer."

"I thought he sounded a bloody little creep, actually."

"Yes," Jurnet assented sadly. It was a familiar disillusion. Violent death so angered him that he invariably flung himself into a murder investigation as if he were inquiring into the Massacre of the Innocents; only to discover that, by and large, the murdered were no more virtuous and no less corrupt than those who died peacefully in their beds. "Though we've only got his Mum's word for it."

"She never said that!"

"Not in so many words. But did you notice there isn't a single one of the boy's pictures up on the walls? You'd have thought she could have found room for one, at least."

Sergeant Ellers frowned.

"See what you mean. Unless it could be young Arthur wouldn't let her. Strange, secretive kid he seems."

"Maybe he had good reason, poor little tyke, with characters hanging about the place with bits of celluloid tucked up their sleeves. I suppose it's the joker with the merry thought of pacing out how far it was to Little St Ulf and Arthur from where hubby mashed himself on the flagstones."

"Same bugger who gave her the slippers," agreed

Ellers, not to be outdone, sleuthwise. "Shouldn't be hard to put a name to him."

"We'll put someone on to it."

The spring sun was taking a leaf out of Sandra Cossey's book, polishing the world to a shine that glinted off the old flints and poured itself into the trumpeting daffodils. This was the business side of the Close; on the one side of the road the eastern end of the cathedral with its great flying buttresses, on the other those equally essential props of righteousness, the Appeals office and the Deanery.

For a moment Jurnet felt inclined to turn in at the latter, have another word with Dr Carver if he was at home; but decided against it. For the time being the two had already said all they could usefully say to each other.

The Dean had been out of the city on Sunday, visiting a country parish. By the time he had returned, there was nothing to see; merely, outside the grey hoarding, a plain-clothes man doing his best to look like a tripper or a worshipper, and not succeeding too well at either.

At that time the photographs had not been printed, so that the Dean had had to take Jurnet's word that a child had been found foully murdered at the tomb of Little St Ulf.

"In the cathedral! The cathedral!"

Pale and shaken, a different being from the confident personage of their last meeting, Dr Carver had moved along the aisle, and into a side chapel where a representation of Christ's Passion glowed jewel-like above the altar.

There, he had sunk to his knees, his head bowed in his hands. Jurnet, close behind, could hear the words, between a whisper and a sob, "In the cathedral!"

Jurnet scowled at the Crucifixion, the bloody wounds. Red paint. He put a firm hand on the Dean's shoulder.

"The boy, sir. Arthur Cossey. One of the choir-boys."

The Dean made the sign of the cross, and got to his feet.

"I know the boy." He raised his head. "You are angry with me. Inspector."

"Not my business to—"

"You are angry with me because I seem more concerned for the well-being of the cathedral than for a murdered child. I admit it. The child has gone to his Maker and will be judged by Him. He is in the hands of a loving God, and neither you nor I nor anyone else can do anything for what remains on earth except bury it with decent decorum. But that the living house of God should be so defiled!"

"As to that," Jurnet returned stolidly, "I can't speak. It's not what you'd call a police matter. But as to young Arthur Cossey, burying him won't be the end of it by a long chalk."

"Of course not," said the Dean. "Foolish of me. I am not myself." He took a deep breath, and said, after a moment, "You are hard on the heels of the murderer, I trust?"

"Early days. I'd be grateful to hear anything you yourself can tell me about the boy."

The Dean's face took on a closed and distant look.

"I find it hard to see how unimportant personal details can be relevant. Surely the balance of possibilities is that any boy would have served equally? The South Door is opened at 7.45 for Holy Communion at 8, and that is celebrated in a chapel quite out of sight of the body of the cathedral. The murderer had only to wait until a boy—any boy—entered, to accomplish his fell purpose."

"In that case, he could have waited a long time, couldn't he? I gather the choir doesn't have to clock in till 10, and by then there'd be far too many people about to try any funny business. Looks more like a meeting by appointment to me—or what's a kid doing in the cathedral at that early hour?"

"Not at all unusual. By tradition, the first door to be unlocked every morning is the Bishop's Postern, the small door in the north transept. It opens directly into the Palace gardens, the thinking behind it being that nothing should impede the Bishop, should he have a mind to it, from entering his cathedral during his waking hours. There is no public access, but there is a footpath from the Cathedral School which the boys have used from time immemorial." The Dean smiled faintly. "I myself, in my time, have come in that way before breakfast, to play marbles or hopscotch in the cloister."

There was no answering smile from the detective.

"If the Cathedrans all know about the Bishop's Postern, so do the Old Boys, who must number quite a few of the public hereabouts. Besides which, your vergers tell me Professor Pargeter and his assistants have a key to that particular door."

"That is so. In order to keep disruption of services down to a minimum, the Professor agreed that as much of the heavy work as possible should be done in the early hours. Of course, no work is done on Sundays at any hour of the day."

"Professor keeps the key in his possession, does he?"

The Dean permitted himself another small smile.

"I hardly think the Professor is that much of an early riser. But I have no reason to doubt the dependability of his assistants. Miss Aste—"

"Ah yes," said Jurnet. "Lord Sydringham's daughter."

"You are still angry with me," the Dean stated without acrimony. "May I ask whether it has anything to do with the fact that your name is Jurnet?"

"I'm not Jewish," said Jurnet, "if that's what you mean. And if I were, it'd be no reason to be angry with you or anyone else. On the other hand, sir, since you've raised the subject, I'll say this. I can't say I think it the best idea in the world to go digging up Little St Ulf."

"Tell me, Inspector," the Dean demanded, "would you be in favour of banning a demonstration organized for some perfectly peaceful and permitted purpose, simply because you had received information that a group of hooligans had plans for breaking it up?"

"That's hardly the same—"

"The analogy is exact. Are we to be denied the chance to elucidate a not-unimportant fragment of the history of this mighty edifice simply on the chance that conscienceless persons may pervert our discoveries to suit their own dark purposes?"

"Not for me to say, sir. The only principle I go on is that a child shouldn't have to be murdered to prove a principle."

"A madman, Inspector! A mindless crime!"

"Mad maybe, but not mindless. Murderers don't stop to carve racist symbols into the bodies of their victims without giving it a bit of thought."

The Dean put a hand over his eyes as if the light had become too strong. He turned back to the altar, to the painted wounds of the dead Christ.

"It is in the hands of God."

"*And* the Angleby Police." Jurnet's tone was uncompromising. "Which is why I need to know anything you can tell me about Arthur Cossey."

"I can tell you nothing. He was a very quiet boy."

10

"Have you noticed," Ellers inquired, as the two passed the Deanery, following the line of the cloister, "how it's always the quiet kids that get done, never the young tearaways you might expect?"

"Don't know about that," Jurnet demurred. "Kid gets done, it stands to reason his Ma's not going to let on he used to kick her up the backside if she didn't have his football socks ready on time."

"Yeah." But Jack Ellers sounded doubtful. "This Arthur Cossey—I shouldn't be surprised if he really was what they say. He doesn't sound what you'd call a childish child."

"His own mates'll be the best judge of that. I intend

to have a word with some of them. For what that's worth, mind you. What's childhood but a closed shop, a show put on to take the grown-ups in? Or are you too old to remember?"

"Me?" demanded the little Welshman, opening his eyes wide. "The pride of Llandrobyneth—the manly little chap, open as a twenty-four-hour petrol station?"

"That's the one. Equally, I don't doubt, the lecherous little so-and-so that was always trying to get the girls into the bike shed to try out his new pump—"

"Any other age, they'd be burning you at the stake for that, boyo! Sorcery, it is! Sauce, anyway."

"No wonder we grow up liars, the practice we've had." Jurnet cast a jaundiced look about the Close. He felt mocked by the budding trees, the flowers. The silly pigeons strutted croocrooing, or else flew round and round the cathedral steeple. Round and round. What was the sense of that, for Christ's sake, when all you did was end up where you started?

The noise in the Upper Close brought him back abruptly to the matter in hand.

There were not a great many more people than usual moving about on the paved space in front of the West Door. It was the noise they were making—a high-pitched hum that might well have gone unremarked by less professional ears—which made the two police officers quicken their steps. That, and the sight of a small group clustered on the grass.

"Jesus!" exclaimed Ellers. "The bloody Fourth Estate!" He groaned as a small white van, with *Eastern Television* painted on it in blue, hurtled through the FitzAlain Gate and braked as if an abyss had suddenly opened an inch ahead of its front bumper. Out of the back tumbled young men with long hair in T-shirts and ragged jeans who, despite their appearance, proceeded to set up a television camera and ready the recording apparatus, with the dexterity of a gunnery crew at the Royal Tournament. "What the hell's going on?"

A police car came into the Close, probably in pursuit of the van, for the two uniformed men who got out of it seemed to be in no doubt whom they wanted to see. But they too, as they started across the grass, caught the strange humming sound and turned, alert, towards its source.

Aware at last that something was up, the crowd in front of the West Door had divided, the voyeurs drawing to one side for safety's sake but staying to see what was to be seen, the rest of the tourists retreating into the cathedral. The remainder—a hundred or so men and a dozen women—drew together in a phalanx, well posed in relation to the cameras, and, at a signal from a man with a sternly noble face who seemed to be in command, produced from beneath coats and jackets, with an efficiency betokening many rehearsals, an assortment of banners and placards.

Only the lettering showed haste in preparation. Unevenly printed, poorly spaced, they read: 1144—JEWS KILLED LITTLE ST ULF. WHO KILLED ARTHUR COSSEY? and: HITLER WASN'T ALL BAD. A third demanded: AVENGE ARTHUR NOW! and a fourth, simply: RITUAL MURDER! Two women held up a large Union Jack. A banner of some white material, flourished aloft on poles by the man and the woman at either end of the front line, proclaimed: THE ENGLISH MEN FOR ENGLAND!

Sick at heart, Jurnet broke into a run.

A child was dead.

Death was an end.

This was a beginning.

The noise expanded to an orgasmic climax. "Rit-rit-ritual murder! *Rit-rit-ritual murder!*"

One of the uniformed men was back at the car, speaking urgently to Headquarters Control. Jurnet ran to the front of the screaming faces and shouted, "We are police officers! It is against the law to demonstrate in the Cathedral Close! Put down your posters and disperse immediately!"

Intoxicated with their own uproar, the demonstrators did not hear him: or, if they did, paid no heed.

"Rit-rit-ritual murder: Rit-rit-ritual murder!"

"The bleeding buggers!"

"Cool it!" Jurnet's hand clamped hard on the little Welshman's shoulders, forcing the heels back to earth. "I see Hinchley's called in. We'll wait for reinforcements." To Hinchley's companion, who had joined them looking angry and rebellious, he directed, "Smile, Bly! We're on telly, can't you see? A nice case of police brutality'd make their day." Jurnet saw that three of the vergers had emerged from the cathedral, one of them, Harbridge, carefully rolling back the sleeves of his gown. "Oh my Gawd, the Three Graces! Get after 'em quick, and let them know if they so much as touch a hair on this lot we'll do 'em for GBH before they know what's hit them."

Bly moved away sulkily, and Ellers muttered between gritted teeth, "How the ruddy hell did they know?"

"The media, you mean?" Jurnet's tone was savage. "The fucking media, protector of our democratic rights and liberties? Because some one bloody told 'em, of course!"

Hinchley came running over from the car with a loud-hailer.

"They're on their way, sir. This any use?"

"I doubt it," said Jurnet, taking the loud-hailer and putting it to his lips.

Immediately the shouting redoubled.

"Rit-rit-ritual murder!"

Jurnet lowered the instrument.

"No point in making ourselves more ridiculous than we are already."

Ellers demanded, "No brutality, OK—but do we have to stand around looking like pooves?"

"Unless you can think of something better."

A young man came running over to them from among the onlookers—a young man with a girl following behind, evidently bent upon dissuading him from his course of action. The young man's exuberant jacket and slacks advertised his transatlantic nationality. His dark, curly hair and dark eyes marked a further allegiance.

"For Christ's sake!" the young man yelled. "Aren't

you going to do something? Are you going to let these goddam anti-Semites get away with it?"

"Mort—please!"

The girl plucked desperately at his sleeve. The young man jerked himself free.

"Don't 'Mort please' me!" To the police officers, "Can't you read what they've got written up on those posters? Can't you hear what they're shouting? Or isn't it an offence in these wonderful British Isles?"

Jurnet replied steadily, "It *is* offensive, sir, I agree. Just as it is also an offence to demonstrate here in the Cathedral Close without permission from the Dean and Chapter. However, in view of the numbers concerned, measures to bring the demonstration to a close may take a little time. We should be in a position to take action very shortly."

"Rit-rit-ritual murder!"

"Jesus!" the young man shouted; and again he pulled his sleeve away from the clutching girl. Even in the midst of his preoccupations Jurnet noticed that she was very young, slim-legged, and elegant in an English mackintosh the way English women seldom succeeded in being. She stood whispering "Mort!" in a horrified undertone as the young man made for the close-packed English Men and, before any of them could divine his intention, drove his fist into the noble face of their leader.

The man went down to a dismayed howl from his followers. One of the women with the Union Jack brought her flagpole down on the American's head. He reeled, enveloped in folds of red, white, and blue. Blood trickled down either side of his nose, but he did not fall. Instead, he lowered his head and butted it into the stomach of the close-cropped youth who held the placard which proclaimed that Adolf Hitler was not all bad.

For further details thereafter, Jurnet was forced to refer to the television company which, later in the day, put on a private showing for his and the Superintendent's delectation. The long-haired boys had done their stuff. The detective shifted in his seat until, bruised as he was, with a couple of strapped ribs, he felt less uncomfortable, and correspondingly less censorious of the young technicians, intent on their job though all hell broke loose about them. True, a little active participation pending the arrival of the reinforcements from Headquarters would have been worth a hundred pictures; but the other onlookers, after all, with nothing to do but their duty as citizens, had done sweet Fanny Adams, whereas the telly men had at least engaged themselves in the useful activity of compiling a record.

There was not much they had missed. The young American disappearing beneath booted feet as the four police officers launched themselves to the rescue; the three vergers whirling like dervishes, their arms flailing; the sun catching brass knuckle-dusters—it was all there, in glorious Technicolour.

Had the onlookers stood by like that, all those years ago, watching Josce Morel and his wife Chera dying slowly in their iron cages on the city wall? Had they craned their necks to get a better view of the good doctor, Haim HaLevi, upside down on his cross?

Even as he posed the questions, Jurnet knew the answers. They had stood by. There were always onlookers.

The Superintendent turned to him in the darkness of the projection room, and asked, with a gentleness that was almost paternal, "You feeling all right, Ben?"

"Bit sore, sir, that's all."

"I don't wonder." The Superintendent returned his gaze to the screen where Police-Constable Bly, in close-up, was spitting out a tooth. "I shall want to know why it took as long as it did to get help to you."

"Don't see how they could have done it any faster," said Jurnet, always the peacemaker: it was what made him so popular back at Headquarters, in spite of his looks. In the darkness the detective smiled up wryly at his own image, one sleeve of his jacket missing, urging the English Men's leader, none too gently, towards the police van.

"Brinton, Briston—what's the chap's name?" the Superintendent demanded.

"Brinston. Claude Brinston. Seems to have a positive genius for teaming up with villains. A born tool."

"One of *the* Brinstons?"

"That's right. Brinston Boots and Shoes. That's why they kicked out Chesley Hayes, their old *führer*. Wanted to get their hands on the Brinston millions. And that's why we now have Hayes's League of Patriots as well as the English Men to contend with— two lots of nutters instead of one."

"So much the better! Only a dustpan and brush needed to clean up little messes."

"Yes, sir."

The studio was filling now with the sound of nearing sirens as earlier, in the Close, they had sounded in Jurnet's ears like the trumpets of the blest. The screen was alive with movement. Police poured out of vans like dogs released for exercise, feet pounded over the ground. Even at second hand you could sense, in the midst of the danger, a tremendous elation, even merriment.

Some of the English Men got away, but not many. Soon it was all over, all that was left of the episode some bunting and bits of shredded cardboard which the three vergers, in torn gowns, were piling in a heap on the paving as if they intended a victory bonfire.

Not quite all. On the grass, watched by the girl in the English mackintosh, a doctor worked over the body of the young American. Pictures that the editor was quick to stress had not been broadcast showed an ashen face, eyes closed, blood trickling from the side of the mouth. The two detectives watched as the ambulance men eased the body on to a stretcher, the girl waiting stiff as the statues on the lawn. When they slid it into the waiting ambulance the onlookers began to drift away, full of what they had seen and of their own luck to have seen it. The ambulance, its siren blaring, passed under the arch of the FitzAlain Gate, and out of sight.

The screen went blank. Somebody turned up the

lights. The higher-ups brought in to fend off awkward questions inquired warily if there were any further way in which they could be of service. They had already confirmed that an anonymous telephone call had alerted them to the imminence of something newsworthy in the Close.

"Naturally—" one of them spread out well-manicured hands in a plausible simulation of innocence—"we assumed that the police were *au fait* with what was in train."

They spoke a little further of the public's right to know: offered sherry, which the Superintendent declined courteously.

"Inspector Jurnet and I have taken up enough of your time."

They did not deny it; escorted the pair to the main entrance, affable now at the prospect of getting rid of them. One of the long-haired young men, something to do with the sound balance, followed them out, and asked, "The American fellow—will he be all right?"

"Doubt it," Jurnet answered.

"The lousy bastards!" The long-haired young man went back inside.

It had grown dark. The street lights gleamed frostily, winter still lurking in the April night. Jurnet, who had dashed home to exchange his ruined suit for his only other one, which was thinner, felt chilled as he and the Superintendent made their way to the carpark. He tried nobly to stifle his resentment towards the Super, strolling comfortably in a twill topcoat.

The Superintendent said, "Impressive, don't you think?" Jurnet nodded, nosing the car out into the traffic. "Quite a trick, it must be—deciding the moment to stop filming and get back to base. Things so seldom come to neat ends."

Not this thing, that's for sure, Jurnet thought, but did not say.

The Superintendent continued, "I thought one of those vergers looked a bit worse for wear."

"Harbridge—I've mentioned him to you. They got him on the old wound he picked up the day the foot-

ball fans came to town. Wouldn't go to hospital. Said
he'd see his GP later."

"Not wise—unless it looked worse than it was. Blood
on television always looks bloodier than blood in real
life." The Superintendent looked sideways at his
subordinate. "I thought you looked awful."

"Lousy make-up man."

"I suppose there's nothing they left out?"

"Not so far as I could tell." Jurnet omitted to mention two small matters which had escaped the intru-
sive microphone and the prying lens. One was a
fleeting glimpse of Stan Brent among the lookers-on:
the other, the pale American girl. The detective had
taken her by the elbow to help her into the ambulance, and at the top of the steps she had turned and
said, "We've been married ten days—no, nine! Tomorrow we'll have been married ten whole days."

Jurnet groaned aloud.

"What is it, Ben?" the Superintendent inquired with
concern. "Something hurting?"

"A bit."

11

By the time Jurnet got to Bridge Street, to the front
entrance into that no-man's-land where Joe Fisher
stockpiled his wares, mist from the water meadows
was drifting across the roadway, blurring the neat
rows of artisans' dwellings on the other side of the
street, which marched up to the humpbacked bridge
over the river. The street lamps, rimmed in dull orange, cast a dim, religious light that was more dis-
quieting than darkness.

The detective felt low-spirited. His ribs ached, the
abrasions on his cheeks stung in the biting air. After
dropping off the Superintendent at Headquarters he

had intended to pop back to his flat, pick up a coat, have a drink, even open a tin or two. There were, he knew, a few cans of beans on the kitchen shelf, as well as some packets of a dehydrated chow mein to which, for a month of gastronomic lunacy, he had been unaccountably addicted. But now, the very thought of the Sino-chemical mess turned his stomach.

He did not go home.

He locked the car, crossed the pavement, and climbed the padlocked gate painfully, listening to his heart thudding against his damaged skeleton.

There was a light in the trailer. Jurnet was about to call out something reassuring when the door opened, a slight figure stood silhouetted at the top of the steps, and that voice, sweet and brainless and so unlike any other, inquired, "Joe?"

Almost, the detective wished he could say yes, just to make Millie Fisher happy. But a second later it seemed that Mr Ben could make Millie Fisher happy too: if not as happy as Joe, happy enough to be going on with.

"Mr Ben! Willie! It's Mr Ben!"

The boy appeared in the doorway as his mother ran down the steps and flung herself at the detective with her usual surfeit of joy. To Jurnet's customary feelings of guilt at her onslaught were added the pains of his hurt body. But when, looking down, he saw Willie, the little face upturned in expectation, he clenched his teeth and swung the child up on to his shoulder the way he always did.

"How's the big boy, then?"

"Mr Ben! Mr Ben!"

Joe Fisher, it appeared, had been and gone. He had brought gifts.

"Will yer take tea?" asked Millie, and this time Willie, jumping up and down with excitement, shouted, "You can, Mr Ben! We got a fast! A vacuum fast!"

Within seconds, Jurnet was seated on the bench, in front of him the "vacuum fast", from which he was adjured to help himself.

"Joe filled it up," Millie beamed, obviously convinced that no one but Joe could work the trick. "An' it stays hot an' hot an' hot!"

"Not for ever, barmy," the boy corrected her. "Not more'n a week, I shouldn't think." He turned to the detective with pride, "An' we got pastries!" He brought a cardboard box to the table and opened it to reveal some cakes somewhat the worse for wear. The child regarded them with passion, counted their number aloud, and inquired anxiously, "Would you like the chocolate one?"

"Just had my tea," said Jurnet, "and I'm full up to here—" drawing a hand across his throat. "But I wouldn't say no to a cuppa, if there's one going."

Joe Fisher had been gone some considerable time, Jurnet surmised, sipping his tea with every appearance of enjoyment out of the screw-cup on top of the flask. The tea was strong and sickeningly sweet. It was also lukewarm.

"Joe back soon?" he asked conversationally.

"He'll have to, won't he, when yer've drunk up the tea? Ter fill it up again." Millie giggled at her own craftiness.

"You're expecting him back tonight, then?" Jurnet put the cup down. Another drop, and he'd bring up the lot.

"You ain't drinking!" Millie's beautiful eyes clouded over.

Jurnet said, "Waiting for it to cool off." He took a deep breath, and swallowed all that remained in the cup.

Millie smiled beatifically.

"Now Joe'll come."

"Well," said Jurnet, who needed to vomit, "I must be getting along."

"You c'n come to tea any time," said Millie, "now we got a vacuum fast."

As, a few minutes later, rid of the dreadful brew, he leaned, shaky but revived, against the nearest Nissen hut, he felt a tug at his trousers—Willie, his straw hair bright even in darkness, his upturned face heavy with importance.

"I know where Joe goes!"

"You've not been following him about?" Jurnet's fears for the boy's safety eclipsed any satisfaction he might have derived from the information. "You'll get yourself run over."

The child drew himself up.

"I go to the chippie, don't I? An 'fer the milk an' the bread? I c'd go anywhere, if it weren't too long t' leave Ma."

"That's what I mean." Jurnet hastily retrieved his error. "You can't stay with your Ma if you're busy following your Pa all over the place."

"I *weren't* following him! I jus' come out of the grocery an' I seen him on the other side o' the street. So I thought I'd ask him for 10p for a sucker. Ma'd said I could 'ave one if there was any change, on'y there weren't any. So I thought, Joe's rich, I'll ask him."

"Who told you Joe was rich?"

The boy looked puzzled. Then, "He just *is*. So I waited till I could get across—" he looked at Jurnet severely. "I'm always *very* careful. On'y by then he was all the way up the street, an' I had to run after him—" The sentence petered out.

"Yes?" said Jurnet, encouragingly.

"I—" The little face creased and uncreased itself as the child struggled to convey feelings he could scarcely register, let alone put into words. The detective forced himself to stay silent, let the boy resolve his dilemma in his own way.

"Then," said Willie, "I didn' feel like a sucker arter all." He looked hard at Jurnet, daring a contradiction. "I often don't feel like one when I've just felt like one. He 'adn't seen me, so it didn't make no diff'rence."

"Did you go on following him?"

"It weren't far. He went down a street, an' then he went inter a house."

"Maybe he went to call on a friend."

Willie made no attempt to hide his scorn.

"He's got a lot o' keys on the end of a chain in his trousers pocket. He took it out, an' he took one of the keys an' went in." In case Jurnet still hadn't caught on, "He never knocked."

"Do you know what street it was?"

Willie's face crinkled up again. This time it was a child crying.

"Yer know I can't read!"

At that, Jurnet swung the boy up on to his shoulders again, the pain in his ribs swallowed in a greater one.

"Know what, young feller-me-lad? We're going for a ride!"

"Ma—"

"The three of us! To show me that street. Think you can remember where it is?"

"Jest 'cause I bleeding can't read it," Willie said savagely, "don't mean I don't know it!" After a moment he demanded, "What kind o' car?"

"Rover. New model."

"Rover!" But the cares were never far away. "Ma—" Willie began again.

"Look—" said Jurnet, setting the child on his feet again, "we don't want Ma to bother her head, do we, with houses and keys and stuff like that. You sit in front and tell me quietly where to go, eh? And when we get to the house itself, if you recognize which one it is, just give me a tug of the trousers, like you did just now, OK? Only don't pull 'em off, will you? Out in the street without my trousers, a police officer! That'd be a fine thing!"

To huge laughter at the thought of Detective-Inspector Benjamin Jurnet caught driving in his underpants, they came back to Millie, and caught her up in their glee. A ride! A ride in a new model Rover!

Upon Jurnet's insistence that the two wrap up warmly, Willie, from under the trailer bench, brought out a fur coat of ambiguous pedigree which filled the detective's mouth with hairs as he gallantly helped Millie into it. Willie himself had a duffle, dirty but warm.

"Jes' wait till I tell Joe!" exclaimed Millie.

The two ran gaily ahead of him, finding their way between the scrapheaps like cats in the dark, Jurnet lumbering behind by torch-light. Their excited voices came to him from the other side of the fence.

"Purple!" That was Millie.

Willie shouted, "Blue, silly! Police cars are always blue!"

Jurnet, unable to discover where the two had made their exit, heaved himself over the gate again.

"It *is* blue, in't it, Mr Ben?" Willie settled himself into the front passenger seat. "I tell 'er, but she won't listen."

"Purple!" cried Millie. Jurnet reflected that tomorrow, back at the police garage, the hairs on the back seat would require explanation.

He switched on the engine, put the car into gear, and pulled out from the kerb.

"You're both right," he said. "Blue in daylight, and purple after lighting-up time. So you're both winners."

"I told yer!" cried Millie, leaning forward and thumping her son on the shoulder.

Willie twisted round in his seat and shouted back triumphantly.

"An' I told *you!*"

Both winners! Jurnet's hands tightened on the steering wheel. Softly to Willie, so that Millie should not hear, he said, "Going the right way, Squire, are we?"

The right way led down Bridge Street as far as Bridge Gate, then veered away from the Close to follow the high wall which enclosed the Bishop's garden. A little before the curving lane widened into a fine ceremonial space facing His Grace's front door, Willie spoke low, and pointed.

Jurnet turned right and, a few hundred yards on in response to a further direction, right again.

He knew where he was now; but drove on nevertheless, so that Willie could have the pleasure of pulling his trouser-leg as they passed Mrs Cossey's front door.

In the back, Millie stretched out her arms luxuriously.

"Wait till I tell Joe!"

12

Professor Pargeter had been in Birmingham. Detective-Inspector Benjamin Jurnet took it as a personal affront that Professor Pargeter had been in Birmingham at the time when, in Angleby Close, events were happening for which, in the Inspector's view, the Professor must bear a large portion of the responsibility.

It had not needed much inquiry to discover where the English Men had come by the knowledge of what had been done to the corpse of Arthur Cossey. Every one in Angleby who could spare forty minutes, and many who could not, made a point of tuning in to the Professor's weekly lunch-hour programme on local radio.

"Pargeting" as it was called, was a combination of chat show, history lesson, and stand-up comedy which was deservedly popular. You never knew what to expect from the Professor—only that, at the end, somehow, along with the gossip and the blue jokes, you could reckon on emerging better informed than you had imagined possible on subjects as diverse as Neolithic droveways and Mayan concepts of time. The Professor—people were always saying it—could get away with murder.

That day he had got off to a good start, opening with the husband-and-wife team starring in a Noel Coward season at the Theatre Royal, a couple so manically intent on burnishing their togetherness image as to be totally unaware that, under the gentle promptings of their interlocutor, their exchanges were becoming bitchier by the minute. As for the closing item, a plea for the preservation of a nineteenth-century lunatic asylum scheduled for demolition, it was impossible to decide whether the Professor were being serious, or guying over-enthusiastic conservationists.

Two good "Pargeting" pieces. Between, the Professor, having noted offhandedly that young Arthur Cossey, murdered in the cathedral, had been mutilated in precisely the same way as Little St Ulf before him—to wit, castrated, and scored from throat to navel with the interlaced triangles of the Star of David—had launched into a compelling five minutes on the fascination of magical signs in general.

"And now for an act of vandalism, perpetrated—would you believe it?—not by some of those disturbed adolescents for whom our hearts never stop bleeding, but by the wiseacres of our local Council—" and so on to the threatened asylum. Listeners were already wondering whether they were meant to grieve or rejoice over the impending fate of "this incomparable Romanesque escape into the East Anglian landscape" when the penny dropped, with all the thud of delayed shock. *What was that again about Arthur Cossey?*

Immediately after the programme, which he always insisted on broadcasting live, the Professor had left for Birmingham to deliver a lecture at the University. Located there and brought to the telephone to receive Jurnet's call, he was cheerfully unrepentant.

"I bet Flossie's wetting his knickers!"

"I haven't spoken to the Dean."

The Professor's booming laugh came over the wire. "When you do, give him a kiss from me."

His voice expressionless, Jurnet said, "A young American tourist was seriously injured and is still unconscious."

There was a silence. Then the voice at the other end said, "Know something, Inspector? Play the clown long enough, it's the only bloody part you know how to." There was another pause. Then, "I hope you don't think I planned that little hullabaloo?"

Jurnet ignored the question. He said, "I think we should have a talk, sir. Today, if at all possible."

"I'll be back in Angleby by 8. Any time after that. I'm sure you know where I live. Inspector?"

"Sir?"

"If you think I had anything to do with the death of that child—"

After waiting, as it seemed to him, long enough, Jurnet asked again, "Sir?"

But the Professor had rung off.

When Rosie Ellers opened her front door to Jurnet, her plump, pretty face lost its habitual aspect of sunny unconcern. She rounded on her husband, shrugging on his raincoat in the little hall.

"Where were you, then, when the stones were flying?"

The little Welshman, rosy and unmarked, gave his wife a resounding kiss and edged round her to the door.

"Small is beautiful. Little fellow like me, he slips into the spaces between one bash and the next." Regarding the Inspector with a pitying eye, "Stand out like a blooming lighthouse, what d'you expect?"

Rosie said, "The Inspector ought to be in bed. Running a temperature, I shouldn't be surprised. *And* out without a coat and all!" She tut-tutted, and finished, "Couldn't Jack run you home, Mr Jurnet, and then do whatever it is needs doing on his ownsome?"

"Looks worse than it is," said Jurnet, who indeed felt terrible. But not as terrible as he would feel at home, on his ownsome.

"At least come in for a hot drink when you bring His Nibs back."

Jurnet was glad to let his subordinate drive. He himself sat slumped in the passenger's seat, watching the familiar streets stream past.

"What are we asking this bloke, exactly?" asked Ellers, troubled by the other's silence.

With an effort, Jurnet pulled himself together.

"We know he let the cat out of the bag after the Superintendent had particularly asked him not to. We've agreed that whoever killed the kid will want the peculiar nature of the inquiries made public, whether to give the old lies a fresh airing, or simply to deflect us from his real motive for murder. So—the Professor deliberately spilled the beans. Sinister, or just fucking irresponsible?"

"Can't see a chap like that hobnobbing with those English Ape-Men."

"Mosley in the '30s was a bart, and look who he knocked bout with."

"Oh, the '30s—"

"What makes you think the '80s are any different? You've read the English Men's manifesto. They've had to wrap it up in gobbledegook to get it past Race Relations, but it's all there—England for the English, and, in their book, that means white Anglo-Saxon Protestant." He looked at the little Welshman with amused affection. "Can't think where that leaves you, boyo."

They were in the outer suburbs now, a well-heeled district that had once been a village.

Sergeant Ellers turned the car out of the main road into a lane where house lights glimmered an expansive distance back from the road.

"Take to the hills, I reckon," he answered, smiling. "You and me both."

"Ever been in Brum?" Professor Pargeter greeted them, glass in hand. He had opened the front door himself and ushered the two detectives into a spacious hall full of bits of broken pottery Jurnet's old mum would long ago have put out for the dustman. "Don't, if you value your life."

Leading the way into a pleasant, book-lined room, he observed over his shoulder, "God alone knows how many bones lie bleaching beneath the Bull Ring, brave youths and beautiful maidens who never made it out of the labyrinth."

It was not an auspicious beginning, and it did not get any better. Jurnet, who was not frivolous by nature, and had never learnt to cope with frivolity, especially the academic variety, full of insensitive assumptions of a shared background, began to feel unwell again.

"Drink?" asked the Professor, replenishing his own glass at a side table loaded with decanters. He turned round and regarded his visitors, still standing, the tall and lean, the short and tubby, and burst out laughing. "Sit down, for Christ's sake! You look like Laurel and Hardy!"

He waved the two towards a deep leather sofa, on whose edge they perched embarrassedly. He did not appear to expect a reply to his offer of drinks, and made no move to provide any. Positioning himself in front of the marble mantelpiece, and waving his glass in a gesture that sent the liquid swirling dangerously, he demanded, without further preamble, "If I told you, Inspector, that the only reason I put in that bit about Arthur Cossey was because my producer asked for a little something to separate the two main items, and I couldn't for the life of me think of anything else on the spur of the moment, would you believe me?"

"Was it the reason, sir?" Jurnet began to feel better as he sensed a certain lack of assurance on the part of his questioner.

"You haven't answered my question, so I'm hanged if I'll answer yours! I'll try again. What would you say if I said I did it as a gesture—call it a blow for freedom—after that self-important dunderhead of a Superintendent of yours—" a blush of shock suffused Sergeant Ellers's face—"had the nerve to try and clap some kind of D Notice on me?"

"I'd say—*did* you do it as a gesture?"

The Professor rocked delightedly on his heels.

"Would you indeed? And if I went on to admit that, actually, the only reason I did it was to put Flossie's nose out of joint—what then?"

Master of himself again, Jurnet returned, "I would say that none of those reasons, nor all three of them put together, would add up to an adequate excuse for instigating a riot."

The Professor finished off his drink and set the glass down on the mantelpiece.

"Tell me—" he demanded. "*Was* Arthur Cossey's body mutilated in the way I described, or was it not?"

"You know it was. We discovered it together."

"Thank you!" An inclination of the head. "So at least you are not accusing me of perverting the truth, only of uttering it." The man's blue eyes were bright and angry. "There is, you must admit, a certain irony in being reprimanded by the police, of all people, for telling the truth."

"Aren't you being a bit naive, sir? It's not as if a lie's the only alternative."

" 'A time to keep silence, and a time to speak,' eh?" The anger faded, to be replaced by a rueful amusement. "Silence! From a professional blabbermouth! You don't know what you're asking!"

Jurnet said, "I reckon you know when to keep your mouth shut as well as the next man."

"I don't, you know." And now the amusement, too, had gone, leaving only the rue. "Know me better, Inspector, and you'll find that I wear my words as I wear my clothes—too loud, too sloppy, but what the hell? Anything to cover my God-awful nakedness." He crossed the room to some shelves from which he took an object smaller than a tennis ball. When he came back to the fireplace Jurnet could see that it was, in fact, a small stone head, reduced by time to a pebble, almost.

"Would it surprise you—" Professor Pargeter inquired, strong brown fingers affectionately tracing a rudimentary curl on the ancient artefact—"would it surprise you to know that the main reason I took up archaeology was because it was so quiet?"

"If you say so, sir."

"I do, Inspector! As you may have noticed, I'm a noisy person—too noisy by half. But the language of a fallen marble column, silent witness of a time of glory—" the man's face took on an earnestness that

Jurnet, who had seen it thus garnished often enough on the box, observed without notable conviction— "charred beams that speak silently of ancient pillage, even the siftings of some humble midden—there you have the essence of communication, once you've learnt to read the signs. Ah, if only the present could be as silent as the past! I'd be out of a job, but what a wonderful world it would be!"

"Silent's the last word I'd use for it, at the moment. Thanks to you, sir, Little St Ulf's shouting his sainted head off."

"Sorry about that. I really am." Professor Pargeter did not sound particularly sorry. He turned away and set the little stone head down, next to his empty glass. Back to the detectives, he inquired, "And the young man? How is he?"

"Not so good."

The Professor turned round. There was a silence. Then, "American, I think you said? How'd he ever get mixed up in something that couldn't possibly concern him?"

"Oh, but it did. It concerned him very much. He's a Jew."

"Is he, by Jove!" There was another pause. When the Professor resumed, his voice held a distinct note of pleading. "I'm sure you understand, Inspector, that one simply has to assume that all men are civilized— all one's countrymen, anyway—much as one has to assume that any aeroplane we board will bring us safely to our destination. The fact that we know perfectly well there are some men who are barbarians, and some planes which will inevitably, in the way of things, fall out of the sky, must not be allowed to dislodge that working hypothesis without which ordered life would be unthinkable. I'm sure you take my point."

"Assume all men are civilized," Jurnet returned stolidly, "I'm the one'd be down at the Job Centre. Anyone who assumes that goons like the English Men are civilized human beings has got hold of the wrong assumption. To put it bluntly, sir, it's all but impossible to credit that an intelligent person like yourself wouldn't have foreseen the possible consequences of that broadcast."

Professor Pargeter's lips twisted under his moustache, sending it a little askew.

" 'All but impossible'—for that pinhole of misgiving, much thanks! It can only mean, I take it, that you are not yet quite ready to arrest me for the murder of Arthur Cossey."

Jurnet ignored the thrust.

"Are you absolutely sure you didn't know the boy?"

"I am absolutely sure, just as I am absolutely sure that my sexual proclivities are not such as to make me the slightest danger to juveniles of my own sex, whether known to me or not. Mind you—" the blue eyes were mocking—"I've often felt that even a modest predisposition to pederasty would have done wonders for my understanding of the Ancient Greeks."

Ignoring the bait, Jurnet said, "I understand you have a key to the Bishop's Postern, the little door in the north transept?"

"I do, and so do Miss Aste and Mr Epperstein. If you tell Flossie I had duplicates made he'll have, *deo volente*, conniptions. Coming into the cathedral by our separate ways, it's been simply not on for only one of us to have a key, with the likelihood of keeping the other two hanging about in the cold of early dawn. And speaking of Miss Aste—" the tone had become measurably less genial—"she telephoned me. Was it really necessary to harass her with your questions the way you did? The child was really upset."

"Detective-Sergeant Ellers spoke to Miss Aste." Jurnet, who had his own, not very creditable, reasons for deputing his assistant to question the Honourable Liz, nodded to the little Welshman. "I hope, Sergeant, you'll be able to reassure the Professor that, despite what he may have been told, no harassment of any kind took place."

"Can't say that, sir!" Sergeant Ellers declared roundly. "Any amount of it! Only, not her—me! All but reduced me to tears. I threatened to complain to the Chief Constable, actually, if she didn't give over."

"Didn't give over what?" The Professor spoke as if he could guess.

"Telling such almighty whoppers."

"Oh, that!" The Professor smiled. "Liz always tells lies. You must never believe a word she says. She tells lies the way some people are left-handed. It's as natural to her as breathing."

Ellers lamented, "And there was I, thinking she was doing it on purpose! I couldn't understand how she could deny she'd even been in the cathedral on Sunday, when she bumped into you and Mr Jurnet on the way out, large as life. Something about picking up some slides, Mr Jurnet said."

"She keeps them up in the triforium," Professor Pargeter said, "along with all the other photographic stuff. The dust down below in the dig would ruin them."

Jurnet asked, "The triforium?"

"The gallery over the side aisles. Liz has been documenting our progress. She's a very talented photographer." The man hesitated, then spoke with a certain urgency. "She wasn't at the tomb, though. You can take my word for it even if you can't take hers. I pressed her particularly, because it seemed to me on the cards that if she *had* gone there for some perfectly innocuous reason, and caught sight of that dreadful carcass, she might well prefer to blot the whole thing out of her consciousness—nothing sinister, a perfectly understandable reaction—and swear she'd never been near the place. But in fact she hadn't."

"Then perhaps," Jurnet suggested, "she also told you what she did with the slides. She wasn't carrying anything she could have put them in when she ran into us, and that dress she had on certainly wasn't hiding anything. If she's the little liar you say, what makes you so sure she was telling the truth to you?"

The Professor said, "I'm the exception that proves the rule. Liz never lies to me. We have an understanding."

"I thought you might."

"Did you, now?" The Professor threw out his arms in a gesture between impatience and amusement, and subsided into an armchair, from whose depths he gazed up at the detective in mischievous contemplation. "Lord, what it is to be a policeman, with a mind like a sewer! Let me tell you, your Little St Arthur could never have put the bite on me, even if he had had ideas in that direction. My life is an open book—only available for perusal in the back room, true, but known to altogether too many readers for any ill-disposed person to attempt to earn a quick buck out of keeping it off the front pages."

Jurnet observed, "Odd that you should think to associate a mere child with blackmail."

"Suspicious, is that what you mean? I don't see why not. I believe the little brats to be capable of anything and everything their elders and betters get up to. But to get back to putting you in the picture, Liz's mother—Viscountess Sydringham as is, Mrs Mallory Pargeter as was—was my first wife. There've been a couple of others since, but not so you'd notice. Laura was the only one who amounted to a row of pins. Only, unfortunately for me, she fancied a title. When Sydringham came along I could no more stand in her way than I'd have expected her to stand in mine if they'd offered me the Directorship of the BM. Very decent chap, Sydringham."

Jurnet waited, knowing there must be more.

"Very decent chap, Sydringham," the Professor repeated. "Devoted to Laura and the children—Liz and her brother Mallory, my godchild. Quite understands that Laura and I like to get together over a cup of tea every now and again, to talk over old times." He arched his fingers together, and pressed the resulting edifice gently against his lips. "I can't be sure about Mallory," he said. "They had a Royal at Sydringham for the shooting. His bag was seventy-five brace of pheasant, six hares, and Laura. But Liz—" He sat smiling.

"She has beautiful blue eyes," said Jurnet, looking down into Professor Pargeter's blue eyes.

"That's not all she has, by God!" The Professor's face shone with pride.

"Does Miss Aste know of your true relationship?"

"Nothing's ever been said, though my guess is she can put two and two together as well as the next person." The Professor chuckled. "Not that it's stopped her trying to get me into bed, just for the hell of it."

"And do you approve of Miss Aste's association with Mr Stan Brent?"

"What makes you think I'm in a position to either approve or disapprove? I have no *locus standi*. But I'll tell you this—" the Professor jumped up, invigorated by the birth of a new idea—"if you're looking for a murderer, there's your ideal candidate!"

"Brent? We've nothing to connect him with Arthur Cossey."

"Go on!" urged the Professor. "Stretch yourself! You can dream up something if you put your mind to it. What if I tell you he's a pimp, supplying choirboys to half the diocese, and that young Arthur demanded an increase in his cut, or else? Or—how's this?—the lad found Liz and Stan having it off on the High Altar, and threatened to tell Flossie." He looked at the detective, and once again the dismaying boom of his laughter filled the room. "Don't look so outraged! I was only illustrating the possibilities of creative detection."

"Not in my contract of employment. We have to stick to the facts, I'm afraid."

"Well may you be afraid! No more dangerous beasts lurk in the undergrowth, lying in wait for the hapless wayfarer."

"They're all we've got," returned Jurnet, losing patience. "Or haven't, as the case may be. A child has been killed, and it's my job to find out who killed him. It's as simple as that."

"I'm glad it's simple." All trace of mirth had vanished from the Professor's handsome face. He paced thoughtfully across the room to a desk placed between two windows; and then, with the sudden movement of one who has come to a decision, bent down, opened a drawer, and took out a small packet which, returning, he held out to the detective.

"What is it?" But already, out of habit and experience, Jurnet had the packet to his nose, sniffing.

"Heroin, I suppose. Or opium. Cocaine? Don't ask me. I've no knowledge of such things, I'm glad to say."

"Where did you get it? You know it's an offence even to have it in your possession, unauthorized?"

"Come now, Inspector! You're a narrow man, but not, I think, a small one. I took it out of Stan Brent's anorak. He was up in the triforium with Liz—helping her fix a camera, or so they said—and then the pair of them went outside for a smoke. After they'd gone, I went up to the gallery to see what they'd been up to—as if I didn't know! It's really not an easy part to play, that of father incognito." His voice sounded heavy as he explained, "She keeps her photographic gear packed round with big squares of foam rubber. Quite a serviceable mattress they make, laid out side by side on the floor. In the circumstances I felt no compunction about going through the anorak pockets."

"You ought to have turned it in to us at once."

"What do you suppose Liz would say to my shopping her fancy boy? I warn you, Inspector—if you now, in your wisdom, decide to make something of it, I shall deny all knowledge of the stuff, and furthermore, make allegations of corruption against you and the good Sergeant here that will sound so convincing you'll end up believing them yourself. No: I present you with this abominable dust merely as my own modest contribution to that hoard of facts by which you seem to set such exaggerated store. Murder in the nave, dope in the triforium: it seems to me not inconceivable that there may be a connection. Cathedrals aren't what they used to be in my young days."

The gravity splintered, the clown reassumed his motley. Unless, thought Jurnet, it was the other way round: the gravity the mask the clown the man. "But

then, with Flossie and his go-go girls at the Deanery,
who's to say what's possible and what isn't?"

13

Jurnet let Jack Ellers drive him back to his semi, but
there he slid gingerly into the driving seat, grimacing
as his ribs came into contact with the steering wheel.
He refused to come in for the hot drink Rosie had
waiting.

"Give me hell, she will," the little Welshman
pleaded. "She's always lecturing me on how the
quickest way to get on in the Force is to suck up to
your superior officers."

"Clever girl! You do that."

"Yes, sir! Even those without the bloody sense to
know what's good for them, sir?"

Jurnet laughed and drove away. He was feeling
much better. The night air had cleared his head. The
pain in his ribs had quietened to an ache he would
quite miss when it stopped altogether. It was even
comforting, in a funny kind of way, to be reminded
of the reality of one's own body; to know one was
more than a dark shadow in a dark car speeding
through a darkened city like something out of Phan-
tom of the Opera.

He wound down the window and enjoyed the wind
on his face. Past the shops and the Georgian houses
that 200 years earlier had been suburbs themselves,
and now formed a silent reproach to the housing es-
tates beyond, Jurnet turned into the driveway of the
Norfolk and Angleby Hospital, savouring, as always,
at the back of his throat, the faint taste of apprehension which dated back to his operation for an appen-
dix ruptured on Angleby Secondary football ground
at the age of fifteen.

In the corridor outside the intensive care unit, the young American girl sat, still wearing her English raincoat. A police-constable a little further along the line of chairs got to his feet.

The girl smiled when she saw Jurnet, and raised a slim hand.

"Hi."

"Hi." The detective returned the smile, and, turning a little away, directed a questioning glance at the police-constable. The man shook his head slightly and, at a gesture from his superior officer, resumed his seat.

The girl said, "He's going to be OK, you know."

Jurnet sat down beside her.

"That's fine! When did they tell you?"

"They haven't—yet. I just know." Reassuringly, "Don't bother with thinking up the right words. I'm not kidding myself along. Mort and I just happen to be on the same wave-length, I guess. We communicate. I guess all people in love are the same."

The stab of envy that pierced Jurnet's chest set his ribs throbbing afresh.

He asked, "Is there anything we can do for you? There ought to be a WPC—"

"Policewoman, do you mean? She's gone over to the hotel to pick up my things. They say I can sleep right here. Everyone's been so kind! I hate to cause so much trouble. Though I guess it's Mort, really, that's caused it. That boy," she said fondly, "he's never happy unless he's setting the world to rights." With a glance at the detective's bruised face, "Too bad he had to get you mixed up with it."

"All in the day's work," said Jurnet, "and I reckon the first blow was struck a good many years before Mort got *his* in. Now—what about you? We can get in touch with the American Embassy, and they'll get on to your people in the States—"

The girl considered, then shook her head.

"I don't think so. If Mort was going to die it would be different. As it is—" she blushed, charmingly. "I guess you would call us elopers, if that didn't seem such a quaint old word in this day and age. My Dad's

mad I married Mort, and Mort's folks are mad he
married me." She turned on Jurnet eyes wide at the
absurdity of it. "Mom was OK, though. She said to
Dad, 'For Christ's sake, honey! It could've been a ni-
gra!' "

Not until he had parked his car outside the synagogue
and noted the light shining from a second-floor window did it occur to Jurnet that the Rabbi might be in
bed.

Just the same, he pushed the bell button.

Immediately Taleh gave tongue, and in a little
while Leo Schnellman, in baggy pajamas, came
downstairs and opened the door wide. The detective's
remorse at having disturbed him spilled over into his
greeting.

"Rabbi—it's past midnight! How many times do I
have to tell you to keep the door on the chain?"

"What is this—testing?" The Rabbi smiled. "Job,
in the land of Uz, had four doors to his house, so that
no one need ever have trouble finding the way in, and
you expect me to whimper 'Who's there?' through the
letterbox?"

Jurnet came into the synagogue lobby, carefully
shutting and bolting the door after him. Already he
could feel comfort spreading like balm through his
battered body.

Leo Schnellman said, "As it happens, I stayed up
for you. I saw the television news, and I thought you
might look in."

"I'd have been here earlier, only there were things
to do."

"Of course." Leading the way upstairs, "The coffee
should be hot still."

In the living-room Jurnet sat down on the leather
pouffe and cradled the mug of coffee in his hands.
Taleh came as usual to lay his head across the detective's knees.

The Rabbi stood, legs apart, on the hearthrug, a fat
man in rumpled pajamas. He made no reference to

Jurnet's bruised face, merely asked, "Is the coffee drinkable?"

"Fine." The detective took one sip and no more. He sat with head bowed, looking into the mug as if he saw something of importance mirrored in the dark fluid. After a little he said, "I'm afraid I'll have to let the lessons go for a bit."

"I understand."

Jurnet burst out, "What gets me is the way the kid's getting lost! Not enough he's dead, he's getting buried under a dung-heap of religion, and politics, and God knows what else. He's become a symbol. And he isn't. He's a kid. A poor dead kid."

"You're wrong." Leo Schnellman shook his head. "He's a poor dead kid *and* a symbol. Denying it isn't going to alter the fact."

Jurnet glowered at him. It was not what he had come to hear. He said, "I knew I could rely on your shoulder to cry on. I suppose you've got it in for me because I had young Master Epperstein over the jumps."

"Don't be stupid!"

Jurnet stared for a moment; then reddened, and looked away.

"I'm sorry. I need to get to bed."

"Yes. But first we'll have some fresh coffee."

Mosh Epperstein had drooped languidly on his chair in the interviewing room, his long arms dangling between his legs, and inquired, "Is it always this dead boring, being run in by the fuzz? Where's the high drama I'm always reading about?"

"You've been reading the wrong books." Jurnet kept his tone impersonal. "And let me put you right. You haven't been run in. We are simply seeking your help, just as we are seeking the help of a great many concerned citizens in order to discover the perpetrator of a brutal crime."

"So that's what it is! You could've fooled me. Just how that confers on you the right to give me the third degree—"

"You *have* been reading the wrong books! Suppose you clear up the misunderstanding by telling us exactly what you were doing in the cathedral on Sunday, and then we can both have the pleasure of bringing this interview to a close."

"I already told you. I'm a Matins buff."

"You were seen to leave the cathedral in what, in that setting, might be called indecent haste. Judging from your facial expression, you were in some distress."

"I was mortified. The Communion wine was plonk, can you believe it? I was on my way to ask for my money back."

Jurnet said, "You're a bit old for this kind of thing."

"OK." The voice was suddenly tired, drained of aggression. "I'd left some notes I was working on at the tomb."

"I see. What did you find there when you picked them up?"

"I didn't. Half-way down the nave I thought, for Christ's sake, it's Sunday: I need to get my head examined. So I turned round the way I'd come."

"What time was it you got to the cathedral?"

"Haven't a clue. The service was on, if that helps."

"I meant, earlier in the day."

"I wasn't there earlier in the day!" Epperstein's voice rose to a fractured treble. "What is this—a trap?"

"No. I understand you have a key to the Bishop's Postern. I merely thought you might have used it, to get some work done at the dig."

"On a Sunday? What d'you take me for—one of the world's workers?"

"Professor Pargeter seems to think highly of you."

"So he should, the old fraud, seeing I do the best part of his work for him."

"Do you, indeed?" Then, "Have a bit of a lie-in, Sundays, do you? Landlady bring you up a nice cup of tea?"

"If you're trying to find out whether I was out of the house early, the answer's yes. I went jogging."

"On your own?"

"On my own. I am," said the young man, "what the shrinks call a loner. It's not an offence, is it?"

"No," Jurnet acknowledged. "I just wondered whether you might not have been out jogging with Miss Aste, because it seems she was in the cathedral at exactly the same time you were."

"So were hundreds of others. Miss Aste," said Mosh Epperstein, "is not the jogging type."

"All the same, did you by any chance bump into her?"

"By no chance."

"Funny thing—" Jurnet rubbed his chin. "You came into the cathedral for some notes and didn't get them. She came in for some slides, and didn't get them either. What do you make of that?"

"I don't make anything of it," Mosh Epperstein said. "I'm not the Philip Marlowe look-alike around here." He stuck a bony hand into the back pocket of his jeans, and brought out a battered cigarette, two-thirds smoked. "Mind if I smoke?"

"Go ahead."

"Got a match?"

Jurnet opened a drawer and found a book of matches, which he tossed across the desk. He watched as the young man drew on the butt, the tight-drawn features under the frizzy black hair relaxing as he did so. All at once the detective's eyes widened in angry astonishment. He snatched the joint from between the archaeology student's lips.

"Of all the bloody nerve!"

Mosh Epperstein, mocking, "I asked, didn't I?"

The second pot of coffee was strong and scalding. Jurnet drank two cups.

Rabbi Schnellman asked, "Do you have to keep him in custody?"

"For crying out loud! We found another ten reefers on him, *and* a tin with traces of snow. He's got a solicitor if he wants to apply for bail. Lighting some grass right under the nose of the police officer interviewing him!" Jurnet calmed down and demanded, "Why? That's the question. Was he half-stoned already and didn't realize what he was doing? Were the questions getting too near the bone, or has he reasons for thinking he's safer locked up in a cell than out free on the streets? Not custody, but sanctuary. What or who is he afraid of?"

"You could have asked him."

Jurnet shook his head.

"I didn't trust myself to."

"You mean, because he's Jewish?" The other nodded. "But surely, in your chapel-going days, you didn't favour Baptists above Christians of other denominations?"

"I don't mean playing favourites—quite the opposite. I was leaning so bloody far backwards to avoid any suspicion of it, I couldn't be sure any more I was doing my job properly." Jurnet moved Taleh's head gently aside, got up, and moved restlessly about the room. "God, I *know* I'm not doing my job properly. There's a kid dead, and all I want is to get away from the side issues, back to the fundamentals—the body, the dick, the murderer, just the three of us getting cosily acquainted, not the re-run of an old movie that got itself an Oscar back in 1144. Just one solitary kid, not a massacre."

The Rabbi said, "One *is* a massacre." He looked towards the patch of night sky visible through the window. "Who could conceive a star if nobody had ever seen one? But once you've seen one of them, what's a galaxy? One comprehends all, which is why we are never more in tune with the Almighty than when we recite the *Sh'ma,* the declaration of His Oneness. All other numbers are an illusion, a mathematical confidence trick."

"There you go," Jurnet objected. "Turning Arthur Cossey back into a symbol again."

"No. The reverse. I'm turning the symbol back into Arthur Cossey."

The telephone rang. Leo Schnellman looked at his visitor.

"Anybody know you're here?" The detective shook his head. The Rabbi lifted the receiver. "Yes—yes—when? I see—are they—? Yes—" To Jurnet, the words were uncommunicative; but the changes in the Rabbi's expression had him waiting impatiently for the call to come to an end.

"Not necessary," said the Rabbi into the telephone. "I have transport. Detective-Inspector Jurnet is with me. We'll come at once."

He replaced the receiver, and announced quietly, "I won't be a minute. I have to get some clothes on."

At the door, he threw over his shoulder, almost casually, "Seems there's somebody in town likes old movies."

14

Lise's Patisserie was in Shire Street, a winding thoroughfare which the Angleby planners, for once repressing their urge to tear down and replace with something in reinforced concrete, had turned into the most delightful pedestrian precinct in the country. During the day the narrow roadway, paved over and set about with seats and shrubbery, resounded to the rat-tat of footsteps and the hum of conversation. It was a pleasant place to shop, to linger, to meet one's friends.

And the pleasantest place to meet one's friends was the pastry shop and café run by the Weisingers.

White-painted, with a green-and-white sunblind curving out from the fascia, Lise's Patisserie promised no more than it delivered. Whether, on sunny days, consumed at tables and chairs set out in the street, or, in less clement weather, eaten within, the Weisingers' apfelstrudel and Sachertorte surpassed anything to be found in Vienna, even in the days when Vienna *was*

Vienna. The coffee was wonderful; a rack of the day's papers was there for the reading; at a white-painted baby grand embowered in potted palms a delicately nurtured lady dispensed the melodies of her prime. The waitresses in their colourful dirndls were obliging, the prices were reasonable, and the Weisingers themselves were the best value of all.

They were a small couple, Lise plump and vivacious, Karl quieter. Angleby natives tended to boast about the Weisingers to visitors to the city, and take them to the Patisserie the way they took them to see the castle and the cathedral. It was invariably these visitors who commented on Karl's hands, immaculate in white cotton gloves, or who, in summer, when Lise wore short-sleeved blouses, remarked upon the number tattooed on her left arm.

Then, with voices kept low out of regard for their hosts' susceptibilities, but with that relish inseparable from having a shocking story to tell, the outlanders would be told that Karl, whose piano playing in the '30s had delighted musical Europe, was, like his wife, a survivor of Auschwitz, where the camp doctors, full of a scientific curiosity as to what made pianists tick, had reduced his hands to talons. According to some versions, Lise, who before the war had already begun to make a name for herself as a singer of *lieder*, had found him after the liberation dying in a ditch by the roadside, unwilling to be rescued maimed as he was; had nursed him back to health and self-respect, and to a love which more than compensated for all that he had lost . . . Though there were others who dismissed this as sentimental nonsense, declaring that the two had suffered enough to be spared the further humiliation of being reduced to characters out of a story in a women's magazine.

Whatever the truth of it, from Auschwitz to Angleby was a long journey: from piano and *lieder* to apfelstrudel and mandelkuchen even longer. True, Lise had never sung a note since the day camp was liberated, and Karl could no longer play the piano, which was a tragedy. Yet look how things turn out!

It was Karl who, notwithstanding his hands, made all those wonderful cakes. He had discovered in himself another form of genius, one which, in different circumstances, would have lain unknown and unused: and who—fingers quartering the plate for the last delicious crumb—were mere mortals to say it may not have been all for the best.?

"I am furious with myself!" Karl Weisinger greeted the two arrivals. He looked smart, even foppish, in a foulard dressing-gown with cravat to match. On his hands were gloves dazzling in their whiteness. "Why on earth did I ask the police-constable to telephone? At this hour of the night! Unpardonable!"

Leo Schnellman put up an admonitory hand.

"Please! I'm grateful. People so seldom permit me the delusion of thinking I can be of help."

Tieless, braces hanging, his black trilby grey with Taleh's hairs, he looked an unlikely candidate for ministering angel. But at the sight of him Lise Weisinger smiled for the first time since, in their flat above the shop, they had been awakened by the noise of the brick crashing through the plate-glass window below.

"No delusion, Rabbi," she said. "To see the face of a friend at such a time—there could be no help greater."

"Oh yes, there could! And Detective-Inspector Jurnet is here to provide it."

Karl Weisinger shook hands with a Continental formality. Jurnet, who knew the couple's history, and had, in Miriam's company, several times patronized their establishment, was pleasantly surprised at their composure. He could only surmise that, after all that had happened to them already, a brick through a window was not all that much.

The husband looked at Jurnet's face, and remarked, "If I may say so, the Detective-Inspector looks as if he could do with a little help himself."

Jurnet grinned.

"Not any longer. I've been visiting the Rabbi."

"Ah! Leo is a source of strength to us all. You were in the affair in the Close? We saw it on the News.

And I suppose—" taking in the mess of glass, the display stands and the candy boxes scattered about the tiled floor, where, among the devastation it had created, lay a raw, red brick—"this is a continuation of the same event?"

"Too soon to jump to conclusions," said Jurnet, who had jumped to them already. "PC Hubbard here tells me he's already taken down particulars, so I won't harrow you with going over it all again. Tomorrow, when you've got over the shock, we'll have a proper talk. Just one thing—after the crash, did you hear anything? Someone running away, or maybe more than one? Footsteps sound loud at night."

The man shook his head.

"We go to bed early, because we must be up early for the baking, and so we were deep asleep. Lise takes a pill—"

Lise Weisinger observed, in a matter-of-fact way, "It is difficult, is it not, when you have just woken up, to know what is reality and what is still the dream?"

"It's too bad!" Jurnet burst out, carried away by his imaginings of what might be the dreams of people with a past like the Weisingers. "That of all the people in the city, this had to happen to you."

"Of all the Jews in the city, you mean?" Karl Weisinger shrugged his shoulders. "It is of no significance. In a matter of this kind, you understand, all Jews are the same Jew."

There was no answer to that, and Jurnet attempted none. Lise exclaimed, "It could have been worse! Nobody has been hurt. What is a bit of broken glass, after all? Now, I am going to make a nice cup of coffee—" (Jurnet, who had already drunk three mugsful at the Rabbi's, contrived nevertheless to look suitably expectant) "—and then we shall all feel better. Karl, fetch some of the streusel kuchen, and make sure there is a table and some chairs with no pieces of glass."

"Are we permitted to tidy up?" her husband asked Jurnet.

"Don't touch the brick. Being so porous, they're not

much use for prints as a rule, but you never know. I'll send a man round first thing. And somebody'll be coming to relieve PC Hubbard—"

Lise Weisinger, bringing cups and saucers from the kitchen behind the shop, put down the tray. It was the first time Jurnet had seen fear in her face.

"You think they may come back?"

"Nothing like that," the detective hastened to reassure her. "It's the broken glass, and that hole in the window. Somebody passing might get themselves cut, or some yobbo with a bit too much beer inside him decide to help along the good work. Tomorrow I can let you have some names. We keep a list at Headquarters of firms that do this kind of work at short notice—"

Karl Weisinger inquired with polite interest, "To mend the broken window, Inspector, or the broken dream?"

Jurnet stared, and stammered, "I beg your pardon?"

One of the white-gloved hands was raised in smiling admonition. "Please! It is we, the dreamers, who should be asking pardon of you for being so much trouble, for forgetting that the essence of a dream— its geometrical proof, as you might say—is that, sooner or later, one wakes up." With a crunch of glass underfoot, the man crossed to his wife's side and put a loving arm round her plump shoulders. "Lise and I, we have been very happy here in England. The English people have been very good to us. But now the dream is ended."

"Just because a couple of louts—" Jurnet began in protest. The other cut him short.

"You really think that is all it is, you with your hurt face from today's doing in the Close? You with the murderer of that poor child still to find?" Karl Weisinger shook his head. "No, my dear Detective-Inspector, do not deceive yourself, and do not ask us to deceive ourselves either. Nothing is changed. The evil that was there still flourishes; a weed which, cut down, merely reappears in another place. It is all be-

ginning again, just as it began all those years ago. And
we are no longer young, Lise and I." Turning to Leo
Schnellman, "You must forgive us, my dear Leo, for
feeling that we really cannot face it a second time."

Braces dangling, the Rabbi still contrived to look
like an Old Testament prophet as he demanded
sternly, "What kind of foolish talk is this? If fear ex-
cused self-murder Jews would have vanished from the
face of the earth centuries ago."

"You are mistaken." Karl Weisinger shook his head
again. His grasp round his wife's shoulders tightened.
"We are not afraid. Fear is a positive emotion. It does
not kill. It reminds you how wonderful it is simply to
draw breath. Do you think that, in Auschwitz, we
could have borne the agony of awaking to another
day and another day if, unbearable as each day was,
it was yet more bearable than the only alternative?"
With a smile of great sweetness, "To be beyond fear
is to be beyond hope, and alas, my dear friend, the
truth of it is that tonight we are beyond hope. Tired."
In a voice so low as to be barely audible, "Tired unto
death."

But at that his wife pulled herself free, her bosom
heaving, her eyes shining with love and impatience.

"Pay no attention to him, Rabbi! Who does he think
he is, that the world must change to suit his convenience? Nothing is changed, the fool says, as if all our
years together have no meaning! As if, given the choice
all over again, I shouldn't choose Auschwitz with Karl
rather than Buckingham Palace without him! *The
dream is broken!*" she repeated scornfully. "Who needs
dreams so long as we have each other?" Unmindful of
spectators, Lise Weisinger embraced her husband with
a passion that aroused in Jurnet feelings of loneliness
and longing. "And now, *Liebchen,* the kuchen. You
are keeping our guests waiting!"

Jurnet had parked his car round the corner from the
pedestrian precinct, and the two walked the short distance from the Patisserie in silence. At the corner the
Rabbi stopped and gazed unseeingly into a shop win-

dow full of the latest in gents' suitings. The contrast between Leo Schnellman's *ensemble* and the high fashion within would have been enough to make Jurnet smile. If he had felt like smiling.

The Rabbi's face, reflected darkly in the plate-glass, looked old and defeated.

He said broodingly, "There was a man called Ishmael ben Elisha, who was martyred in the reign of the Emperor Hadrian, and who wrote a commentary on the Book of Exodus. It is called *Mechilta*, which means 'Measure', and it is the measure of many things. What worries me are some words of Ishmael ben Elisha. Words which warn Israel not to treat the Almighty the way heathens treat their idolatrous images; praising them when something good happens, and cursing them when things don't turn out right. God, Ishmael ben Elisha points out, doesn't operate that way. *'If I bring happiness upon you, give thanks: and when I bring suffering, give thanks also.'*" His voice suddenly harsh and despairing, the Rabbi said, "I am finding it very hard to give thanks."

Jurnet unlocked the car and held the front passenger door open.

"I'll drive you home." With as much conviction as he could muster, "Things'll look better in the morning."

The Rabbi got in obediently. Jurnet had set the car in motion, reversing in the narrow lane to go back the way he had come, when the Rabbi suddenly cried out "No!" and opened the door without waiting for the detective to stop.

Jurnet jammed on the brakes and said severely, "That was a stupid thing to do."

"Yes. I'm sorry. I have to go back."

"What's up now?"

"Karl. He may not be afraid—but I am." The fat, lumbering man swung his legs round, fumbled with his safety belt. "How do I get this thing undone?"

"Hang on," Jurnet objected. "PC Hubbard's on duty. There'll be someone there right through to daylight."

"Your police-constables can't follow them into their bedroom."

"Neither can you," the other pointed out reasonably. "Let me get you home, Rabbi. Mrs Weisinger won't let her husband do anything silly."

"Love," said the Rabbi, "as you yourself may have noticed, incorporates every other quality except judgment." Having found the release point for the belt, he got his feet down on the ground at last and levered himself out of the car. "No need for you to wait, Ben."

Jurnet said nothing, but parked the car once more straight with the kerb. He caught up with Leo Schnellman as he turned the corner again into Shire Street.

"What the—!"

Music sounded along the street, dimly-lit save where light spilled out from the Weisingers' wrecked shopfront. The two men could see the police-constable standing on the pavement, his face turned towards the interior, his mouth open.

Was it music, though? There was something odd about the sound; a jangling, not quite a tune, yet that tune vaguely familiar. And now somebody was singing, a woman, in a voice that was a ruin haunted by the ghost of a glorious past.

Leo Schnellman was murmuring something under his breath. Hebrew, Jurnet thought, though he could not be sure. The music grew louder, the woman's voice more confident. In the upper storeys along the street lights were appearing, curious faces at the windows. By the time the detective and the Rabbi reached the Patisserie the Weisingers had swung into full stride. Karl sat at the white-painted piano, his hands bouncing up and down the keyboard with energy and determination. His white gloves lay on the floor, tossed among the broken glass. One hand on his shoulder, his wife stood behind him, peering forward at the sheet music, part of the delicately nurtured lady's repertoire, open on the stand.

"*Picture you upon my knee—*" Lise Weisinger sang,

tears, of which she appeared unaware, coursing down her cheeks. *"Tea for two and two for tea—"*

Her husband at the piano seemed to be watching what his dreadful claws were up to with the amused indulgence of a disinterested spectator.

*"Me for you and you for me
Alone!"*

On the *Titanic*, Jurnet reflected, watching from the shadows at once exalted and humbled, they had opted for a hymn tune. No one could say there wasn't a wide choice of music for a shipwreck.

Lise bent down and kissed the back of her husband's neck. Karl turned over the page and the two launched themselves into a spirited approximation of *Lazybones*. Infected by the prevailing joy PC Hubbard joined in the chorus in a resounding baritone. At an upper window someone clapped.

The Rabbi's face was radiant, and now Jurnet could hear the words.

"If I bring happiness upon you, give thanks: and when I bring suffering, give thanks also."

As if by common consent, the two men turned away together, without making their presence known. Ensconced in the car again, driving back to the synagogue, Jurnet could not resist asking, "And if He brings suffering and happiness together at the same time, what then?"

"That's easy. Thank Him twice over."

15

"I've been having a word with the Chief," the Superintendent began urbanely. It was the opening move of a game Jurnet could have played blindfolded, so many times had the two of them played it together. "He says you'll have to have help. What do you think?"

"Whatever you say, sir."

The Superintendent looked as though he could not believe his ears.

"You feeling all right, Ben?"

Jurnet, though not in humorous mood, permitted himself a smile. What he ought to have said, abiding by the rules, was, "I believe Sergeant Ellers and myself can cope, sir,"; from which point on the exchanges would develop gracefully towards a conclusion acceptable to all participants, the Chief Constable included. Jurnet, who hated to work with anyone beside Ellers, would agree to join forces with Inspector So-and-So and Inspector Such-and-Such; the union being postponed for a period long enough, with luck, to enable the Jurnet-Ellers team, unaided, to bring the investigation to a successful close.

Today, for all he cared, the Superintendent could put his murder where the monkey put his nuts.

"I said you should have taken sick leave."

Jurnet, who knew that, in actual fact, he would howl blue murder if the Superintendent took him off the case, pulled himself together. "I'm OK, thanks. It wasn't the murder itself I was thinking about. More the attendant circumstances."

The Superintendent got up from his chair and strolled over to the window. He pushed it open and let in the sound of birdsong.

"I know what you mean. Child killings are usually the simplest. Sex and domestic violence—and there you've got 99 percent of them. But not Arthur Cossey. He's a pebble, thrown into a pond and making ripples that spread wider and wider." He came back to his desk and sat down again. "What I had in mind was this: to bring pebble and ripples, if I may mix my metaphors, under one umbrella, the handle of which will remain firmly in your hand. That should give at least the appearance, if not the reality, of a team at work. Which I trust—" the Superintendent finished with an air of demure mischief—"will prove satisfactory to both you and the Chief Constable."

"Thank you, sir."

"Hale and Batterby are already dealing with the demo. You'll have to fill them in on this brick-throwing caper. By which I mean, have a jar with them from time to time. Even make use of their services, if you can bring yourself to do it."

"Yes, sir."

"Get along with you!" the Superintendent exclaimed. "Don't take any longer than you have to."

"No, sir," replied Jurnet, repressing the urge to say more. *The bloody twit!* How long did he think he intended to take?

"By which I mean, I know you won't take a minute longer than you have to."

One of the best, the Superintendent.

With the best will in the world, Mr Hewitt, who had been Arthur Cossey's form master, was not being very helpful.

"His friends?" repeating Jurnet's query. "D'you know, offhand, I can't think of a single boy—" He broke off, a rueful expression on his good-natured face. "I take it as a shocking reflection on my own performance. Hang it, it's my business to know who a boy's friends are!"

"Unless there aren't any."

"Oh, come now! We may not be entirely a happy band of brothers, but there's a team spirit, a camaraderie." Mr. Hewitt finished, a little forlornly, "He was, of course, a very quiet boy."

"So everyone tells me. Bright, was he, at his school work?"

The schoolmaster pursed his lips.

"Difficult to say. Mediocre, so far as marks went, but one had the impression of a lively intelligence at work, if only he could be persuaded to use it. He was good at art, but hopeless at games—" Mr Hewitt's tone left no doubt as to which of the two activities he considered the more important—"and then, of course, there was the choir. Mr Amos always said we hadn't had a Song Scholar with a voice of that quality in years." With dawning relief, "Mr Amos is the person you should be speaking to, really. His relationship with the choristers is, in the nature of things, so much more personal than is possible in the Cathedral School proper."

Jurnet came out of the Cathedral School into the Upper Close, his ribs responding with a sympathetic twinge to the sight of the late battlefield. There seemed to be rather more visitors about than usual. The Dean and Chapter were on to a good thing, had they only the sense to take a lesson from history: 50p to see where the deed was done: two sainted little buggers for the price of one, half-price for children and senior citizens. Just let some old biddy cry out that her arthritis was cured, and they had it made.

The detective joined the thin stream of people filing into the nave, his face turned resolutely away from the memorial inscription in the corner by the door. The vergers moved about busily, looking, in their long gowns, as if they rolled on casters. At the bookstall Miss Hanks had as much business as she could handle.

A rumble sounded from the organ loft, followed by a fluting chord, and then another, heavy with authority. Taking the sounds as an invitation, Jurnet made his way along the north aisle, past the grey-boarded enclosure whose admonitory "Private" was now fortified with a corral of hurdles lashed together with lengths of chain. A large notice proclaimed uncompromisingly: NO ADMITTANCE.

The door to the organ loft was open. Jurnet went up the stairs as quietly as he could, hoping to find at the top the man he was looking for. Presumably there were others besides Mr Amos who came out of the woodwork from time to time to tootle on that oversize tin whistle.

As the detective came out on to the floor of the organ loft, Mr Amos swung round from the console.

"I'm afraid nobody's allowed—" He broke off, blinked with eyes slow to read just from the concentrated light over the keyboard. "You were with the Dean—"

"You've got a good memory."

"No," Mr Amos replied, with a simplicity that had Jurnet completely off-balance. "It's simply that you have a memorable face. Just the same—" he wagged a finger in reproof, as Jurnet could imagine him wagging it at his choristers—"the organ loft is strictly out of bounds to members of the public."

"I don't know that I'd qualify as that, exactly. My name's Jurnet. Detective-Inspector Jurnet. I'm a police officer."

"Oh dear!" said Mr Amos compassionately. "How awful for you!"

"There are worse fates."

"I'm being silly," Mr Amos declared. "It's my besetting sin. Do please stop me if I do it again. It always happens when I'm preoccupied."

He half-turned back to the console, and ran a loving hand over the manuals. "Something's not quite right with the General Cancel. And I'm not all that happy about the Great Tomba either. And now—" as if giving his attention to some other mechanism not functioning as smoothly as one might wish—"you want to ask me some questions about that poor murdered child."

"A few, sir, if you please. What I'd like to have from you first, though, is a bit about the choristers' Sunday routine. What time they have to turn up, and how it goes from then on."

"That's easily told. Morning service starts at 11, and I require the choristers to be in the Song School, robed, by 10 sharp. We've never had any difficulty. The boys are often here early, either to play games in the cloister, or to do their prep. So far as I'm concerned, however, to rush hotfoot into the House of God at the last minute, and expect to sing Tallis or Aylward as they should be sung, is simply not on. There has to be an interval, however brief, between the Kingdom of Earth and the Kingdom of Heaven."

"In that interval, what do you do?"

"We have a little under an hour, usually. The Song School is at the far end of the cloister. We have to allow sufficient time to organize ourselves into a crocodile, walk the length of the cloister to the door in the south transept, and take our places ready to process with the clergy to the altar and the choir-stalls. To make the most of such time as we do have, I generally begin with a few exercises to clear the throat and head. We may sing a few bars of an anthem or a canticle. Nothing set. A calm, relaxing time that always seems to end too soon."

"What do you do—you yourself? See the choristers into the stalls, then nip up here to play the organ?"

"Gracious, no! The procession has to make a proper introit, so that everybody in the cathedral is made aware that something wonderful is about to happen. Once I've made sure the choir has assembled itself in proper order I leave them, and hurry here to play the procession in."

"It can't be the easiest thing to play the organ up here and conduct the choir down there at the same time."

Mr Amos gave his jolly laugh.

"It's lovely! Only wish I could do it all the time." Explaining, "I'm only the Vice-Organist. Dr Hurne, our Organist, is touring the Continent, giving recitals. Last Sunday—" the man's utter lack of envy was indeed lovable—"he played in Cologne Cathedral! What do you think of that! Everybody says it was a triumph! You really should make a point of coming along to hear him when he gets back. Oh dear—silly me again!" Mr Amos sighed. "I do apologize. I had no right whatever to assume you were not a regular cathedral-goer."

"Not all that regular," Jurnet returned, poker-faced. "You cathedral people, on the other hand," he went on, turning the other's *faux pas*, rather cleverly, he thought, to his own purpose—"obviously you have to attend when you're needed, feel like it or not. But how many services do you attend that you don't have to?"

"Such as last Sunday morning's Communion you mean?" the little man stated, rather than asked. "Yes, I was there, at 8 o'clock, in St Lieven's chapel." He added, "I expect you will also be interested to hear that I was in the cathedral a good deal earlier than that. Not much past 7."

"Indeed, sir? Any special reason?"

"For the very special reason that I would rather be there than anywhere else in the world." Mr Amos looked at the detective with eyes of a transparent candour. "I live in the Lower Close—one of those houses which were recently turned into flats. I have no wife, I live alone, and I am a confirmed early riser. Once awake, I find that my thoughts invariably turn to this place, and, more often than not, as soon as I have got myself dressed, my feet also. These spring mornings—" his eyes brightened just to speak of them—"the cloister is absolutely delightful! Shadow and chill at first, and then comes the moment when the sun clears the eastern wall—magic!" In the voice of one promising a great treat, Mr Amos exclaimed, "You really must come one morning and see for yourself!"

"I must do that." Then, "How do you get into the cloister so early?"

"From the Song School. I have keys to both doors, of course—the one that opens into the Close, and the one on to the south cloister."

"What about the cathedral proper? Could you get into that, if you wanted to, before it opens for business?"

"Certainly. I also have a key to the Prior's Door into the south transept. Not that I used it on Sunday. The cloister was so lovely, and so quiet. For once, none of the boys was there to play their games—traditional, but so noisy! I sat until it was almost 8 o'clock. By then, the Prior's Door was unlocked anyway, and I went directly to Communion."

"Did you notice anybody about in the nave as you crossed the transept?"

The Vice-Organist shook his head.

"I'm afraid I can't help you." Again he lifted to Jurnet eyes that were disturbing in their utter lack of guile. "I was on my way, unworthy as I am, to partake, if only symbolically, of the body and blood of

Our Blessed Saviour. Called to such a feast, do you really expect me to notice who was and who wasn't about in the nave?"

Somewhat at a loss, Jurnet turned away and looked over the chest-high panelling which fenced in the organ loft, discovering that, from that vantage point, it was possible to see down into the Little St Ulf dig. The actual excavation was cut off by part of the hoarding, but the table was visible, and some bowls and sieves piled haphazardly in a corner. Turning back to Mr Amos, who had followed the direction of his gaze, the detective was taken aback to see that the man's eyes were full of tears.

Jurnet said awkwardly, "It's hard to accept the violent death of a child."

Mr Amos nodded, and a tear fell down upon the sandy hairs that coated the backs of his strong little hands.

"Even a boy like Arthur," he said.

"I can see," Mr Amos said, "that I must get this over and done with. Otherwise you'll be wondering whether it was I who killed him." The Vice-Organist looked down at his clasped hands, his head a little to one side. "Poor Arthur! Poor little boy, so odious and corrupt!"

Startled, Jurnet said, "If that's what you thought of him, I don't know what you're so upset about."

"To be cut off in sin, with no possibility of repentance—is not that the most terrible fate of all? To die young and still not innocent?"

Jurnet demanded, "What did he do?"

"He never was an attractive boy—" the other appeared to go off at a tangent. "A pale mean look and a mean, slope-shouldered body. Hard to believe a frame so unlovely could house a voice of such angelic purity. If you had heard him in Tallis's Canon—!" Mr Amos broke off and shook his head in affectionate bemusement.

The detective, trained to listen, said nothing. The Vice-Organist, exactly as if the other had made some observation, went on, "Ah! You've noticed I began by talking about Arthur's looks, and I imagine you find that suspicious—understandably so, you who must spend so much of your time in dark places. So when I say further that not only do I love my boys for their divine gift of song, but that I find the physical beauty, equally God-given, of the well-favoured ones as great a delight to the eye as the other is to the ear, I may well confirm your worst fears." The man regarded Jurnet comfortably. "You will think me ridiculously naive, I'm afraid, but Arthur was the first to bring home to me the construction the outside world might put upon my unthinking admiration of young male beauty."

"Threatened you, did he?"

"Please!" Mr Amos put a protesting hand. "Now you're thinking badly of him, when pity is what's called for. For myself, I'm immensely grateful to him for trying to blackmail me as a homosexual. It really doesn't do, does it, to go through life a moral simpleton?"

Jurnet refused to be deflected.

"So he asked you for money?"

"He importuned me to buy him an easel and a set of oil paints. If I didn't, he said, he would write to the Dean and complain that I was sodomizing the choristers."

"What did you do?"

Mr Amos opened his eyes wide, as if the question astonished him.

"Nothing, naturally."

"You didn't think of having him up in front of the Dean as a lying little so-and-so?"

"But then he would have been expelled without a doubt. And his mother is a widow, of very modest means. I could not bring myself to jeopardize a boy's future on account of a youthful venality which, with God's help, he might outgrow. Especially as I felt myself in some degree culpable, in having behaved in such a way as to put the idea into the child's head in the first place."

"So what happened?"

"Oh, he wrote his letter, just as he said he would. Anonymously." Mr Amos looked at the detective hopefully. "I think that was a good sign, don't you? It showed, wouldn't you say, that he already had some misgivings? A stepping back from the brink?"

Jurnet chose not to leave the man that comfort.

"Gave himself an out, is how I'd interpret it. In case things went against him. What did the Dean do?"

"He sent for me, of course. To ask if I had any idea who might have written it."

"Not whether the charges it contained were true?" Mr Amos bowed his head.

"That too."

"And you still didn't give the boy away?"

"How could I? When challenged directly on the point, I had to say I thought I knew who was responsible; but that, equally, I did not feel able to pass the name on."

"And how did the Dean take that?"

"He was not pleased." Mr Amos's troubled expression deepened. "Will he have to know now that it was Arthur?"

"It wouldn't surprise me if he's put two and two together already. You understand," Jurnet insisted, "that I myself am quite unable to give any undertakings of any kind."

"I understand." Mr Amos sighed. "It's just that it seems such a pity, now that he's dead and can do no more harm."

"That remains to be seen," said Jurnet. "He's not doing too badly so far."

16

"Wet," said Christopher Drue. In the shadowy cloister the boy's voice had an odd, sweet resonance. "If you really want to know, Arthur Cossey was the most awful drip."

Jurnet said, "I really want to know."

The boy hesitated and then—or so it seemed to the detective—decided to give his questioner his trust. Jurnet, who saw the decision mirrored in the vivid young face across which thoughts and impressions chased each other like clouds before the wind, was foolishly glad of it.

"I know we're not supposed to speak ill of the dead," the boy went on, "and I *am* awf'ly sorry for him. I'm sure I shouldn't like to be murdered, whatever sort of drip I was—but it wouldn't be honest not to tell the truth to a police officer, would it?"

"It wouldn't be honest not to tell the truth to anyone."

"Oh, yes, sir! But especially a policeman. I mean, you could do things if I told lies."

"Like shutting you up in a dungeon and putting you on bread and water? Let's hope it won't come to that! Mr Amos couldn't think of anyone who had been what you might call real friends with Arthur; and you were the nearest thing he could get to it. Mostly, I think, because you walk in line together in the choir. So don't worry. I'm not expecting to hear you two were like David and Jonathan, if you know who they were."

"Yes, sir. The Bible. Jonathan got killed too, didn't he?"

"So he did. I should have known they teach you

scripture in the Cathedral School. What Mr Amos did say was that whatever you might think of Arthur, he had the impression that Arthur thought the world of you. Was that right?"

Christopher nodded gravely. A dark lock of hair flopped over his forehead. "He had a crush on me. He followed me about everywhere, like a dog. Even if I went to the loos. It was an awful bore. He'd never take no for an answer."

"Why didn't you want him for a friend?"

The boy concentrated with drawn brows.

"I didn't like him in the first place because he was who he was in the first place. I mean, you can't like a drip, can you? Nobody can."

"It *is* hard," Jurnet conceded. "Just the same, were there never times when you let him join in with whatever it was you were all doing?"

"We let him play marbles with us. He was rotten at it, but he used to buy all the special kinds—not the ordinary 35p a bag ones, the big ones you buy separately. Some of them cost 35p *each*! Arthur was the only one with money to buy marbles like that." Christopher chuckled. "We always won them off him, though."

"Where did he get the money from, do you know?" The boy looked startled, as though the question had never before occurred to him. "I mean, his mother's not well off, from all I gather."

"He had a paper round," Christopher suggested doubtfully. Then, with a brilliant smile, "But you'll find out about it, won't you, being a detective."

Jurnet grinned.

"I'll do my best. Now, what about weekends and school holidays—did you ever see him then, out of school?"

"Not if we saw him first! Sometimes, if we were standing about with our bikes, he'd come up and want to go riding with us. Do you know, he had the best bike of anybody in the form—seven speeds—and he still couldn't keep up for toffee!" The child laughed merrily. "It never took us long to give him the slip!"

This glimpse into the jungle of childhood prompted Jurnet to observe, though with careful detachment, "That must have upset him a bit."

"Upset Arthur!" Plainly, the possibility had not occurred to his school fellow. "Nothing upset Arthur. He was always smiling. We once thought of asking his mother if he smiled when he was asleep, but we were afraid she might not like being asked. Mr. Hewitt was always on at him to take that silly grin off his face." Coming so close to the detective that a rosy cheek rubbed against Jurnet's jacket, he added, a little breathlessly, "Why, he even smiled when—"

"When what?"

"I don't know whether I ought to tell you." Then, "Will you tell Mr Hewitt?"

"I shouldn't think so."

"Or Mr Amos?"

"So long as you aren't going to tell me it was you who killed him."

"It was something worse, in a way," Christopher asserted solemnly. "Well, not worse, but—" He broke off and tried again. "It was only because he was always saying how much he liked me and how there wasn't anything he wouldn't do for me—"

"So?"

"So one day when he said it we were in the Lower Close, and a lady was there, walking her dog. And just as she went past us the dog sat down and did its business."

"Well?" demanded Jurnet.

"Well, I was so sick of hearing there wasn't anything he wouldn't do, so I said—" the boy's face was completely hidden now, pressed into Jurnet's jacket— "so I said, if you mean it, then eat the dog's do." Another pause. "And he did. *And* he was still smiling. It was all over his hands, and some of it was smeared round his mouth, but he was still smiling."

"Are you very angry?" the boy ventured at last, when the silence had been prolonged. The cloister lawn sparkled in the sun. Had the old monks, Jurnet won-

dered, been allowed out there, or had they been con-
demned to promenade these freezing alleys, mortify-
ing the flesh for the love of God? Had they loved God
enough to eat dog shit in His Name?

Did he, Jurnet, love Miriam enough to do it, should
she call for such a bizarre proof of his passion? He
knew he never could; and he stood, silent, shaken with
envy for the great love Arthur Cossey had borne for
the boy at his side.

Jurnet said, "I'm not angry at all."

"Just the same, if I'd known he was going to be
killed, I'd have tried to like him. I don't know if I
could, really, but I'd have tried."

"No one can say fairer than that," said Jurnet, returning, with an effort, to the matter in hand. "The
choir, now—let's chat about that a little. It must mean
a lot of extra work."

"I don't mind. I like the singing, and learning about
music. And I quite like going into the cathedral in a
procession and dressing up in a cassock and ruff and
a white surplice on Sundays." With a rueful little
laugh, "One thing—I won't have to tell Arthur about
his ruff now." He explained, "We have to bring our
fresh things to Saturday morning practice so everything's ready for Sunday. Only my mother—she's a
lecturer at the University and too brainy for house-
work—doesn't understand about starch. Some weeks
my ruff's so stiff it's like a board; and other times—
though she's used exactly the same amount, that's the
amazing thing—it flops all over the place, and you'd
swear, if you didn't know, it hadn't been starched at
all. Well, last Saturday was one of the floppy days, and
Mr Amos gets into such a stew about floppy ruffs you
can't imagine. So when I came into the cloakroom on
Sunday and saw Arthur's still hanging on his peg I
thought he must be staying home with one of his colds—
he was always getting sniffles—and so I borrowed it."

"Taking a chance, weren't you? It could have been
he was just later than you arriving."

"And then he'd have been stuck with my floppy old
thing and have to lump it!" Christopher giggled. "He

wouldn't have minded—because he had such a crush on me, you see. Anyway, Arthur was never late. I'm the late one, 'specially on the Sundays Mummy and Dad drop me off on their way to golf." After a little, "I hope Mrs Cossey won't mind. I put the ruff back after the service, but of course she'll have to launder it, now it's been worn. She does them so beautifully I wanted my mother to pay her to do mine at the same time as she did Arthur's, but Mummy thought it might hurt her feelings, I don't know why. She does cleaning for some people we know in the Close so I shouldn't think she'd mind."

"Do you know Arthur's mother?"

"Not really. I went to tea with him once. He kept asking till I had to." At the sight of the boy's face, screwed up in an expression of humorous disgust, Jurnet suppressed a smile. "It was awful!"

"Grub below par?"

"Oh no—quite the opposite! There was ham, and trifle, and at least four kinds of cake and pastries—"

"Doesn't sound too bad to me."

"It was so *fussy*! Mrs Cossey had put a lace cloth on the table, and there were fancy serviettes and she was all dressed up—and I mean, it wasn't as if it was a party. It was only me!"

"Perhaps *you* were a party to Arthur and his mother, if nobody ever wanted to go home with him."

The boy reddened. There was a quiver in his voice as he said, "I'm sorry now, truly I am. But then—"

"Then he was just a drip with a crush on you. Don't blame yourself. We all do things we're sorry about afterwards. After all, you did go in the end."

"It was awful!" Christopher said again. "After tea we went upstairs to his room so he could show me his pictures. Can you think of anything more boring? Every time I said I ought to be getting home he'd bring out another lot. I said I'd be honest. Well—" the curly head came up, the thick-lashed hazel eyes looked solemnly at the detective—"even if I'd known he was going to be murdered, I don't think I could ever have gone there again. It was so boring I thought I'd die."

"Never mind," said Jurnet. "At least you can console yourself with the thought that you did Arthur a good turn while he was still alive to enjoy it."

"I *think* he enjoyed it. At any rate, he kept on smiling."

17

Mr Harbridge, peering through the glass panels let into the upper half of the Prior's Door, saw Jurnet making his way up the worn steps from the cloister. He opened the door and let the detective into the cathedral. In his wide-skirted gown with its broad black belt and white tabs at the throat, the verger looked damaged but dependable, his face only a little less bruised than Jurnet's. A plaster was still in position on the back of his head.

He looked out over Jurnet's shoulder and across the cloister to the south-east corner where the sturdy form of Christopher Drue could be seen disappearing through the entrance into the Song School.

"Young Chris been chatting you up, I see."

"Or vice versa. He's a live wire all right."

"That he is. Any mischief afoot in these parts, ten to one he's at the bottom of it."

The tone was affectionate, and Jurnet, who had also felt the powerful charm of the boy's personality, looked at the man with a kindly regard.

He demurred nevertheless. "There've been a few things happening here lately that are hardly child's play."

" 'Kids' jokes, I mean. Like the time someone stuck price tags on a couple of hundred kneelers we'd piled up in the north aisle during cleaning. 'Reduced to

£1.75'—that's what some joker put on them. Poor Miss Hanks, nearly driven mad she was with people wanting to buy'em."

"And that was Christopher's doing?"

"Can't say it was, can't say it wasn't. But it don't stop me having my own opinion." The verger chuckled. "Caught him out red-handed, though, couple of weeks ago. Not to say green and yellow an' sky-blue-pink!"

"How's that again?"

"Coloured chalks. Caught him colouring one of the tombs in the ambulatory. It's got a design of leaves and such, and to tell you the truth I thought it quite an improvement. Brightened it up something wonderful. Still, we can't encourage that sort of thing or there'd be no stopping the little perishers. So I made him fetch a dwile and a bucket of water and wash it all off. Stood over him till he done it, even if he did miss his games period."

"He couldn't have thought much of that."

"Oh, he took it all as a great joke. That's the kind of lad he is. 'No hard feelings, Harby,' he said to me when I finally let him go, and he stuck out his hand to shake, cheeky as you please. You can't help liking him, even when he's driving you up the wall with his merry tricks."

"Not like young Cossey. Not the most popular boy in the school, so far as I can make out."

The verger said, with a certain truculence, "Arthur was a very quiet boy."

"So everybody says. That's what makes it so puzzling."

"I shouldn't 'a thought myself," said the verger, his voice heavy with sarcasm, "that the maniac as did for Arthur examined him first to find out how he was for conversation."

Jurnet objected, "I don't know why not. Once you dream up your madman there isn't anything he mightn't do, since you've already made up your mind he's off his rocker to begin with. If it's a madman you want," he concluded amiably, "make sure he behaves like one. Unreasonably."

Harbridge stared.

"You think what was done to Arthur reasonable?"

"Definitely. Sick but sane. The product of a reasoning mind. Little St Ulf's grave, the star of David, the mutilation—in my book it all adds up to a deliberate composition, a work of art designed to evoke a carefully programmed response. So let's forget the maniac, shall we? Which brings us back to my original question. If Arthur was such a quiet little boy, minding his own business, what possible reason could anyone have for killing him?"

After a pause, during which a large lady, all agog, asked the verger to point out exactly where the little boy was murdered, Harbridge said, "I could think of a few."

In the FitzAlain chapel they were safe enough from interruption. Visitors to the cathedral tended to keep to the main routes, treating the byways with the distrust of motorists coming upon a road not marked on the map. Smiling in his sleep, Bishop FitzAlain slept on his tomb undisturbed.

Jurnet, looking about him, nodded in the direction of the brown paper still cellotaped to the wall. "Might as well get rid of that now. I've been meaning to tell the Dean, but what with one thing and another—" The verger made no comment. "Ever since I found out what an artist Arthur was," the detective went on, "I can't help wondering if that wasn't some more of his handiwork. What do you think?"

Harbridge said with bitterness, "Nothing about that little stinker'd surprise me. There! I'm glad it's out." The verger looked at the detective, a line of anxiety deepening between the eyes. "Thing is, I don't want to say nothing that'll hurt Sandra."

"Oh, Mrs Cossey! I didn't know you were on first-name terms."

"What name terms d'you reckon a man ought to be on with his own sister-in-law?"

Jurnet said, "Don't be so prickly. No one's getting at you. Just don't expect me to be psychic. Nobody told me Arthur was your nephew."

"Not by blood he weren't! Twenty-eight years ago come September I married Beryl Cossey. Wasn't to know, was I, Arthur'd come into the bargain."

"So your wife's Vincent Cossey's sister?"

"Was. Died five years ago next July the 15th." The sparse intelligence encompassed a world of loss. "Different from Vince as chalk from cheese. Leave it to me, I wouldn't have had Vince on the doorstep, let alone ask him in. But you know women. Vince was her little brother, all the family she'd got, and families have to stick together even if they hate each other's guts. Never could see the point myself."

"Know what you mean. How did your wife feel about Mrs Cossey—Sandra?"

"They got along all right. Not that Sandra didn't drive her round the bend with her finicky ways. But she made Vince a good wife, far as he gave her the chance. He was all bets, booze, an' birds before he got married, an' he didn't see no cause to change after."

"Wonder a chap like that ever married at all."

Harbridge smiled for the first time.

"Oh, that was Sandra's doing. Got herself in the family way."

"You don't say! Wouldn't have thought her the type myself. Anyway, I didn't think that one worked any longer."

"Maybe not, outside of the Close. Here, we still keep to the old ways. Sandra said, if Vince didn't make an honest woman of her, she'd go to the Dean and Chapter and tell them what he'd been up to, out of working hours. Vince was a first-class mason. I'll say that for him, making good money at the time—that was when all that work got done on the presbytery, it must be fifteen, sixteen years ago—and he didn't want to risk losing his job. He felt the way we all do. Once you've worked in the cathedral you don't want to work anywhere else."

"Fifteen years! Then it couldn't have been Arthur—"

" 'Tweren't nobody. Sandra had a miscarriage when they come an' told her about Vince's accident. At least, that's what she said."

"Which accident was that? I thought—"

"Not the one that did for him good an' all. Bit o' stone flew into his eye and made a right muck of it. They give him a glass one, an'—you know what?— though his own natural ones were dark brown, he had 'em make it blue. Said he's always fancied beautiful blue eyes, and one was better than none, even if it weren't real! That's the sort of chap he was. When he was killed, Sandra would've had it buried with him, only young Arthur begged to be let keep it, as a re-membrance of his Pa. Morbid, I call it, but there! Arthur could always twist his Ma around his little fin-ger. He kep' the eye in his pocket—said it had magic powers, like in the fairy stories. Did you ever hear such nonsense! Rub it an' make a wish, an' your wish was granted. Pathetic, really. As my Beryl always said, if you c'd make a wish, who'd wish to stay Ar-thur?"

"Quiet little Arthur."

"Tha's right." The verger's mouth set in a thin line. "Never a peep out of him when he was a baby, even. You never heard him cry. But there was something about the way he used to look at you. It's hard to explain. My Beryl always said he was a creep before he could walk."

"Very witty," commented Jurnet, and was re-warded with a gratitude that lit up the man's face. "Still, his Ma and Pa must have loved him."

"Sandra was never one to go cooing and kissing. But I'll say this for her—she kept that kid looking like he'd just stepped out of a bandbox. Vince give him a cou-ple of thick ears when he'd had too much to drink, but nothing out of the ordinary. Said it got on his nerves, the way the kid followed him round the house like a puppy, only never making a sound. 'If on'y it'd give a little bark once in a while,' he said to me one time, 'at least I'd know it was human.' "

The verger looked at Jurnet with a perplexity that was directed more at himself than at the detective.

"You'll be thinking we were a flint-hearted lot, and we weren't so at all. My Beryl, never mind me, had a heart as big as a house. But there was something about Arthur—" He frowned, concentrating. Then he went on, as if in explanation, "Sometimes, when the four of us were sitting downstairs talking, and he was up in his room, all of a sudden you'd hear 'im singing, and it was like an angel. I don't know why, it made your blood run cold."

"Oh ah." Feeling, for the moment, that he had had as much of young Master Cossey as he could take, Jurnet transferred his attention to Bishop FitzAlain; sauntered round the tomb, aware for the first time that its sides were not walled in but balustered, the spaces between the barley-sugar-twist pillars filled in with mesh grilles, through which it was just possible to discern that under his bed, as it might be a chamber-pot or dust overlooked by a slatternly house-maid, the Bishop harboured a skeleton.

Ugh!

With no desire to make a closer inspection Jurnet came back to his starting point, and remarked in an offhand way, "I suppose he was blackmailing you, too?"

"What you mean, *too*?" Harbridge's relief was un-disguised.

"Don't worry. You weren't the only one Arthur tried it on with." Jurnet sat down on one of the chairs lined up facing the little altar. He patted the seat next to him. "Sit down and tell me all about it."

The verger preferred to stand. He began, "I can't think how you found out—"

"I didn't," Jurnet admitted. "Once I realized what kind of game little Arthur was playing, it didn't take much to work it out. Something to do with that fire, was it?"

A spasm twisted the verger's face.

"The nasty little toad! Said the reason I didn't answer the bell and open the gate for the fire engine was
because I'd been drinking and because I was in bed
with his Ma." His voice rose in a horrified astonishment, as if he still could hardly comprehend that such
a suggestion had indeed been made. "His own Ma!"

"He was after money, of course?"

"Wanted me to fork out for some special kind of
easel he wanted, and some other stuff to do with his
painting. I was too bowled over to take in the details.
An' once I took them in—" the man's fists clenched
until the knuckles showed white—"it was all I could
do not to wring his scrawny little neck then an' there."
He took a deep breath and relaxed. "He said if I didn't
cough up he was going to write to the Dean an' tell
him all about it."

"And did you—cough up?"

The amused pity in the verger's face was answer
enough.

"Only to be expected," Harbridge conceded, "living
out in the city, an' doing the job you do. Here in the
Close—" he spoke without embarrassment—"we live
closer to God. I often think that's why it's called that.
It don't mean we're any holier than folks outside the
gates, or any less sinners. Just closer, somehow—to
His judgment seat and His everlasting mercy."

"I take it," responded Jurnet, cool to the presump-
tion that the Close possessed something denied to his
beloved Angleby as a whole, "that what you're saying, in your own peculiar way, is that you didn't give
Arthur a brass farthing?"

"Give 'im! I told him, go ahead an' see what good
it'll do you. Write your bleeding letter and see what
happens!"

"And what did happen?" It was the first time in
their acquaintance, Jurnet noted with interest, that
the man had used anything approaching an expletive.
"What did Dr Carver say?"

"Better ask him! Never said nothing to me. Never
heard another word from that day to this."

"And you never once asked the boy: 'Look here, did you or didn't you write to the Dean?' "

"Wouldn't lower myself. Bad enough I had to see him, day in, day out, trotting along in his cassock, looking like butter wouldn't melt in his mouth. And when he sang solo!" The verger shook his head, and ended, with a simplicity that Jurnet found unanswerable: "Makes you wonder, don't it, how the Lord could cause such a cracked bell to ring so true?"

"Did you know that Mrs Cossey has a lodger?"

The verger looked pleased.

"I been telling her ever since Vince died! But she never would. She was afraid the neighbours might get the wrong idea."

"Ideas or not, she's got one now."

"Not before time. Always said, criminal to let that nice little room go begging when she could do with the extra. So long as your conscience is clear, I said, and you choose carefully who you take in, the neighbours can think what they like."

"Do you happen to know a scrap merchant name of Joe Fisher?"

"You mean down by the river?" Jurnet nodded, and angry astonishment flooded into the verger's face. "She's never taken in *that* riff-raff?" Jurnet nodded again, and the man exclaimed: "What she want to go an' do that for?"

"I suppose she decided the extra money would come in handy, like you said. And as to choosing carefully, it surely depends on what you're choosing *for*?"

"A respectable chap, that's what I told'er! Regular pay and habits."

"Ah! But that'd be your choice, not Sandra's. From what you've told me about Vince, I reckon she likes a man to have a bit of the devil in him."

"But he's already got a wife down there in that caravan, soft in the head, *and* a kid!"

"You're as bad as the neighbours."

"All the same—" in retreat, albeit unwillingly— "that no-good! She should have thought of Arthur—"

"Perhaps that's exactly what she was doing. Extra

money for Arthur to get his easel with, and his paints
and such."

"You must be joking!" the verger exclaimed in de-
risive contradiction. "Oh, I'm not saying she didn't
look after the boy—always dressed decent and plenty
of food on the table. But 50p a week was all he ever
got by way of pocket money—*when* he got it. Anything Sandra has over from the housekeeping goes
straight into the Building Society. Evenings, she'll sit
with that passbook on her knees like it was the family
Bible. Anything Arthur wanted over 50p he had to
earn himself or whistle for it."

Jurnet asked: "What's the going rate for a paper
round these days? More'n it was when I did one myself as a kid, that's for sure. But enough to fit up a
proper artist's studio? To run to a bike with seven
speeds? Enough to buy glass marbles at 35p a time,
and splash'em around like there was no tomorrow?"

The verger said: "Whatever it is, Sandra took the
best part for his food an' clothing. You'll have to keep
asking around, won't you? All I can say is, he never
got nothing out of me."

The chapel was stuffy, with a frowst of disinfectant
which seemed to mask rather than eliminate an un-
dercurrent of something less salubrious. Harbridge,
with the air of daring a refusal, said, "I've got to be
getting back to my job." The detective, who was more
sensitive to bad smells than was convenient to one
who, in the course of the working day, was often
called upon to poke his nose into malodorous places,
remarked, "You could do worse than make a start
here. Pity those windows don't open."

The verger, his housekeeping in question, looked
distressed.

"It's this blessed floor! Tufa, they call it. Only
chapel in England paved with it, so I've heard, and
no prizes for knowing why. Sops up everything like a
sponge, an' then keeps it hanging about inside it like
it can't bear to let it go."

"Wonder you don't shut the place up for a bit and
give it a proper fumigation."

The verger jerked his head in the direction of the tomb.

"He's the one says it has to be open. The ol' Bishop. And what he says goes. When you've done as much for the cathedral as he has, I reckon you've got a right to call the tune. One of the terms of the FitzAlain Bequest says the FitzAlain chapel has to be kept open in perpetuity."

Jurnet took another look at the Bishop. Not the plump cleric serene on his stone pillow, but his *alter ego*, the skeleton in the lower berth.

"Perpetuity's a long time. What do you do when Old Bony down there needs a wash and brush-up?"

"The grille behind the head's made to lift out. He gets a proper spring-clean every November 6th, Founder's Day."

The tomb rested, not on the tufa itself, but a few inches below it, in a shallow pit which seemed to have been hallowed out to receive the sarcophagus. A gully, finished off with a simple beading, separated the tomb from the surrounding pavement.

Jurnet peered down into the narrow space, bent and picked something up. Held it out on the palm of his hand without a word.

The man looked at it uncertainly: uncertainty that turned to annoyance when the detective first set the tiny object down carefully upon the Bishop's chest, and then, in a few swift steps, was at the head of the tomb, down on his knees, and tugging at the metal grille with all his strength.

"Not like that! You'll have it in pieces! Lever it out gentle!"

Jurnet, still saying nothing, obeyed instructions. The grille lifted easily from its anchorage.

Seen from behind, the skeleton's cranium looked formidable, a carapace to house a brain of size and power. To have provided such a lordly receptacle with a pillow would have been an insult, and the sculptor had had the good taste not to do so.

But someone else had.

Jurnet reached in and removed the bundle wedged

under the skull. He brought it out carefully, and swivelling round on the floor, unrolled what he had found: a boy's blazer, trousers, and socks wrapped round a bloody knife and a pair of buckled shoes. Not until he had lifted the shoes clear of the enveloping cloth did he realize what he had found beside: up-ended first the left shoe, then the right, and watched with reluctant fascination as, out of the second, something sticky and abominable slowly emerged, and slid with horrid deliberation down to the heel.

Jurnet got to his feet, leaving Arthur Cossey's clothes and what had once been his penis where they lay. He went round to the side of the tomb again; took out a small polythene bag, teased open the edges, and into it dropped with care the wheaten-coloured sliver he had picked up from the floor.

"Did you know—" he asked of the man who stood, his face the colour of ashes, one hand to his mouth— "did you know he'd rather eat sugar crispies than sweets any day?"

18

The meeting was held in the station on Market Hill, in a room of whose very existence Jurnet had been unaware. A bit of architectural left-overs, too big for a broom closet, too small for anything else. It contained some metal chairs and a round table which was undoubtedly the reason for the Superintendent's choice of venue. At a round table no one was above the salt, no one below: all equal, like King Arthur and his Knights of Old. This typical example of the Superintendent's exquisite consideration for the feelings of his inferiors made Jurnet want to puke.

Sergeant Ellers took in the lay-out at a glance.

"Where's Guinevere?" he inquired cheerfully, scarcely bothering to keep his voice down.

"What's that, Jack?" The Superintendent had already seated himself. In front of him, a virgin notepad and a gold pen of distinguished pedigree proclaimed where power lay as loudly as the Mace before the Speaker of the House.

"Cosy den in here," Ellers translated shamelessly. "Sir."

"A bit on the small side." The Superintendent smiled impartially at the four men ranged hesitantly round the dingy walls. "Sit down, you chaps. You're making me uncomfortable."

The police officers seated themselves, the Superintendent looking on benevolently. He knew how hard it was for men who had been out in the world, using their own initiative in what was, when you came down to it, a damn rum business altogether, to be summoned at the snap of an authoritarian finger back into a rigidly structured society where every dot over the i, every cross of the t, had to be accounted for in triplicate.

Let them take their time. It needed, as he knew from experience, only the briefest period of readjustment before the initial disorientation gave way to the blessed relief of being home among one's own kind, among brothers with whom problems could be shared, or on to whom, with a bit of luck, they might even be unloaded.

When he judged the moment right the Superintendent began without introduction.

"Professor Pargeter has identified the knife as one in use at the excavation, and customarily left lying on the table at the end of the day's work. Examination shows the blade and handle to have been wiped clean of fingerprints. So—we have the weapon with which the mutilations were done. Which, I am sorry to say, gets us very little farther."

Jack Ellers spoke up: "At least, unless it was one of those Ulf-diggers themselves, it shows the murderer didn't arrive kitted out for the job. For murder perhaps, but not the embroidery. The Little St Ulf bit could have been a sudden inspiration, come to him on the spur of the moment."

"Hm." The Superintendent pursed his lips discontentedly. Then, "And the Bishop's tomb, Ben. I can't see that gets us much forrarder, either."

"If you say so, sir." Jurnet nodded agreement, and proceeded to disagree exactly as if the words had never been uttered; a habit of his which he would have been astonished to discover irked the Superintendent every bit as much as any of the Superintendent's little idiosyncrasies annoyed *him*. "Dr Colton says that the boy was killed between 6.45 and 8.15. My guess is that it has to be earlier than 8, because I reckon the killer would want to get rid of the clothes without wasting a minute and by 7.45 people were already arriving for the Communion service."

Sid Hale, long-faced and melancholy, wanted to know, "What time does the cathedral open officially?"

"Our information is that the vergers take it in turn to open up—one week on, one week off. Sunday, it should have been Mr Quest, the head verger, only his daughter's ill, and Harbridge stood in for him. Apparently, the drill is to come in at 6.30 and unlock the Bishop's Postern—that's the traditional bit so the Bishop can get in soon as he has a mind to; then at 7 on the dot the verger undoes the south transept door to let the cleaners in. They don't work on Sundays, but it seems to have become a habit to open up at 7 anyway. At 7.30 he unlocks the West Door—or rather, the little door at the side of it—and the doors into the cloister, and that's it." Jurnet paused and corrected himself. "Not all of it. Professor Pargeter and his helpers each have keys to the Bishop's Postern and so, theoretically, could come and go at any hour of the day or night. Mr Amos, who's in charge of the choir, can also get into the cathedral any time he fancies, from the Song School. On top of that, the cathedral keys are kept in the vestry, in the south transept—except that the verger on duty for the week takes the key of the South Door home with him at night, otherwise how's he going to get in next day in the first place?"

"Wonder they bother locking up at all!" the Superintendent exclaimed. "I can see we'll have to send our Security Officer round for a chat with the Dean."

Jurnet said, "My understanding is, they put their faith in a higher authority. But what it comes down to, sir, is, that a stranger wouldn't have time to go looking for a hiding place on spec. He'd *have* to know it beforehand."

"Which narrows the field to how many, would you say?"

Jurnet, absorbed by this thesis, failed to pick up the hint of danger.

"An insider. Someone who knows the cathedral intimately. I won't go further than that."

"Just as well, Ben." The Superintendent picked up a paperback he had placed ready on the table. *"Cathedrans and the Cathedral,"* he read out the title printed in Gothic lettering above a representation of the FitzAlain crest. "Author, the Reverend Doctor Oswald Delf-Polesey. Published 1901. Reprinted 1979. The publishers tell me some 7,000 copies of the later edition have been sold. I purchased mine at the cathedral bookstall. Splendid value for 95p."

Aware that Batterby, who lived for the day when he would be head of the CID, was looking smug, Jurnet kept his voice carefully non-committal.

"What does it say, sir?"

"Merely that all Cathedrans, almost from the time the good Bishop's tomb was erected, know about that removable grille. It seems that in less sceptical times the boys had a charming custom of sticking petitions into the skeleton's eye-sockets, thereby inviting its intervention with the powers above to get them a good mark in their examinations. About 150 years ago, some dear little fellows had an even better idea." The Superintendent thumbed through the pages, seeking the quotation.

" 'At the beginning of Michaelmas Term, 1823, a boyish prank had unforeseen consequences. A new boy named Andrew Kettleby, a connection by marriage of the Buckworths of Hannerton Hall, was either invited or induced to enter the lower portion of the tomb, being assured that it was the practice of all new boys so to do; one that unfailingly brought them good luck and success in their studies. Once young Kettleby was within, however, his thoughtless schoolfellows replaced the metal grille (which could only be removed from without) and, whether by accident or design, did not return until the following day, by which time the unfortunate boy had lost his reason, and was obliged to spend the rest of his life in an institution for the insane.' "

The Superintendent looked up from his reading as Jack Ellers burst out, with Celtic passion, "Gagged him, they must have, or he'd have yelled the place down! Hope they thrashed the little buggers from here to Christmas."

"The reverend doctor is silent on the subject. Merely that—" referring anew to the text—" 'As a result of this regrettable incident Lord Buckworth felt compelled to withdraw his annual Good Conduct prize to the School of books to the value of fifteen shillings and sixpence.' "

"So you see, Ben—" the Superintendent leaned forward, friendliness itself once the boot was in— "anybody who spends 95p at the bookstall can learn all about the secret of the Bishop's tomb. What's more, the editor of the 1979 edition—who, by the way, is none other than the present Dean—adds a helpful footnote specifying exactly which grille is the operative one, and letting the reader know that it remains in operation to this day. Of course, anyone who is, or ever was, at the Cathedran School will know without being told."

Batterby put in demurely, "Claude Brinston's an Excathedran, as a matter of fact."

"*And* Chesley Hayes," added Hale.

The Superintendent observed, "I'm sure I don't know what we've done, here in Angleby, to be cursed with, not just one, but two native sons who are professed fascists and the leaders of political parties dedicated to racial and religious intolerance of the crudest and most objectionable kind."

"Is there any other kind, sir?" Jurnet asked, all innocence.

"Quite right, Ben!" the Superintendent admitted instantly. "The sins one commits in the interests of a well-turned phrase! How about it, Dave? Have you turned up anything to suggest that either the English Men or the League of Patriots might be involved?"

Dave Batterby said, "Nothing you could call solid." Admitting failure was not something that came easily to him. "Both organizations are getting maximum footage out of Arthur Cossey's death, the way, you might say, the Nazis did over the Reichstag fire. Since the punch-up in the Close the English Men've been acting like wounded heroes. Chaps that weren't within five miles of the place have been going about with their arms in a sling—"

"At least, with luck, we'll get some of them put away for a bit."

"Fines and bound over, I'll take a bet!" Batterby's face mirrored his disgust. "Everyone saw on telly how that young American fellow started it."

Jurnet, who had driven out to the hospital earlier that morning to find the pale, golden girl sitting by her unconscious husband's bedside, reading aloud to him the news of the day, said nothing; not even when Batterby, unable to purge his voice entirely of hope, added, "If he kicks the bucket, of course, that's a different ball game." Demonstrating what a good fellow he was basically, Batterby went on, "It was Ben put us on to Joe Fisher. Not that he wasn't an old acquaintance, only politics was a new line, so far as we were concerned. Once Joe found out it wasn't a load of scrap I wanted to see him about, there was no stopping him. Seemed to think membership of the English Men gave him the Good Housekeeping Seal of Approval as a pure-blooded Englishman, none of your foreign wogs with pig's piss in their veins—I'm quoting Joe's own words, sir." The Superintendent bowed his head in acknowledgment. "But as to an actual link with the boy—" Batterby smiled at Jurnet across the table as he dumped the problem back in his colleague's lap—"once I found out Joe was lodging at Mrs Cossey's, I reckoned Ben would know what to do about him without any help from me."

The Superintendent looked pleased.

"That's what I call a team! Everyone doing what he does best, and no treading on each other's toes! Only thing—" the tone hardened, the words took on an incisiveness that made his subordinates sit up straighter in their seats—"we've got to get a move on—you all know that, don't you? Not just because a child is dead, and we don't want any more dead like him. Not just because we've got reporters buzzing round the door like bluebottles on a bit of cat's-meat; but because, while we're hanging about, taking our time, the whole city's going bad on us, as if the last eight and a half centuries had never happened. As if the question is: is Angleby, or is it not, a civilized place for civilized people to live in?"

As always, when the fair name of his native city was called into question, Ben Jurnet was moved to protest.

"Sir, if the whole shoot of'em, English Men and League of Patriots together, comes to more than five or six hundred all told, I'll be surprised."

"Six hundred rotten apples are more than enough to turn the other 120,000 rotten, given them the chance. I tell you, there's an atmosphere. Don't tell me you haven't noticed."

Sid Hale took out a sheet of paper.

"I've noticed," he said. His face was that of a man saddened by the world's ways, but never surprised by them.

The sheet of paper was a poster, jag-edged from having been ripped from its moorings.

ENGLAND FOR THE ENGLISH!
WHO KILLED ARTHUR COSSEY?
WHO NEEDS THE JEWS?

Hale said, "There were twenty-seven of 'em stuck round the Market this morning."

The Superintendent instructed him, "Tell the others about Mr Cecil Baumann."

Jurnet looked up sharply. Mr Baumann was the chairman of the honorary officers of the synagogue, a twinkling little man with a store of Jewish stories which Jurnet, as a candidate for conversion, could not but feel were some kind of test. The detective always laughed, whether he saw the joke or not, lest Mr Baumann raise the imsuperable objection: how can we let anyone become a Jew who doesn't understand Jewish humour?

Sid Hale turned over the pages of his note book.

"He owns a dress shop in Bullen Street. This morning, while his wife was out buying stock and his assistant had gone across the street to get some coffee and sandwiches, two girls accompanied by a youth entered the shop. As Mr Baumann caters exclusively for outsizes he immediately told the girls there was nothing there to interest them. Their answer was to start pulling clothes off the hangers and throwing them on the floor. When Mr Baumann remonstrated, the youth gave him a black eye, and then took out a flick knife with which he threatened to slit his throat if he called for help. At that point, the sales assistant, returning with the coffee and sandwiches, found a second youth outside the shop engaged in spraying the word YID on the shop window. Taking in the situation she prised off the top of one of the coffee cartons and flung the contents over the youth's head. His screams brought the other three running out on to the pavement, where PC Bly, who had also heard the noise, was able to apprehend the scalded youth and one of the girls. At the station, the two refused to give their names, merely stating that they were members of the League of Patriots making a gesture."

Dave Batterby commented, without noticeable regret, "Chesley'll cry. Chesley always cries when something goes wrong."

"Wrong?" echoed the Superintendent. "I should

have thought, that, from Hayes's point of view, it's gone completely right. Acres of publicity, hundred of pounds worth of damage, a Jew terrorized— No, I shouldn't have said that—" He broke off with a chuckle. "Do you know what Mr Baumann did when I arrived at his shop, and saw the mess, and was properly horrified? One eye was out like a balloon, a couple of his front teeth were missing, and he slapped me on the back and said, 'The grass is still green, the sun still shines. Don't *worry*!' "

Sid Hale persisted, "Chesley will, though. Worry. It doesn't take much to make Chesley take on. Like that brick through the Weisingers' window. From what I hear, that was League of Patriots too."

The Superintendent said, "Hearing's not enough, Sid."

"Don't I know it, sir! What I meant was, they were all set to go public. Phone the papers, claim responsibility. Seems Chesley nearly bust a gut when he saw Brinston and the English Men making the big time on TV and felt he had to dream up something pronto to put the L of P on the map. Trouble was, he chose the wrong target. Apparently it dawned on him too late that the Weisingers are so well-thought of locally that claiming the credit for wrecking their place would only do him and his outfit more harm than good."

"Speaking for myself and off the record," said the Superintendent, "as one who believes the Weisingers' petits-fours to be a foretaste of heaven, I'd give a lot to get the mindless lout who threw that particular brick."

"Not mindless enough, sir, that's the trouble." That from Batterby. "There's at least two shopkeepers live over their premises in Shire Street who heard the breaking glass, looked out of the window and saw who it was running away. Two men, they say—and that's all they say, because they know the louts aren't so mindless that, if they say any more, they won't get a brick through their own windows, if not worse."

"That's why we've got to get our hands on whoever killed Arthur Cossey. To put a stop to all this once and for all." The Superintendent looked round at his helpers. "Or even if it doesn't."

19

The Market Place, as ever, was full of life and colour. Stalls with striped awnings; fruit and vegetables in mouth-watering heaps; pots and pans and plastic tat; T-shirts swinging in the breeze. Wah-wah of pop music; twitter of budgerigars; patter of the travelling men who sold crockery and yard goods as if they were rehearsing for the halls: Norfolk voices curving up and over towards the end of every sentence like combers homing to the beach. Vinegar-spiced cockle stalls; chips frying; flower fragrance; rotting cabbage leaves.

Glad that he had left his car in the station car-park, Jurnet drew a deep breath.

Nothing had changed.

Everything had changed.

He felt a great need for Miriam, for love and reassurance, and settled for what was available.

"Fancy a bag of chips?"

"Rosie'd kill me," Sergeant Ellers replied. "The way she goes on about calories, you'd think they were catching. I could screw every WPC on the Force and there'd be less of a carry-on."

"Please yourself." Jurnet stopped at the chip stall, made his purchase, added salt and vinegar, and took his first bite. Hot and tasty, if it wasn't as comforting as love, it was a good deal less demanding. He finished the chip and took a second.

Jack Ellers mewed plaintively, "I thought you were going to cajole me!"

"In full daylight! I don't see why I should get into Rosie's bad books on your account. If you want to sell your soul for a mess of chippage, let it be on your own conscience."

"On my conscience," returned Ellers, "I wouldn't worry. As my old granny used to say, we are all sinners, the Lord be praised. It's on my bloody waistline! Ah well—" the little Welshman reached for a chip, ate it, and helped himself to another—"we can't all be tall, dark, and handsome."

"Oh ah," said Jurnet.

The detective felt considerably cheered. Wonderful what a few slivers of spud dunked in hot grease could do for your *weltanschauung*, if that was what it was, or even if it wasn't. Who the hell did the Super think he was, to label the lovely city, as it might be an old map, "Here be Corruption"?

The euphoria lasted until the chips were gone, and for some distance thereafter. It was only when following round the walls of the Close, all the buildings turned inward, their backs to the city like an architectural insult, that the uncertainty and the unhappiness flooded back in full spate. Bits of cathedral roof, turrets and pinnacles, filled in the random spaces; while, above, the pigeons still circled the steeple, all going clockwise, like time itself.

"What makes you think he'll be in?" Ellers asked suddenly. "Man of affairs, Joe. You haven't made an appointment?"

"Next thing to it. I got Hinchley after him to let him know I'd be calling at Mrs Cossey's round dinnertime, and he'd better be at home to visitors if he knew what was good for him. Not to make him frightened—he's not one to take fright easily—but to make him curious. If I read his mind correctly, he'll be staying home to grill us, not the other way round."

As it turned out, Joe Fisher was staying home, or so it appeared, to put the dinner on. The man had barely opened the front door to the two detectives before he let out an anguished "Fuck!" at the sound of something boiling over in the kitchen. The gas lowered, he returned to the little hall to scream a companion "Balls!" at the sight of the linoleum.

"For Christ's sake! Why'n't you bring in the frigging dog with you and be done with it? Don't they run to doormats down at the nick?"

"You should know," answered Jurnet. Just the same, he went back to the door and scraped away with a will. "Your turn, Jack."

Joe Fisher snapped, "Fat lot o' good that'll do now! I'll have to get some paper."

When he had cleared up the mess to his satisfaction, he allowed the two through into the little living-room, indicating which chair each was to occupy; rushed back into the kitchen to pop a rice pudding into the oven; and only then put himself at the police officers' disposal. It dawned on Detective-Inspector Jurnet that Joe Fisher was a very happy man.

"Sandra's always late getting back from Canon Greenaway's. Holy old humbug, pays her for three hours an' keeps her bes' part o' four. Can't think why she stands for it, 'cept she reckons working in the Close gets you a free pass at the Pearly Gates."

Jurnet asked acidly, "And who's helping out Millie?"

"Don't gi' me that." The man was quite embarrassed. "Millie's right as rain, and well you know it. Fish an' chips fit for a belted earl, that's what she's tuckin' into this very minute, as we sit here gassing. I give young Willie the money last night. So don't give me that."

"If you're going to treat her like an animal—feed her at intervals and then forget she even exists until feeding time comes round again—you might at least muck her out occasionally. I don't recall seeing you messing about with doormats and old newspapers down by the river."

"Millie don't know what clean means." Joe Fisher rose from his seat, picked a thread off the carpet, and sat down again. "An' she don't want ter know. Once I give that trailer a coat of emulsion an' she took on like I'd knocked off her best friend."

"She manages to keep Willie clean."

"Willie keeps hisself clean. Look 'ere, Mr Jurnet—"

the man rose again, to stand square and bulging on the hearthrug. "Is that what you kept me in all morning for? To gi' me a lesson how to look after Millie?"

Jurnet said, "You know why we're here, right enough."

"Oh ah." Joe Fisher resumed his seat, lowering himself carefully on to the buttoned dralon. "That bloody kid. What you think I can tell you about the little squirt you don't know already?"

Jurnet said, "You just told us something. Squirt. Not poor dear little Arthur."

"You must be joking! Don't tell me you lot been snufflin' round this long, and ain't found out yet what Arthur was really like? Makes you wonder what we pay rates for."

"Couldn't hardly expect you and him to hit it off," Jurnet conceded. "No kid likes it when his Ma brings a fancy man into the house."

"You ought to have your mouth washed out!" There was no doubting that the anger was unfeigned. "Apparently you could be as hung with balls as a Christmas tree and still be as pure as the driven snow."

Jurnet said, "My mistake. I'll try again. How much did the boy take you for?"

"Arthur? Take me? I'd see the little bugger dead first!"

"Got that down, Sergeant Ellers?" Jurnet's tone was crisp, professional.

Joe Fisher stared.

"Don't talk so daft! Can't you reckernize a figger of speech when you see one? You arst me did I give that little shit money an' the answer is no, I did not give that little shit money. So why should I knock him off and get Sandra all upset? It stands to reason."

"If you refused to pay blackmail, all the more reason for shutting him up permanently."

Joe Fisher ran his fingers through his hair.

"Gawd preserve us from dumb cops! Blackmail! Injure my spotless reputation? Don't make me laugh!"

"Something in that," admitted Jurnet, always willing to concede, even to the opposition, a point well taken. "Unless, of course, you had something big in the pipeline, and Arthur said pay up or I spill the beans."

"If yer want to know—" Joe Fisher spoke with dignity—"the on'y big thing I got on at the moment is politics. An' fer that, as you know as well as I do, the more publicity the better."

"Thinking of standing for Parliament, are you? Come to think of it, I heard somewhere you'd joined the League of Patriots."

The man's face darkened to purple.

"Tha's a bloody libel for starters! The English Men, didn't Mr Batterby tell you? Not that pissy League of Pansies!"

"That's very interesting." Jurnet sat back and crossed his legs. "Sergeant Ellers and I have often wanted to know what the English Men stand for, exactly. Now you can tell us."

" 'S not what they stand *for*," Joe Fisher pronounced. " 'S what they're *against*. Contamination of our pure English blood, kikes an' blacks out, an' so on."

"Fascinating! Some time we must have a long talk. As time's a bit short, perhaps you'd tell us this—if you didn't hand over any payola to Arthur, where d'you reckon he got the bread to pay for his bike and all that stuff up in his room. Not out of his paper round."

"Course not! Sandra took that. I asked 'im once why he kept it on at all, seeing he never seemed short of a penny."

"What did he say?"

"That he liked bein' out on the streets early when they was quiet an' nobody about." Joe Fisher leaned forward confidingly. "Don't let on to 'is Ma I said so, but the kid was a freak."

Jurnet persisted. "Where do you think he got the money from, then?"

"Out o' the cathedral collection, for all I know. Never 'ad two words to say to him myself when one 'd do."

"Was that a fact?" Jurnet waited a moment before

pouncing. "At least you exchanged enough chat to find out where he kept his little nest egg."

"What's that supposed to mean?"

"Only that when Sergeant Ellers and I were here before, we found that a drawer in Arthur's room had been forced open."

"I never—!"

"Can it, Joe. Next time you do a job, don't leave your tools behind. I'm willing to believe you did it because Sandra asked you. His Ma, after all, and could do with the money. Only I need to know how much you found—the truth, mind!—to get at the proper scale of Arthur's business activities, whatever they were. Otherwise, I'll have no alternative than to assume you handed over hush-money after all, and were only taking back what you thought of as yours—" The detective finished, offhandedly, "After you killed him, that is."

"I—" Joe Fisher began huskily. He cleared his throat and began again. "Four hundred and fifty nicker," he said. "In fivers."

Sergeant Ellers said, "And I was beginning to feel sorry for the little runt! Poor little blackmailer, trying so hard to make a dishonest penny, and everyone saying 'Nothing doing, sonny!' Pathetic! But four hundred and fifty!"

"Where'd he get it, that's the question."

"One of 'em's bloody well lying. Take your pick."

" 'What is truth? said jesting Pilate: and would not stay for an answer.' First sentence of Bacon's Essays," said Jurnet, "and don't ask me what comes next because that's as far as I got." After a moment he added, "Far as anyone's got."

The two detectives walked on in silence. In the Close, azaleas were taking over from the almond blossom, whose petals lay about in drifts as if a wedding procession had passed that way. Tulips and wallflowers were opening among the tiring daffodils: on the lawns, illicit dandelions flowered like mad while the going was good. An elderly canon had come out daringly in his light clerical grey, and from the Deanery emerged a young priestling full of a seemly joy.

Jurnet said abruptly, "I'm going to pop down to the river."

"To make sure Willie got the fish and chips?"

"Certainly not. You heard what the Superintendent said. 'Get on with it.' I propose to get on with it by proceeding with all haste to the Water Gate to satisfy myself that the PC we stationed there hasn't fallen in."

PC Blaker, guarding the Water Gate against all corners, sat on the staithe feeding bread to a cluster of assorted waterfowl. As he scrambled to his feet at the detectives' approach, a gull, yellow legs dangling, swerved past and snatched the piece of bread he held in his hand.

"Cheeky—" PC Blaker began, and blushed in the presence of his superiors.

"Ah, George!" The young constable blushed redder, gratified to be recognized thus informally. "Making friends with the locals, I see. Very commendable, even if that bloody herring gull has just made off with your dinner."

"Oh no, sir! My Mum give me a bag for the birds. This is the second day I've been down here, an' I told her—" The red on the downy young cheeks became positively fluorescent as PC Blaker stammered, "And, begging your pardon, Mr Jurnet, it weren't a herring gull. Lesser Black-backed, sir—"

"You don't say!"

"Yellow legs, sir—that's how you can tell. Herring gulls are a dirty pink."

"You learn something new every day!" Jurnet smiled at the young policeman. "This lot your only callers?"

"Couple of tourists from the cathedral, took a look and went straight back. Courting couple and a young chap on the towpath. Bit early in the year for much to be doing down by the river."

"Let's hope it stays that way."

A smart cabin cruiser, every polyurethaned surface

gleaming, came slowly upstream, its engine purring expensively. The elderly couple in the cockpit stared at the three men on the staithe with the undisguised curiosity common to children and the old; the woman letting her knitting drop into her lap as she leaned forward to make some observation to her husband.

"Taking a look at the natives," said Jurnet, noting that Jack Ellers, aware of being under surveillance, was well up on his toes. The boat went past, and the little Welshman's feet resumed contact with *terra firma*. "Didn't pay for that little toy out of their old-age pensions."

"They'll be back in a minute, you'll see." PC Blaker predicted confidently. "Couple of 'em yesterday, the same thing. Get round that bend and all of a sudden it isn't pretty any more, not entertaining. They see those old huts, and the rubbish dumps and they turn back."

Jurnet said sympathetically, "You're a bit short on entertainment yourself, down here."

"Oh no, sir! I quite like it, what with the birds—" PC Blaker stopped, and blushed again.

"Yellow legs, Black-backed. I must remember that."

"*Lesser* Black-backed," was the anxious correction. "The *Great* Black-backed's got pink'uns, just like the herring gull."

"I know when I'm licked!" Jurnet threw up his hands humorously. "From now on, far as I'm concerned, gulls are gulls pure and simple, and to hell with the colour of their socks! Come on. Sarge! Keep on with the good work, Constable."

"Yes, Mr. Jurnet." Seeing the direction the two detectives were taking, the young policeman added, "You can't get far that way, sir. The path stops a little way on."

"Thought we'd try to get across country." Jurnet was not anxious to advertise his private back door into Joe Fisher's estate. He took a few steps, and immediately drew back, his face blank.

Stan Brent came along the river path not at all disconcerted to find himself in the unexpected company of three police officers; at first, or even second, glance a clean-limbed English lad in his uniform of jeans, T-shirt, and anorak, his red hair trimmed to an acceptable shortness, the knapsack on his back khaki and serviceable. A cool customer, Jurnet thought again, feeling his face tighten with an annoyance that was no less strong for the realization that sexual jealousy accounted for a good part of it.

"Well, well!" he greeted the newcomer. "Look who's here! Gentleman Jim!"

"Don't shoot!" Stan Brent cried. "I'll come quietly." He grinned, completely at ease. "Don't tell me the three of you've come all this way looking for little me!"

PC Blaker, young enough to resent any detraction from his professional dignity, addressed Jurnet in his most official tone, "Sir, he's the one come past twenty minutes ago."

"Oh good show, Watson!" Stan Brent exclaimed; and to Jurnet, "Eagle-eyed, that one. He should go far."

"It's a public footpath," Jurnet pointed out, refusing to be drawn.

"Lonely, though," the young man rejoined. "Just the spot for a quiet rape."

At that Sergeant Ellers rose up on his toes and said, "I'm splitting my sides, laddie."

"Don't do yourself an injury on my account," the red-haired young man begged earnestly. "You'll be glad to know I've left some clues. Orange peel, a Coke tin, and the wrapping off a Mars bar. In the wastepaper basket, of course. I wouldn't want to be run in for something really serious, like litter." Tiring of the game: "Permission to go, sir?"

Jurnet said, "I was thinking you must be feeling lonely to stay this long."

Which must have unwittingly touched a chord, for Stan Brent said, with a wistfulness which, except for what had preceded it, would have convinced his hearers utterly, "Maybe I am at that. It's watching that blasted river. All that water flowing past and you high and dry on the bank, not going anywhere."

As he spoke, the cabin cruiser came slowly into sight again, as PC Blaker had prophesied. Passing the staithe, the elderly man at the wheel waved shyly, and the woman looked up from her knitting and smiled, as at old friends. Both of them examined the red-haired young man, the addition to the group, with the same inoffensive curiosity they had earlier directed at the three police officers; and again, the woman let her work drop into her lap while she leaned over to speak to her husband.

"Look at that!" Stan Brent exclaimed. "Enough to make you throw up! Beautiful little boat, could cut through the water like a knife, going five miles an hour with a couple of geriatrics!"

"Knots," PC Blaker, red with earnestness, corrected him. "Boats go in knots, not miles."

"You don't say! And you can get knotted too, mate."

It was suddenly all so young, so schoolboyish, that Jurnet, against his will, nearly laughed aloud. He remarked, "If you're that fond of boats you could always join the Navy."

Stan Brent said, "I went on a training cruise on the *Winston Churchill*. I was sick as a dog the whole week."

"So was Nelson, and it didn't stop him winning the Battle of Trafalgar."

The young man stood watching the cruiser diminishing in the distance. When he spoke again, the yearning was still there; but all the innocence had gone out of his voice.

"I'll tell you this much—when I go to sea it'll be as the bloody admiral, not swabbing the decks like some bleeding char."

"Oh ah," observed Jurnet, not sorry to be back on the old footing. "Works out a bit pricy that way. Unless, of course, you've got plans to marry into the aristocracy."

"Considering it." With a last look downstream,

Brent turned away from the river. "Look out for the announcement in *The Times*."

As he passed Jurnet by, the detective took him suddenly by the wrist, sliding the anorak sleeve up the bared arm. The skin was firm, unbroken. Jurnet let the arm drop.

Stan Brent said, "Sorry to disappoint."

"A syringe isn't the only way."

"Not for me." The young man spoke in a way that carried conviction. "Filling your body full of dirt like it was a dustbin." He shook down the sleeve. "Drugs just aren't my scene."

"I heard different."

"Then you heard wrong." There was no heat in the disclaimer. "The effing Efferstein, I suppose. In trouble himself, tries to get out of it by shopping his mates."

"Can't say I got the impression Mr Epperstein counted you among his inner circle. What's more, so far as I know, he has made no specific allegations of any kind against you."

"He'd better not! Why don't you ask him how he tried to get me hooked? Pressing the stuff on me for free—let me roll you a reefer, old pal. Try a snifter of snow, does wonders for the liver. That's the way pushers work, in case you didn't know. Get you curious, try it for a laugh, and before you know what's hit you they've got themselves another customer. Nice little operation Mr Mosh Eff's got going. I don't suppose he told you about that, either."

"We'd be glad to hear from you."

"Split on a friend? Not cricket, by Gad!" Grinning hugely, "Especially as it's all a load of cock and bullshit anyway."

"Oh ah? You and Miss Aste have a game on, have you? Which can tell the biggest whopper?"

"Liz? I'm not in her class." Brent moved away, towards the Lower Close. "I'll tell her you were asking after her."

Jurnet let him go a little way. Was it that swagger

of hips that made him call out then, "You never told us what you've got in that knapsack."

"Thought you were never going to ask." The young man turned back at once, and slipped the knapsack straps from off his shoulders.

"I never said take it off," Jurnet snapped, angry with himself, and aware of Ellers and young Blaker watching. You could hardly demand of others standards you fell short of yourself. "That path seems on the short side for a hike, that's all."

"Small walk, large knapsack. My God, Watson, if that isn't suspicious I don't know what is!" Stan Brent burst out laughing. "How many miles d'you have to cover, Officer, before it stops being suspicious behaviour and becomes healthy exercise?" He hoisted the knapsack back into place between his shoulderblades. "Since you've been such a gent—I've been shopping, and a carrier bag just isn't me. So, there's some Coke, a couple of bags of crisps, a box of those nasty little cheeses with the silver paper you can never get off—oh, and some baked beans. You're welcome to look. You're welcome to a packet of crisps, if you want. I can't say fairer than that."

"No thanks."

"Can't say I blame you. They're prawn. Taste like sick. Actually I'm a salt-and-vinegar man, but the prawn were 2p off. Of course, when I marry into the aristocracy—" Stan Brent finished with a broad smile—"I'll send out the butler."

20

Jurnet sat on the leather pouffe, drinking tea angrily out of the dainty china that was part of the late Mrs Schnellman's immortality. Having driven with all haste to let the Rabbi know that a request had just that afternoon been received from a consortium of Jewish and other organizations for permission to hold a demonstration and a march through the city, it was disconcerting, to say the least, to learn that Leo Schnellman had in fact been approached some days earlier to serve on the committee planning the event.

"You mean, you've known about it all the time, and never said a word? As if we haven't got enough on our plates, here in Angleby as it is, you want to bring in coachloads of outsiders to stir up more trouble!" The detective jumped up and returned his cup and saucer to the table with a thump and a rattle of teaspoon that had the Rabbi rising agitatedly from his chair. "They're OK. No harm done." Jurnet calmed down, and his host sank back in relief.

The detective went on, unrepentant however, "And it's not because I'm a copper, either. Like anybody else with his brains the right way round I'm fed up to here with do-gooders who think they've a God-given right to snarl up the traffic, inconvenience citizens going about their lawful business, and leave behind a ton of litter to be paid for out of the rates—to say nothing of damage to property and to people, the police included, likely as not."

Unperturbed by the outburst, the Rabbi inquired goodhumouredly, "Am I to take this, Inspector, as official notice that our request is turned down?"

"Only wish it were! Let's hope the Chief has as much sense as me. Blessed ego-trips! By the time they're actually out on the streets and marching you need a microscope to make out who it is that's demonstrating for what—Neo-Nazis, Reds, or Old-Age Pensions for One-Parent Cats. The minute they start chanting those moronic slogans like a lot of ventriloquist's dummies, they all sound like *Sieg Heil* to me, whatever they're saying. I must say, Rabbi—" the detective finished, a little dismayed by his own vehemence—"I never expected to see you taking part in one of those jamborees."

"Strictly as a backroom boy," Leo Schnellman assured his guest. The Rabbi leaned back in his chair, taking in the lean height, the dark good looks of the man. "Believe me, Ben, if I looked half as good as you do, I'd be out there, slogans and all, leading the parade. But what kind of advertisement for racial tolerance d'you think I'd make, a fat slob like me, the prototype of the cartoon Semite? You might as well expect to sell ladies' tights using a picture of a bow-legged octogenarian with varicose veins! Even tolerance has its limits. One mustn't expect too much of people, too soon."

"You couldn't look worse than some of the types that are bound to be turning up," responded Jurnet, only partly appeased. "The nuts and the weirdos, all the slimy things that normally stay quiet under their stones—"

"Nothing," Leo Schnellman pointed out crisply, "that wasn't there already. You think Angleby was a Garden of Eden before all this happened? As a policeman you know it wasn't. As a minister of religion I know it wasn't. Indeed, so long as you won't pass it on that I said so, I'll go so far as to say I have my doubts there ever *was* a Garden of Eden. Without evil I find it hard to conceive a purpose to Creation. If there are no choices to be made, we are nothing."

Jurnet said wearily, "You'll have to excuse me, Rabbi. I'm not feeling up to such high-toned metaphysics. Or low-toned ones either. I'm sorry if I went off the deep end. All I can think of, these days, is Arthur Cossey, and how I'd give my eye-teeth to get my hands on the bastard who killed him."

"You must have some suspicions."

"Too many! Arthur was a nasty bit of goods. Young as he was, he'd made enough enemies to last a lifetime—which, come to think of it, is exactly what they did."

"You've spoken to them all?"

"All I could find, anyhow."

The Rabbi said calmly, as one resolving a difficulty, "One of them will have lied to you."

"I'd be surprised if the whole darn shoot hadn't."

"In that case, you must look for the truth you have

overlooked." The man heaved himself out of his chair. He stood looking down at the detective with the encouraging air of a schoolmaster for a pupil who needed to try just that little bit harder. "Think about it. It will come to you. And now I'm going to make you a hot, fresh cup."

He was still in the kitchen when the doorbell rang.

"I'll get it," Jurnet called, and went downstairs to let in Mosh Epperstein.

When he saw who it was, the detective almost left the house then and there. Instead, he turned his back on the new arrival without a greeting, ran upstairs and said to his host, "Thanks just the same, Rabbi, but I've got to be getting along."

"Unclean! Unclean!" The archaeology student came into the room. He looked thinner than ever, the dark eyes sunken in their sockets.

Leo Schnellman put the tray down on the table, and handed Jurnet his tea. "You aren't going to waste it."

"Give it to him instead."

"Now, Ben, don't be childish. Would it surprise you to know that when I looked out and saw you parking the car I telephoned Mosh to come over?"

"Nothing about you would surprise me, Rabbi," said Jurnet, obstinately ignoring the proffered beverage. "That doesn't mean that, just because you tell me to, I've got to sit down and make polite conversation with a man who's out on bail on a serious charge."

The Rabbi opened his eyes wide.

"Who said anything about polite conversation? Mosh wants to tell you what he was really doing in the cathedral the morning Arthur Cossey was killed, that's all."

After the Rabbi had fetched a cup for his second visitor, Jurnet demanded impatiently, "Well? I'm waiting. What *were* you doing in the cathedral? What time was it, Sunday, you went there?"

The archaeology student took a sip of the hot liquid, then set the cup and saucer down on the table. "I didn't. I went Saturday. I was there all night."

"All night! That needs a bit of explaining."

"That's what I'm here for, just like the Rabbi says. It's very simple, really." The young man's voice sounded near extinction. "Liz asked me to stay. She often has night-long sessions, up there in the triforium, with Stan Brent. Fancied a change, I suppose, or maybe she'd had a row with lover boy and wanted to show him he wasn't the only fish in the sea. Liz says it turns her on to screw in such holy surroundings."

Jurnet said, "You're having me on."

"Ask her yourself."

"I mean, the cathedral. There are vergers who make sure the place is empty before they lock up for the night."

"That's just where you're wrong, then. That place is like a park at closing time—the keepers go round the main paths, but they can't look under every bush, there're too many of 'em. The ground floor's easy enough, but upstairs—"

"How do you mean?"

"Don't tell me you haven't noticed it isn't a bungalow! In a way, the way it's built, it's a building within a building. The outer walls form a sort of shell, and inside there's another wall altogether, except that it's pierced through with arches. Marvellous how they figured it out, all those years ago. Between the two, on every level, there's a walk, a gallery, an arcade— a tribune, a triforium, if you want to talk posh—all the way up to the roof. And that doesn't include the tower and the spire. The vergers'd never get home if they had to go through that lot every day."

"The doors to the stairs must be kept locked."

"Must they, indeed? Then you won't want to take my word for it that at least two of the doors—there may be more, for all I know—haven't got any locks on them at all, just bolts on the outside anybody can draw. One stair doesn't even have a door at all—just a red cord like in a cinema and a *No Admittance* sign.

Anyway, Liz has a key to the stairs back of the organ loft, so what difference does it make? All official and above-board. She keeps her cameras and stuff up there. So no problem."

Jurnet pondered what he had been told, then commented, "You looked as if you had a problem or two when I saw you next morning, on your way out."

The young man paled, if that were possible. He shut his eyes, either to cut off the physical presence of his questioner, or the better to see the remembered images of which he spoke.

"We went up to the triforium just before closing time. There was nothing to it, coming in as we did by the Bishop's Postern. You can slink along the wall in shadow all the way, and bob's your uncle. Once upstairs, we peeped over the edge, and there, down below, were the vergers looking for Reds under the bed. It was a bit of a giggle, really. Down at ground level you simply don't realize how much room there is up there. You don't even have to crouch down to stay out of sight, so long as you stay well over towards the outer wall.

"Liz didn't even wait till the vergers had gone to take her clothes off. All she had on was jeans and a sweater and a sort of G-string anyway. She took off everything, shoes and socks as well. By then, they'd turned off all the big lights, and there was just this silvery glow coming through the windows—was there a moon, I don't know, maybe it was the stars—and she just stood there, naked." The private vision became the only reality in the hushed room. "So beautiful I knew, whatever else it was, it couldn't be bad to be with her, like that, in that place, even if it was a church. It couldn't be a sin."

As if in instant derision of his own fantasy, Mosh Epperstein continued coarsely, "I had a hard on, you could have hung your jacket on it. I stripped off in such a hurry I broke the zip of my jeans. I took off everything, the way she had, and—it was the darndest thing—" the eyes opened wide with the wonder of it—"the stone floor under my bare feet was not at all cold, as you'd expect. In fact, my whole body was as warm as toast, and it wasn't because I was feeling randy as all hell either. It was as if all the holiness had risen up from the ground floor and got trapped in those galleries, how I don't know. Only that it was wonderful."

Mosh Epperstein smiled, and Jurnet thought of Miriam, naked by moonlight.

"I was mad to have it off with her then and there," the young man went on. "But she took my hand, with a gentleness you wouldn't believe, knowing Liz, and said, 'First I want to show you.' Anything she wanted was what I wanted, and we set off together, along the gallery, our bodies touching. It happened," said Mosh Epperstein, "but it was a dream. Corridors, and arches folding into other arches like the figures of a dance. Pillars like tree trunks so tall you couldn't see the branches, and the two of us walking naked hand-in-hand like it was through a jungle or some cavern under the sea.

"She'd taken a torch with her, but we didn't need it. She moved like a princess of her kingdom. She turned off into the gallery over the north transept and then led the way up a spiral stair and through a little door into the tower. The bells were hanging there, so black and powerful they seemed the real gods of the place, not that skinny guy down below hanging on his cross—"

Troubled, Leo Schnellman interrupted, "You don't have to go into every detail, Mosh—"

"Oh, but I do! Right, Inspector?" Jurnet nodded. "You see? He has to hear it all just in case there's something that doesn't jive with the rest, or in case, in a moment of absent-mindedness, I let down my guard and make some seemingly trivial remark that gives the game away, and gets me booked, not just for a little civilized pot-smoking, but for murder as well."

"That's right," said Jurnet. "You were in the tower. I must assume you went either up or down."

"O rare sleuth!" the other exclaimed. "Up it was.

We climbed out on to the tower roof. There was only the spire above us, and she didn't suggest climbing that, though, in the state I was in, I'd have followed her to the top of the weathercock if that was what she'd had in mind."

Mosh Epperstein paused; and Jurnet, against all his principles, felt a premonitory twinge of compassion.

"Up there, at night, it's not at all what you'd think. It doesn't seem the top of a tower, or of anything else. It doesn't seem joined to anything either—more a queer kind of raft anchored in space, an unidentified stationary object. It wasn't cold, or if it was I didn't feel it. There were just the two of us on this raft in the middle of the sky. Just Liz and me and a cartload of birdshit into which, being the born clown I am, I had to fall flat on my back!"

His two listeners said nothing.

"Oh, that was the peak all right! Everything afterwards was, literally, downhill all the way. Liz pretended it didn't matter, but I could see how her nose wrinkled. Hell, if I could've walked out of my own skin, I'd have done it, I smelled so awful. When we got back to where Liz kept her cameras—to where, that is, she keeps the squares of foam rubber and the sleeping bags—she fished out a towel from somewhere and I did what I could with that." There was a final hesitation before the man continued, with an incisiveness born of relief that at last the whole of it was out, "What I couldn't do a damn thing with was my bloody cock. It had gone as limp as old flannel. I can't tell you how I—" He swallowed. "Liz couldn't have been sweeter. Said not to think twice about it, she was tuckered out anyway. She kissed me and got into one of the sleeping bags and was asleep in a minute, like a child.

"I took longer. I lay there, looking up at the arches and thinking, of all things, about Little St Ulf. About how, in the story, he had been found castrated, which, in a kind of way, was what had just happened to me. When I finally dropped off, though, I must have slept like a log, because when I woke up it was broad daylight, there were noises coming from down below, and there was Liz, all dressed up in flowered muslin, bending over me."

"Noises from down below?"

"For Christ's sake!" Epperstein said. "I'm establishing an alibi. Noises. Voices. People about, passing the time of day. Definitely nobody being murdered, not even by me."

Jurnet asked, "Have you anything more to tell me?"

"Only to wrap it all up, like in the fairy stories. What Liz did then was lift up her dress and she had nothing on underneath. Not a stitch. And again, just in case you didn't think my cup was full enough already—" the lips twitching, the bony hands tense— "I couldn't do a bloody thing. I hardly dared look her in the face, but when I did, when I saw the sheer, relishing triumph in those beautiful blue eyes—that was when it came to me that it wasn't Little St Ulf who'd made me impotent, nor J. Christ either, for having the cheek to go screwing on his licensed premises, but Liz, my lovely Liz—that she and Stan had probably dreamed the whole thing up between them as an amusing way of passing an evening when there was nothing much going on in town."

The archaeology student got up to go. His ordeal over, he looked down at Jurnet with a smile that was almost friendly. "If, when you saw me, I looked anything like I felt, I can't blame you for wondering what I'd been up to. You weren't all that far out, either. What you saw was the face of a murderer."

"Except that you didn't kill her," Leo Schnellman put in quickly.

Epperstein said sadly, "Do you have to rub it in?"

21

The evening exodus of cars from the city centre had already begun when Jurnet drove his car on to the Chepe, the open space outside the FitzAlain Gate which had been Angleby's market place before even the Normans arrived to shift the commercial centre of the city into the shadow of the Castle. The detective parked, and switched on his radio, missing the opening sentences in the roar of homeward-bound engines revving up to left and right. Then the words got through.

". . . the League of Patriots headquarters in Farriersgate. What is believed to have been a petrol bomb was thrown through a ground-floor window, causing considerable damage to the three-storey building. A member of the League has been taken to hospital with burns which are not thought to be serious."

How they must be blessing Little St Ulf at the Norfolk and Angleby!

Jurnet had already, contrary to the rules, rendered himself incommunicado so far as Headquarters Control was concerned. He made no attempt to reconnect the umbilical cord. Let Hale and Batterby get on with it, and the best of British luck to them.

The detective got out of the car, locked it, and strolled through the FitzAlain Gate.

What was it the Rabbi had said? *"In that case, you must look for the truth you have overlooked."*

Easy enough to say! Something flitted teasingly through the dark recesses of Jurnet's consciousness, just beyond grasping. What the hell was it he had deposited there without filling in a paying-in slip? Something somebody had said? Or a moment of silence whose significance had passed him by; a lacuna more pregnant than words?

It was no use. The detective lifted his head and stared mindlessly at the West Front, magnificent in the evening light.

"Never interrupt a man lost in thought," announced a voice at his side. "The shock of finding himself back without warning in the irrational universe could bring on the bends."

Professor Pargeter raised his moustache like the trapdoor of a silo and launched his great laugh into the air. Startled pigeons rose in flight; and Dr Carver beamed at his old schoolfellow with a tolerant affection.

"I'm particularly glad to see you, Inspector," the Dean said, his gold-rimmed glasses flashing in the last of the light. "We'd be happy to have your opinion. The Professor and I have been discussing what, in the circumstances, should be done about the Little St Ulf excavation."

"Like hell we have!" growled the Professor. "Flossie's been handing down a *diktat*. He's giving us our cards. Fill in the hole and call the whole thing off. Did you ever hear such balls?"

Flushing like a boy, the Dean began, "The Bishop—"

"Don't try that one on me!" Professor Pargeter interrupted. To Jurnet, "You know, of course, there *is* no such animal—merely a cardboard cut-out worked by strings which they bring out on high days and holidays: a gaitered alibi for Flossie to hide behind, cloaking the awful tyranny with which—" jerking a thumb at the cathedral—"he runs that petrified wedding-cake."

"The Professor," said the Dean with Christian forbearance, "will have his little joke."

"Never more serious in my life!" the Professor declared. "Just because some pimply juvenile has the ineptitude to get himself bumped off, this Philistine is proposing to close the books on the third greatest object of pilgrimage in medieval England."

"The Inspector," stated the Dean, with some satisfaction, "has already made known to me his feelings on the subject. I know quite well he does not blame me. I only blame myself for not having had the imagination to conceive, before ever the project was embarked upon, what the possible consequences might be."

Professor Pargeter grumbled, "You'll be wanting us to shift our stuff."

"No hurry," the Dean assured him, happy to make a concession.

"I'll have to speak to Liz. She's got a lot of valuable gear up there in the gallery that she'll have to move out bit by bit. She's going to take this hard, Flossie. She's loved working in the cathedral."

The Dean smiled in acknowledgment of the aristocratic compliment. Jurnet, for a wild moment, was tempted, but restrained the impulse, to let the man know what went on in his patch after business hours. The Dean would have to be told one day. But not now, and certainly not in the presence of Pargeter who—in Liz Aste's interest, if no other—would be bound to turn the girl's nocturnal cavortings into a tremendous jape.

The Professor regarded his old schoolmate without love.

"If she's back to bumming round the discos for lack of something to do, we'll know who to thank for it."

"She could always help out at the bookstall," the Dean said, without apparent guile. "I'm sure Miss Hanks would be delighted to have her lend a hand." He turned his attention to Jurnet, with that mixture of innocence and authority the detective found so disconcerting. "And you, Inspector? I only wish I could say, in the nicest possible way, that we could dispense with your services equally."

"Couldn't wish it more than I do myself, sir."

Suddenly, whatever it was that had to be remembered shot upwards towards the light, only to subside once more into the amniotic darkness. He bade goodbye to the ill-assorted pair, the one in clerical black, the other in his bookie tweeds, and walked the length of the daisied lawn, from one stone general to the other. Turning the corner by the Song School, he came upon a little cluster of parents waiting by the Song School door; choristers emerging in ones and twos, their voices merry in the spring dusk.

Some of the older boys, wheeling out their bicycles, showed their contempt for the babies who were being called for; but even these sophisticates, the detective was glad to note, were careful to keep together. Not one departed into the gathering dark with only his fears to keep him company.

Arthur Cossey was not yet forgotten.

Jurnet was level with the door when Christopher Drue came running out, to hurl himself at a slender woman with a triumphant shout. "I'm to sing solo. Mr Amos says I'm to sing solo!"

As the woman laughingly disengaged herself, and smoothed down the boy's unruly curls with a gesture that said more than words, Jurnet studied her with curiosity and a good deal of pleasure. Mrs Drue was good to look upon. She was possessed of a spare and shapely beauty that, admirable as it was, might have been a little forbidding were it not for the wide-spaced eyes, as eager and loving as her child's, and the gentle curve of her lips. Her dark suit was like herself, being well cut, well made, and instinct with an understated elegance.

The detective watched Christopher tugging at his mother's hand as they moved towards the road.

"You'll have to do my things perfectly, as I'm to sing solo. Even my shoe buckles, though nobody could possibly see them, could they? Mr Amos says he has to see his face in them. And I'm to go to him after school on Friday for extra practice, so don't worry if I'm late, and Mr Amos says he'll see me home—though why can't I go home myself? I'm tired of being met as if I was still in kindergarten. Clive Langford's mother's letting *him* bike to school again, so why can't I? Is there anything in the car I can eat? I'm starving!"

The torrent flowed on. Before Mrs Drue could attempt an answer to any part of it, the boy shouted, "The policeman! He's the one I told you about. Do you want to speak to him? He *is* a policeman even though he doesn't look a bit like one, does he? Hello, policeman!"

"Hello, young fellow!" Jurnet came forward to where, in the fading light, the widely-spaced eyes could pass judgment on him. "How are you getting along, then?"

"I'm going to sing solo!" The exuberance burst out afresh. "If you come to Service Sunday after next you can hear me. I'll be the one sings highest. Arthur used to do it, but now he isn't alive any more Mr Amos says it's to be me. It was between me and Clive Langford. Mr Amos says Clive's voice is stronger, but mine's sweeter—" The boy stopped short, his face suddenly aflame. There was something both charming and touching in the way he hung his head, looked upward through the forward-falling curls. "I didn't really ought to be glad, did I?" Mrs Drue put a reassuring arm round the sturdy young body. "It's like being glad Arthur's dead, and I'm not, I'm not!"

"Of course you aren't, darling." His mother's voice was warm and comforting. "It doesn't mean you can't be pleased about the solo just the same." She passed her hand over the boy's hair again. "There's a Milky Way in the car. It's not locked. Just so long as it won't spoil your tea. I'll be along in a minute."

"It won't spoil my tea, or my supper, or my breakfast!" the boy sang out, and ran off to a Volvo parked a little further along the way. "Ta-ta, policeman! Or my elevenses!"

"Lock the door!" Mrs Drue called after him. She looked hesitantly at the detective. "As a matter of fact, I wanted to have a word with you, Mr—Mr—"

"Jurnet. Detective-Inspector Jurnet."

"Well then." She acknowledged the introduction with a brisk little nod. "My husband—we—" Not much good at aggression, she subsided into a question,

"Is it right, Inspector, is it even legal, to question a child without his parents' prior knowledge?"

"If I *had* been questioning him," Jurnet returned, not without some disingenuousness, his conscience being not all that clear on the subject, "it would certainly not have been all right. As it was, all we did was pass the time of day. No note taken, nothing like that. At Mr Amos's suggestion, as a matter of fact."

"Mr Amos," she said dismissively, "never sees any wrong in anyone."

"I hope you don't see any in me, for wanting to find out who killed Arthur Cossey."

"Oh dear!" Mrs Drue exclaimed. "Now you've put *me* in the wrong, when all I meant was—" The woman studied the detective's face; decided she liked what she saw. "I'm sure it was all right, really. I only hope Christopher was able to help."

"I was trying to find out how Arthur Cossey's friends saw him. What I found out was that he didn't have any."

"It doesn't surprise me." She spoke without sentimentality. "Children who look the way he looked aren't usually the ones who are popular."

"I gather he very much wanted to be friends with your young 'un."

"Oh," she said, with an honesty Jurnet had already perceived to be characteristic of her, "Christopher's lucky. He's the type of child who makes friends easily, and with whom everyone wants to be friends, even when he drives them mad with his winning ways." She smiled, and added, "That last is so I shouldn't sound too much like a besotted mum."

"I'm quite sure you aren't that. Did Christopher ever speak to you about Arthur?"

"Only that he was a drip and he wished he wouldn't keep bothering him. I could have wished him to be kinder, but that's how children are, isn't it? Being sorry for someone's a poor basis for friendship anyway."

"Yes."

"Besides," Mrs Drue went on, a delicate blush tinting her pale cheeks, "it was a bit embarrassing. Mrs Cossey works for some people I know, and—well, it was difficult. I was afraid, if Christopher snubbed Arthur, she'd think it was us being snobbish—or, if he *did* make friends with him, that we were being condescending. Either way we couldn't win. So I never made an issue of it. Just the same, I suggested to Christopher more than once that he ask him back from school for tea. But he always said airily, 'Some other time!'—and now it's too late."

For a moment the death of a child lay between them, the coldness of it, the terrible waste. Then the woman spoke urgently, the colour gone from her face. "Please, please, hurry up and find out who did it. I'm afraid. Every mother in Angleby's afraid, so long as there's a man going about who could—" She shivered and left the sentence unfinished. "Having to call for a boy Christopher's age! If it goes on much longer he's going to become frightened too, and that's what's so awful. Goodness knows there's little enough time anyhow to be a child and enjoy the world without fear."

Jurnet, who remembered his own childhood as a valley of shadows from which he had escaped with amazed gratitude for his deliverance, said, "That youngster of yours has too much going for him for you to need to worry. Sunday after next may be the first, it won't be the last time he's going to land the solo part, not by a long chalk."

"Has Christopher told you?" The jolly voice of Mr Amos rang out behind them. "He's to sing the solo in the Monteverdi." Wrapped round with an old college scarf whose fringed ends reached nearly to the ground, the Vice-Organist shook Mrs Drue by the hand, and greeted the detective with apparently equal pleasure. "The Inspector! Are things going well, my dear sir? I hope and pray things are going well."

"Our inquiries are proceeding," Jurnet replied, feeling a right clot.

"Excellent!" exclaimed Mr Amos. The evening breeze stirred his meagre hair. "Though what on earth shall we do with the murderer once you have caught him?"

"Lock him up, I should hope," Jurnet returned grimly, "where he can't do any more harm."

"You talk of his body," rejoined the other. "I meant his immortal soul. Will our faith, I ask myself, be strong enough to love him as the receptacle of the Divine Spirit, despite the terrible thing he has done?"

"Speaking for myself," said Jurnet, "the answer is no. If you'll excuse me—" this to Mrs Drue—"I must be getting along."

"He thinks me silly," Mr Amos announced sadly. "And of course he is quite right. Even after what has happened to Arthur, I still find it all but impossible to believe in the reality of evil. My dear Mrs Drue—" he took the woman's hand again, cradled it between his own that, strong and stubby-fingered, did not seem the hands of a musician—"whatever must you think of such a silly-billy presuming to instruct your son?"

Christopher's mother withdrew her hand with a smile.

"As you've given him a solo to sing, you have my permission to be as silly as you please."

"How kind! Especially as I fear you are bound to be disappointed with the result. Christopher's voice isn't a patch on what Arthur's was."

She was a very gracious woman. She said, "To his mother it will sound sweeter than nightingales."

22

At a tall house set in a waste of builders' rubble, Mr Amos said good night, and Jurnet continued on his way to the river, still worrying about whatever it was that eluded him. Worried too, at another level, about a Vice-Organist of Angleby Cathedral who did not believe in the reality of evil and who therefore, it followed, might not feel himself constrained by the moral considerations that kept men with less faith in God's allpervading goodness from going off the rails.

But would Mr Amos have killed the boy with the sweetest voice in the choir?

The river, by day so soothing to the spirit, by night compounded Jurnet's uncertainties. A fragile cage of mist encased the solitary lamp on the footpath; and the tarpaulined boats, moving fretfully at their moorings, made small noises of frustration as the water moved past them, whispering.

Beyond the prefabs and the scrapheaps, the trailer light shone invitingly. But for once, when Jurnet mounted the steps, calling out as usual to forestall alarm, no Millie came rushing forth in ecstasy.

The detective pushed the door open to discover Joe Fisher in the bosom of his family, and Millie in the bosom of Joe Fisher. Willie sat glum and as far away from the two as it was possible to get in that enclosed space.

The man, bundled up in a stained robe of terry-towelling—donned, Jurnet guessed, to protect his underlying finery—greeted the visitor with evident relief. Millie murmured blissfully, "Joe's here!" and Willie began to cry, tears too large for the small face to accommodate.

"What's this, then?" Jurnet edged himself past the lovers. "Here's a fine welcome for an old pal!"

Achieving his goal, he lifted the boy on to his lap.

"That kid—" Joe Fisher said, "he don't know what he wants."

"Hush!" soothed the detective, rocking the child to and fro. He had a sudden picture of Mrs Drue stroking her son's hair. "What a carry-on!" Glaring at the boy's father, "He had any tea?"

"Joe bought us Chinese." Millie raised her head proudly. She kissed her husband full on the lips. "Didn't you bring us Chinese, Joe?"

"Now then!" the man admonished. "You're making the Inspector blush. Chinese it was, £5.79 of it, straight off the sampan." He pushed the small, ripe body to one side, and stood up. "Time I was hitting the road." And to Jurnet, "I'd be glad of a few words outside, squire."

Millie began to wail, "Don't go, Joe!" Jurnet lifted Willie from his lap, disengaged the child's arms with great gentleness, and whispered in his ear, "Back in a jiffy!" He joined Joe Fisher outside the caravan, not sorry, after the fetor within, to breathe again the cool evening air where curlicues of mist dangled like streamers at a ghostly carnival.

Joe Fisher removed his outer garment to reveal a natty sports jacket, with shirt and slacks to tone. Then he announced, "I want to give you some money."

"One more word," warned Jurnet, "and I'll have you down at the station, Millie or no Millie." He began to walk away.

"Not what you think, Mr Jurnet!" The man's hand clamped on the detective's arm like a band of iron. "When did I ever try to sweeten *you*? I'd need my head examined!"

"Take your hand off my arm or I'll have you for assault!"

Joe Fisher released his grip. The detective, his lips a thin line of anger, strode away towards the river.

"Have a heart, Mr Jurnet!" the man cried, hurrying after. "Give a chap a chance!" Jurnet stopped, but kept his face averted. "Thing is—I got t' be away on business, an' I can't hardly ask Millie to go into the bank an' cash herself a cheque, now can I? Any more 'n I can trust a kid Willie's age with a handful of ponies. You always make out you're so fond of 'em, is it any wonder I thought—"

Jurnet turned round. "Handful of ponies? Planning a world cruise, are you?"

"Don't be like that!" the other protested. "You're the one always on at me to take better care of 'em, and then when I try to do it, look what happens! All it is, there's this house to be cleared other side of Ely—"

"Nothing to stop you getting to Ely and back in a day easy."

"There's good stuff there. Fetch a right old price in London. I reckon to take it on to a friend I got works the Portobello Road market—"

"So? That needn't make it more than another day, all told. What's the sudden need of an hon. treasurer for a couple of days?" Grabbing the man by the lapels, "Not thinking of shedding your responsibilities, Joe, are you, by any chance? Skipping it, with or without Mrs Cossey? Because if you are, I'll have you brought back, I promise you, if it's from the wilds of Patagonia, and if I have to do it myself!"

The man tried to back away, found himself held fast.

"You're a fine one to be talking about assault!" Jurnet let him go, contemptuously. "An' as fer Sandra, she don't even know I'm going." Joe Fisher straightened his crumpled lapels with tender hands. "You got a dirty mind, Mr Jurnet, tha's what you got."

Jurnet asked quietly, "Then who are you running away from?"

"Don't be daft!" Even to himself the disclaimer must have sounded unconvincing, for the man suddenly changed tone and tempo, the words tumbling over each other in his haste to set the record straight. "Do I look like a hit-man, I ask you! Me and my polonies!" Spreading out fingers which indeed justified the metaphor. "Handle a gob of jelly with that lot an' I'd be a headless wonder afore you could say penny for the guy. But think *they* want to know? Joe Fisher went on bitterly. "All because, couple o' nights ago, in the Lord Nelson, I happened to say, jest making sociable conversation over a few jars, that, if you arst my opinion, the whole bleeding bundle of faggots ought to be blown to smithereens. Me! What couldn't even blow a smithereen to smithereens!"

"Now I see!" Jurnet exclaimed, light dawning. "We're talking about that attack on the League of Patriots—that's it, isn't it? Do I gather that you're denying you threw that petrol bomb through their window?"

"Don't you start on me too, Mr Jurnet! When I get my hands on the joker what passed on my innocent words—" Joe Fisher stopped, and began again, disarmingly. "What I'm saying is, if they come after me here, it's not on'y me that'll suffer. It'll be Millie an' the kid, right? An' as fer Sandra, she'd do her nut if that bunch of oicks turned up and started turning her place over. I 'aven't the heart to let it happen. I got ter get out!"

Jurnet looked past him at the mounds of junk that made up Millie's Garden of Eden. In the thickening mist some rusting refrigerators shone virginal and mysterious.

In the flat voice that told his intimates when he was deeply moved, he said, "Know what, Joe? You're a louse. You've got the money. You could have bought Millie a house years ago, and put in someone to look after her—"

"Don't you think I've tried? I even spoke to Sandra about taking on the job—took her to see a bungalow I got out of the *Argus*. Bathroom an' two lavs, with low flush. Fit for a king! But she turned it down flat. Couldn't let down that Holy Joe of hers in the Close, would you believe it?" Joe Fisher thrust his face close to the detective's. "Millie's happy here, in't that right? An' Willie—that kid's got a head on him like a man o' forty. He'll keep me in my old age yet."

Jurnet observed with satisfaction, "He hates the sight of you."

"On'y natural, in't it?" The man chuckled indulgently. "My ol' man, I'd'a cheerfully drowned him in his bath for a Mars bar, on'y he never took one." He tugged at his jacket pocket, and brought out a wad of ten-pound notes. "Fer Willie's sake—" he pleaded.

"Put them away, or I'll chuck them in the river and you after."

"I been frank wi' you, Mr Jurnet. I'm desperate. *You* tell me what t' do."

"Ask the Citizen's Advice Bureau."

"Mr Jurnet!" There was hurt and reproof in the man's voice. When he spoke again, after a measurable pause, there was something else that the detective was unable to put a name to. "In that case, I got no alternative, have I? I'm givin' myself up."

"So you *did* throw that bomb!"

"Don't talk daft!" Joe Fisher said. "I told you about that. I'm givin' myself up for the murder of Arthur Cossey."

23

"Well, Ben, what do you think?" The Superintendent, wearing evening clothes, sat back in his chair looking beautiful.

Jurnet, without being aware that he was doing so, glowered at his immaculately turned-out superior officer. Nothing could have convinced him, tired and unkempt as he was, that the Superintendent hadn't got himself up like that on purpose; one more skirmish in the undeclared war that was, in some way he had never quite been able to fathom, a mutual declaration of love.

He answered the question. "Hard to say. I'm sure his first thought was to find somewhere safe to hole up—and where safer than the nick? Then, too, he wanted to make sure the League of Patriots wouldn't go gunning for him either down at the scrapyard or over at Mrs Cossey's. Once they knew he was out of reach, where they couldn't touch him, the heat was off, for the time being at least."

"The news-flash only said that a man was helping with inquiries."

Jurnet said, "I had to keep to the usual form. What I've done, though, is have a word with a couple of blokes who, by now, will have spread it round town, and in the Lord Nelson and the Cock and Crow in Farriersgate in particular, that the man we're holding is none other than Joe."

The Superintendent considered.

"I suppose that *is* all that needs to be done?"

Jurnet's hostility evaporated. One thing about the Super: you could count on him to say the right thing at the right time.

"I've sent Hinchley and Bly down to Bridge Street, just in case; and a chap to Mrs Cossey's, on the chance the Patriots know Joe lodges there. PC Blaker's off duty, but he tells me he intends to be down on the staithe anyway tonight, birdwatching. Seems a long-eared owl's been seen down there, and he's offered to keep an eye out on the side. Actually, I reckon it needs eight to ten men to cover the Fisher place properly, what with the river one side and the playing-fields at the back—"

It was too much to hope for.

"Watch it, Ben!" the Superintendent advised, the kindliness thinning to let the underlying iron show through. "You're letting your heart run away with your head again. You've let it be known that Fisher's in police custody, and therefore not to be got at, and that should be enough." He leaned back in his chair, seemingly in no hurry to get away to his golf-club dinner. "You'll pass all this over to Hale and Batterby in the morning, of course?" Chuckling, "I suppose you know, Ben, anywhere else but here, you wouldn't last ten minutes, the way you hog everyone else's job without so much as a by-your-leave?"

"Can't see why you should say that, sir, when I've just brought in a fellow says he murdered Arthur Cossey."

"Congratulations." With a smile that took away all offence, almost, the Superintendent tapped the type-written pages in front of him with a well-manicured nail. "He says he killed Cossey because the boy threatened to go to the authorities with some trumped-up story about having seen him beating his son, and he was afraid the child could be taken into care. Does that sound plausible to you?"

"Plausible that Arthur Cossey could have made the threat?" The other nodded. "Only too much so. He seems to have regarded the world as full of potential dupes."

"How right he was, the little monster!" The Superintendent tapped the pages again. "Now tell me if this confession is worth the paper it's written on."

"It's that, all right. For what it doesn't say, maybe, as much as for what it does. Mightn't be a bad ploy, assuming you'd done a killing, to make a confession with more holes in it than Swiss cheese, so no one'd take it seriously."

"Does Joe Fisher have enough brains for that?"

"Oh, he's quick, especially with a spot of danger to set the grey matter churning. A safe house and a clean bill of health at one go. Not bad, if you can bring it off."

"What are the holes, would you say? You noticed the bit about the boy's clothes?"

"Where he says he dumped them on the floor? One of the deliberate errors—who knows? He'd know about the state of the body, thanks to Professor Pargeter's radio chat."

"But the tomb? Could he have known of that as a potential hiding-place? I must confess I don't quite see him as one of the Reverend Doctor Delf-Polesey's readers."

"Arthur may have mentioned something about quaint school customs. Harbridge, the verger, could have spoken of it to his sister-in-law, Mrs Cossey, at some time or other, and she could have passed it on. What interests me more, though, is what he says about the broom."

"I missed that."

"I might not have noticed either, if the Professor and I hadn't almost fallen over it when we found the body. It had been left just inside the door, and it was pretty clear that the murderer had used in on his way out to brush out any of his footprints that showed up on that bit of drugget. The handle was tested for prints, but there was nothing. Now, when Joe describes what he saw at the dig—the table, the measuring sticks, and so on—he says there was a broom, lying across the table. And later on, after he'd killed the lad, he says that on his way out he scuffed about a bit to make sure he hadn't left any prints behind in the dust. Nothing about using the broom to get rid of them."

"Proof of innocence or another deliberate mistake?"

"That's the sixty-four-dollar question. I haven't forgotten I saw him in the cathedral before the murder ever happened, asking where Little St Ulf was buried."

"Meaning he could have had a good look round then, and seen enough to be able to give a plausible description without having even been there on the day of the killing."

"Exactly. If it wasn't for that broom, that is. Because when I was having a word with Harbridge, earlier on, he told me it was getting on his wick, the way Pargeter and his lot were mucking up the north aisle and leaving it to the vergers to clear up after them. So, he said, he'd put a good hard broom on the table, where they'd be sure to see it, in the hope they'd take the hint and clean up their own mess from then on, instead of tracking it in and out all the time."

"I can't see how that conflicts with—"

"Put it there Saturday night, Harbridge said, after closing time. The night before the murder."

Rosie Ellers's cooking, like Rosie herself, was full-flavoured. Miriam, who regarded the discovery of fire as a male conspiracy to keep women chained to the kitchen stove, had once labelled it pornographic. If his wife should ever do in public what she did in the privacy of her kitchen, she had warned Sergeant Ellers, he, as a police officer, would have had no choice but to run her in for corrupting public morals.

For Jurnet to sit down to such a love-feast without his love by his side was a kind of gastronomic masturbation, an activity he had little taste for. Rosie watched with growing concern as the detective mashed his pâté diligently, fiddled about with the roast duck so as to make it look that he had eaten some, and begged off her justly famous crème brûlée on the unconvincing ground that he was full up to there.

"Ribs still playing you up?" she wanted to know.

"Nothing I can't ignore, nine-tenths of the time."

"In that case," Rosie declared bluntly, "if you aren't ill, you're too old to be dying of love."

"You don't have to tell me."

"You go on that way," Mrs Ellers continued pitilessly, "the boys are going to stop calling you Valentino. Jack—" she appealed to her husband, sitting back rosy and replete, his waistband undone—"can't you take him down to the station and stick a tube down him like what they did the Suffragettes?"

"Don't go by the way he looks," Jack Ellers replied callously. "He's tougher than old boots, actually. 'Tisn't love the Inspector's dying of: it's aggravation. Once he finds out who bumped off Little St Arthur, he'll be as beautiful as ever he was."

Jurnet said, "The Sergeant seems to have overlooked the fact that we already have a man in custody who has confessed to the crime."

"Oh ah," returned Sergeant Ellers, unimpressed. "The day Joe Fisher confesses to something he actually did they'll be crowning me Prince of Wales." The little Welshman belched delicately behind his hand, and continued, "You'll no doubt be wanting to hear how I got on with the Honourable Liz."

At that Rosie, like the well-trained police wife she was, got up from the table and went to do the dishes; leaving the kitchen door ajar, however.

Jurnet said, "You lived to tell the tale, at least."

"Only just! Next time, I promise you, I'm going to put in for danger money. Aristocracy, too!"

"Spare me the lurid details. Just tell me—did she confirm Epperstein's story?"

"Did she not! Once she got going on the subject of

that poor mutt's performance—or, more properly, lack of it—there was no stopping her. I hardly knew where to put my face, let alone various other portions of my anatomy. It was what you might call an illustrated lecture, see? Everything but the magic lantern slides. In the end I just shut my eyes and thought of England."

"So long as you didn't shut your ears as well. I want to know what she was up to while Epperstein was asleep."

"You'll find it hard to credit, but what she says she did, once our ramshackle Romeo had finally dropped off, was shin over to the gallery in the south transept where it appears Master Stan Brent was dossed down for the night, and have an extra good screw with him, to make up for what she'd missed out on over the other side of the premises."

"You're joking! What's the Dean and Chapter running there in the Close, for God's sake? A C of E knocking shop?"

"Just what I thought myself. I s'pose, though, if it could never occur to you in a million years that such and such a thing could possibly happen, you can't hardly be expected to take precautions against it. What the lady—and believe me when I say I use the word loosely—says she did next morning is, she and Brent waited till the Communion service started, and then slipped out of the South Door; went down to the river, to that café at the marina which always opens up early on Sundays. After they'd eaten, Brent went off. Liz says she doesn't know where, and she came back to the cathedral to rouse Mr Epperstein from his slumbers."

He paused, and Jurnet asked, as if he had expected more, "That the lot, then?"

"Not quite. After I left the Aste ancestral pad, I went down to the marina myself. I figured wiping the Hon Liz out of your memory wasn't like wiping the coffee-mug rings off the table tops, and I wanted to have a word with whoever was on at the café early on Sunday. It was on the cards he, or she, might remember something."

"Any luck?"

The little Welshman grinned.

"It turned out to be an Eyetie, and you know what they are. He remembered Liz so well he could have painted you a picture if his name'd been Leonardo da Vinci instead of Marcantonio. But what he remembered was that she and the bloke with her had a blazing row over the Early Morning Special—so much so that the fellow stamped out, leaving her to pay the bill."

"From what I've seen of Mr Brent, that bit's in character, anyhow. Did your Italian gather what the row was about?"

"His English isn't too hot, unfortunately. He just had the impression the girl was pressing the fellow to do something or other, and he wouldn't buy it."

"Mm." Jurnet filed away the information along with all the other pieces of the puzzle for which, as yet, he could find no place. "Funny thing, though. When I saw her a little later that morning, coming down the nave, she certainly didn't give the impression of a girl who'd just had a blazing row with her beloved."

"Well, she wouldn't, would she? If what Mr Epperstein says is true, making a monkey out of him must have set her up for the day. Lovely girl, Liz. Praying Mantis to her friends."

Rosie came back into the room with a cut-glass bowl full of fruit, which she set on the table. With an expert hand she peeled apples and pears, cut oranges into segments, apportioning them between small plates, along with grapes and bananas; placing her finished work before the pair at the table without inquiring whether they wanted it. She herself selected a bright green Granny Smith into which she bit without bothering to peel it. A trickle of juice oozed at one corner of her mouth, and Jurnet, who had been watching her mindlessly, suddenly reddened, looked down, and took a piece of orange from his piled-up plate.

Ellers, with genteel dexterity, spat grape pits into a cupped palm and inquired, "How are Millie and the kid going to manage with Joe in the clink? I suppose it's bring on the social workers at long last, eh?"

"Not if Joe can help it. He phoned a solicitor—bloke by the name of Fendale, from Hiller, Upton's—"

"Hiller, Upton's," echoed the Sergeant, in a tone that spoke volumes.

"Now, now," Jurnet returned reprovingly. "Someone has to represent the villains. They have their rights like anyone else. Fendale seems a decent enough chap. He'll see Willie gets money for food day by day, and generally keep an eye on things." Guilt rose in Jurnet's throat, mingling with the taste of the orange. He had promised the child to return in a jiffy. And he had not returned.

Rosie discarded her apple core and started in on a banana.

"Jack's told me about them. Anything I can do?"

"Ta. I'll bear it in mind."

"Seems a lot to put on a child's shoulders, that's all. How old is he, exactly?"

"Officially, coming up to five and a half. Provided you don't tell the Education Authority, seven."

"Poor little mite!" Rosie was exclaiming when the telephone rang on the sideboard. "It doesn't seem fair."

Jack Ellers took the call.

"It isn't," Jurnet agreed. "But then, what is?"

Jack Ellers held out the receiver to his superior officer, stretching the cord to its limit.

"You'd better hear this, Ben."

Jurnet took the phone; listened, and heard.

24

When they got to the scrapyard the trailer was still burning. Nothing to what it had been before the fire engine arrived, one of the bystanders assured them, sounding aggrieved that the show was nearly over. Someone had sheared through the chain on the metal gates, and they stood open. A hose snaked from a hydrant, figures moved dark against the flickering light, or bright in the headlamps of the fire engine parked beside a small mountain of rusted bedsprings. An ambulance waited, a little further along.

The trailer was dying noisily as its wood warped, its metal twisted in the heat. A sudden crackle splayed a plume of sparks against the night sky.

PC Hinchley came limping to meet the pair, a sleeve of his tunic charred to a sticky web, the arm showing through blistered and swollen.

"I tried to get inside, sir. It went up like a ruddy bomb."

He turned his face away from Jurnet's bleak gaze, and the detective saw that the skin down one side was scorched and angry.

"Go and get that seen to!"he commanded harshly. And, on a softer note, "I'm sure you did what you could, Bob."

PC Bly came up, having heard the last words.

"More than anyone could, short of Superman. Thought we'd lost him as well, for a bit." Perhaps the man imagined some critical appraisal in the detective's eyes: perhaps his own conscience troubled him, for he burst out, "The devil himself couldn't have got in there, Mr Jurnet. By the time we were out of the

173

car and across the street, flames were shooting out everywhere. Those two never had a chance."

"No." After a moment Jurnet asked, "Did you see anyone about?"

"Not a soul. Couple of cars passed earlier, young fellow called for a girl at one of the houses, and they went off towards the river. Otherwise, nothing. Blaker, down at the Water Gate, called in to say it was quiet as the grave over there too—except that, about ten minutes before the fire started, he came on, happy as a sandboy, to let us know some bloody owl was tuwhit-tuwhooing it up in some tree or other."

"You kept the trailer under surveillance at all times?"

"Yes, sir." The constable jerked his head in the direction of the street. "You can see where we're parked. The trailer windows were lit up all the time—that is, until a couple of minutes before the place went up, when we reckoned they'd turned out the light to go to bed. The curtains were drawn, but they were thin, and the light showed through. Every now and then someone seemed to be moving about inside, but the curtains weren't all that thin you could be sure."

"I shall want a full report."

"Yes, Mr Jurnet."

PC Bly watched as the detective strode away towards the fire engine, followed by Sergeant Ellers: stiffened, wondering what more was in store when the tall, lean figure suddenly checked, turned, and came back.

Jurnet said, "I want you to know I'm satisfied you did everything possible in the circumstances."

"Thank you, sir."

The chief fireman, a square, strong man, pursed his lips doubtfully.

"Bomb? Could be, I suppose. More likely a gas cylinder. Wouldn't be the first of *them* we've been called out to, nor the last."

The contents of Joe Fisher's pockets, for which he had been given a receipt at the police station, had not included the "gas bit". (*I'll be back in a jiffy, Willie!*)

Jurnet asked tonelessly, "How long before you'll be able to get at the bodies?"

"Take a bit of time. That metal's been white-hot. Two of them in there, so I hear."

"Yes. A woman and a child."

"Ah. Did something silly, I reckon, like leaving the stopcock open. Some people never learn till it's too late." The fireman sighed, and got back to business. "We've had a look already, far as we can, but there's such a tangle there you couldn't see an elephant, if there was one. They'll be underneath—what's left of them."

"Jack—" turning to Ellers—"will you call in for a van?"

The thought of Millie and Willie, barbecued on the bone, packed into polythene bags like some new convenience food, was suddenly more than Jurnet could bear.

He moved away from the trailer, past the fire engine, and the ambulance waiting to no purpose, into a darkness fitfully illuminated by the flames dying reluctantly behind him. Among the jagged ziggurats of waste metal a pyramid of perished tyres loomed suave and surprising. Several freezer chests lay on their sides, like dominoes flung down by a petulant giant. On one of them, a sign in shocking-pink fluorescent paint read: *Happiness is a Baccaloni Lik-Stik.*

The detective was not aware of grief. He felt empty, hollow, which was no more than he deserved, having done such poor justice to Rosie Ellers's cooking. Burrowing further into the dark, he became aware of the small night noises of the scrapyard, the scuffle of mice and rats and whatever other creatures had staked out a territory for themselves among the rubbish. An owl hooted down by the river. PC Blaker's pal, no doubt.

Nearer, some larger animal—a cat, perhaps, caught in iron ganglia from which it had been unable to free itself—breathed shallowly, in little mews that were beyond despair. Jurnet took out his flashlight and played it over the nearest pile. The light caught some flattened petrol cans with a pretty iridescence, but no creature in distress announced itself.

He went round to the other side and found Millie.

She lay, her cotton dress ripped open from neck to hem, staring up at the sky above a strip of rag tied over the lower part of her face. Her body was scratched and bruised, her thighs dark with dried blood. When Jurnet shone his torch into the beautiful grey eyes they blinked, but otherwise did not interrupt their incurious perusal of the heavens. Every now and again she mewed like a trapped cat.

"Millie!" The detective knelt down in the dirt, removed the gag, and slid a hand gently under the girl's head. "It's Mr Ben!"

She gave no sign of recognition and, swallowing down the bitterness of saying it, he whispered into her dirty and delicate little ear: "Joe!" and again: "Joe!"

For once the magic password had no effect. The girl lay inert. It looked as though Millie Fisher's marvellous luck had run out at last. Unless, indeed, she had achieved yet another miraculous victory against all the odds: escaped into some world of her own choosing, where joy still reigned unconfined, and Joe, darling Joe, was forever at hand to look after her.

Jurnet ran back towards the trailer; fetched Jack Ellers and the ambulance men, needed after all. With expert ease they moved the girl on to a stretcher, wrapped her in a blanket; lifted their burden ready to depart.

Jurnet bent over the battered face.

"Willie!" he begged. "Where's Willie?"

"Leave her be!" one of the ambulance men exclaimed, not at all in a friendly way.

"Willie!" he persisted.

No answer.

After an hour of searching, Jack Ellers said, "We'll have to come back in daylight. It's the only way to be sure we haven't missed anything."

"They may have done him over. He may need medical help. We've got to keep on looking." Jurnet glared at the little Welshman, missing completely the concern incised on the chubby face. "No one's stopping you from knocking off, if you feel you've had enough."

"Don't talk daft! All I'm wondering is if he didn't do the first thing you might expect—take to his heels and get the hell out of here. In which case he could be anywhere."

Jurnet shook his head.

"He'd never leave his Ma."

"The kid could have been too frightened to remember he ever had one. Getting away would be all he could think of."

"Not Willie."

"OK," Ellers agreed wearily. "In that case, I take it, you'll be wanting me to call in to tell the lads to stop looking for him in the city. Tell Mr Hale and Mr Batterby they can go back to bed." Jurnet looked at him without saying anything. "Look, they may simply have dumped him in the river. Or he could be in the caravan after all. The firemen say they can't be sure till morning. An incinerated kid," the Sergeant finished with calculated brutality, "doesn't take up all that much room."

After a moment, Jurnet said, "I'm sorry, Jack. Find Bly and Blaker will you, and tell them to call it a day. You go along with them, and take Hinchley with you. Get him to the hospital, if you have to do it by force."

"I'm not leaving you here on your own."

"That's all right, Sergeant." The Superintendent was standing there, still in his evening clothes. "I'll keep the Inspector company." To Jurnet with, for once, no acid corroding the concern, "You should have let me know earlier, Ben."

Jurnet smiled, inexplicably soothed.

"Hardly thought you'd be dressed for it, sir."

"Quite right," said the Superintendent. "So we'd better find the boy quickly, hadn't we, before I get myself messed up."

•　•　•

They began at the beginning, and worked their way back from the chain-link fence along Bridge Street as methodically as if no one had covered the territory before them. Aware of how small was the space into which a desperate child could compress itself, they circled each scrapheap at a snail's pace, peering along the torch beams that penetrated the dark interiors beyond their reach. They lifted sodden mattresses and rotting cisterns, handling the revolting detritus with the exquisite care accorded to ancient artefacts, lest their prying precipitate an avalanche in which Willie might perish at the hands of his would-be rescuers.

Jurnet's cracked ribs sent thuds of pain through his tired body. The Superintendent worked on imperturbably. Crafty fellow that he was, a born leader of men, he had produced from the boot of his car gum boots and a boiler-suit in which he looked not much less elegant than in his evening clothes. Jurnet would not have been surprised to see emerge from that cache, should the circumstances call for it, anything from deep-sea diver's equipment to an astronaut's space suit.

"I take it—" the Superintendent remarked when, the last scrapheap accounted for, they drew breath in front of the first of the row of prefabs—"that whoever was responsible for what was done here tonight was safely holed up in the caravan before Hinchley and Bly even took up surveillance?"

"Probably. Three of 'em, I reckon. Four at the most." Jurnet omitted to specify the basis of his calculation: one to take care of Willie, one or two to hold Millie down; one to take his turn at rape. "If they'd come after, the light spilling out when the trailer door was opened would have given them away—even though, from the car, the PCs hadn't what you could call a marvellous view of the door."

"And how was that?" the Superintendent inquired, in a tone that boded little good to the departed constables.

"Not their fault," Jurnet countered, quick as always to come to the defence of his brothers-in-arms. "The way the trailer was positioned made it impossible to park in Bridge Street and get a full frontal. I reckon that's how, in the couple of minutes the trailer light was out and before the place went up in smoke, the bastards were able to slip out, and get Millie and the kid out—" he steeled himself to interpolate, "*if* they got the kid out—without being spotted. Hinchley and Bly chose the best spot they could find in the circumstances."

"Nothing to stop them getting out of the car and crossing the road for a better look."

"So they did, from time to time. But I'd particularly warned them to keep a low profile. If anyone *was* planning something, I wanted it to be along the street, where we could control the situation and nip it in the bud." The same loyalty that impelled Jurnet to defend PCs Bly and Hinchley operated to prevent the detective from reminding the Superintendent that it was he who had disallowed protection round the entire perimeter.

"My fault as much as theirs," declared the Superintendent, a wonderful man. "It isn't as though you didn't warn me."

"I'm the one told the kid I'd be back in a jiffy."

"Let's not compete in breast-beating, shall we?" The Superintendent bent his head under the low lintel and entered the first Nissen hut, Jurnet following. The place was stacked with bags of cement, most of them soaked with damp and oozing their contents in a grey slime that overlaid the floor.

"One mystery at least I intend to clear up," the Superintendent stated, sending torchlight in great sweeps round the walls, "and that's how Mr Joe Fisher makes his living. This stuff hasn't been touched for years."

Willie was not there among the cement, nor yet among the scaffolding poles, the wire-netting, the mouse-nibbled sacks, the offcuts of hardboard that filled Joe Fisher's many mansions. The last building was full of old deckchairs, stacked layer upon layer like the early Christians in the catacombs. One day Jurnet meant to ask Joe Fisher to explain their presence and their preservation. In the meantime, their task almost at an end, the detective poked fiercely at the splintered frames, pushed aside frayed canvases stamped variously The Lido, Great Yarmouth BC, and Jacks of Cromer.

And found Willie.

The child was crouched in an angle of the building, in a space Jurnet had missed completely first time round, so well was it hidden by the piled-up chairs. He looked up, squinting in the torchlight, but showing no particular pleasure at being discovered.

"Willie boy!" Jurnet scooped the stiff little body up into his arms. "Are you all right?"

"Ma?"

The boy struggled to be let down. Jurnet set him carefully on his feet, and said, with an artificial jollity it sickened him to hear issuing from his own mouth: "We've been looking for you all over!"

The Superintendent heard voices, came over, and exclaimed: "Thank God!"

Willie asked again, "Ma?"

Jurnet said, "She's going to be fine."

Great gusts of grief shook the child.

"I run away!"

Jurnet picked the child up again, held him against his shoulder, and rubbed the thin little back. A baby to be burped of guilt, as it might be wind.

Pro that he was, even so preoccupied, the detective's eyes were intent on the beam of the Superintendent's torch, sweeping the child's hiding-place in a meticulous quartering; a care rewarded when it came upon a knapsack propped against a deckchair set on its side.

Jurnet, who thought he recognized the knapsack as the one he had seen on the back of Stan Brent, said nothing: rocked Willie gently to and fro and awaited developments. The Superintendent set his torch down on the floor and, kneeling, undid the knapsack straps. From within he drew out a package wrapped in black PVC which he lifted gingerly by one corner and allowed to unroll itself. Out tumbled a little heap of honeycombed plastic strips, together with a number of small, semi-transparent envelopes, the kind used by stamp collectors.

Not only by stamp collectors. Each envelope contained a small amount of a white crystalline substance. The Superintendent picked up one of the plastic strips and studied the tablets encased in them.

Jurnet said, "Acid."

"Several thousand pounds' worth, by the look of it." The Superintendent transferred his attention to the envelopes. "And that's not counting the heroin." He gathered the little haul together and repacked it before picking up the torch and getting to his feet again, the knapsack dangling from his hand. "So now we know how Mr Joe Fisher keeps the wolf from the door."

"Not only Joe Fisher."

"Oh?" The Superintendent was alert, questioning. But Willie, worn out with grief and guilt, had gone to sleep at last, and Jurnet, putting a finger to his lips, made no reply.

25

Sergeant Ellers came into the Incident Room and placed a typed list on Jurnet's desk. Unlike that of his superior officer, the little Welshman's chubby face gave no hint of the strains and stresses of the previous night. Well up on his toes, he waited to be told he had done well.

Inspector Benjamin Jurnet, hollow-eyed and ill-shaven in the misty sunlight that filtered through the windows as if uncertain of its welcome, glanced down at the paper and made the effort to smile.

"You've been up with the lark."

"Open early, newsagents," returned the Sergeant, glowing in the other's approval. "Got him while he was still parcelling up the papers for the boys to take out."

"Did you manage this time to get a word with the boy who's taken over Arthur Cossey's round?"

"Not necessary, once I'd spoken with the boss—Mr Doland, that is. Before, I didn't know what questions to ask. But now—! What he said is that no one's taken over Arthur's round—not *in toto*. If you'll look down the list you'll see why."

The Sergeant's self-satisfaction was so artless that Jurnet, out of sheer affection, pretended not to see.

"You tell me."

"The addresses, boyo! What'd make a fellow in Reresby Road, for instance, get his papers from a newsagent in Palace Plain, the other side of town? Must be at least half a dozen newspaper shops that are nearer. Or somebody in Market Lane who actually lives on top of the W. H. Smith's? And there's a bloke halfway to Cromer—well, maybe that's a bit of an exaggeration, but you know what I mean—gets something called *Practical Pig Management* once a month, and that's all." The rosy face became redder. "*Practical Pig Management!* Laughs himself silly at his own wittiness, I shouldn't wonder!"

"How did Mr Doland explain his far-flung customers, and how Arthur could be expected to cover such a large area delivering to them?"

"Said they were all customers the kid brought in off his own bat. Said he was surprised himself that anyone would want him to deliver from so far away, but so long as Arthur was willing, who was he to complain? Always first in and last back, he said, but that was the kid's business. The boy told him they were all people he knew, and so he assumed they did it to do Arthur a good turn. The chap runs some kind of bonus scheme for the delivery boys, and any boy who brings in a new customer gets so many points which he can use up in the shop as credit for sweets or iced lollies or whatever. Come to think of it, Mr Doland's just about the only one in this whole bloody investigation to put in a good word for Arthur. Newsboy of the

Year nothing—Newsboy of the Century! Says no other boy came within miles of bringing in so many orders, not in all the years he's been in business. And never a complaint from a customer till the day he died, when they were all phoning in asking what the hell. Seems Arthur missed his last delivery altogether. Took the papers out, but that's the last anyone saw of them. Or of him either, for that matter." The Sergeant leaned across the desk and pointed. "The ones with a tick against the name, they're all Arthur's lot."

"Hm. Not all of them out in the sticks. Some are quite close to Doland's."

Jack Ellers grinned. "Shouldn't be surprised they moved there for that very reason, with our lad collecting his cut for the lettings from the landlord or the estate agent. I tell you, if young Master Cossey hadn't been cut off untimely, he'd have ended up running the bloody country!"

"Done better as he is. Saint must surely rank above Prime Minister in the pecking order." Returning to the list, "Any of these names familiar to you? I seem to recognize a couple myself."

"Some. I've put a cross against them. And Mr Batterby—I run into him in the car-park and he took a quick gander. Reckons there's at least four he's had to do with in the way of business, one time or other. I've dropped a copy off at Records, for them to fill in the form, if any, on the whole shoot." The Sergeant shook his head in reluctant admiration. "Milk, newspapers, delivered to your door—so why not acid and pot and snow? That's progress, man! You've got to hand it to him!"

Jurnet inquired mildly, "And who's him, when he's at home?"

"Joe Fisher, of course!" But the little Welshman, alive to the other's every nuance of expression, faltered even as the name was spoken. "You mean, it isn't Joe?"

"He swears he never even knew the stuff was down there by the river. And that he'd no idea Arthur was doing any deliveries."

"Oh—" said Ellers, recovering his aplomb. "He swears!"

"Joe doesn't deny he's obliged a few friends from time to time with the makings of a joint. Nothing more. And he says he always got that from Stan Brent. The one time—still to oblige that anonymous pal, naturally—he asked Brent to get him some LSD, the answer, Joe says, was a punch on the hooter." Jurnet sat back reflectively. "Taking into account that Joe looks like he could gobble up a couple of Brents for breakfast and still find room for his bacon and eggs, that would seem to indicate a certain strength of feeling, wouldn't you say, on the part of Mr B?"

"That shit! He wouldn't recognize a feeling if it stuck him up the rear end with a hatpin!" Ellers weighed the possibilities, and ended by asking, "What do you think, Ben?"

"I think we'll have a further word with the shit in question."

The detective chose not to expatiate on his interview with Joe Fisher. Breaking the news of what had happened to Millie, he had watched the man shrivel in a way he could never have believed possible had he not witnessed it with his own eyes: reduce in size so that the clothes he had filled like a character in a blue movie were all at once too large for him. Jurnet had driven him to the hospital, but left it to PC Blaker actually to accompany the prisoner to Millie's bedside. He had chosen, instead, to wait in the car, appalled at the monstrosity of love, a deformation that could make a human being deflate before your eyes like a pricked balloon, give a child the fortitude to munch dog's turds and keep on smiling, and encourage himself, the logically-minded Detective-Inspector Benjamin Jurnet, in the delusion that, with Rabbi Schnellman's help, he would one day be able to accept on trust a God capable not only of engineering such humiliations, but of actually conning His victims into believing that He did it in their own best interests.

From the hospital they had driven to the children's home where Willie, sedated, tossed on his pillow, the little white face above the white sheet contorted with dreams that had Jurnet moving forward to shake the child free of them, only to be restrained by the disapproving hand of the nurse on duty. On the way back to his cell, Joe Fisher had begun to bawl like a child himself, and it had cost Jurnet all his self-control to stop himself from slapping the self-pitying bastard across the kisser. It was suddenly almost a pleasure to reflect that Millie, albeit the hard way, had learnt at last to do without him.

Sid Hale came in, sad-eyed, and Dave Batterby, inflexibly determined to get his man, the right one if possible, otherwise the best that offered. Telephones rang, young constables with clipboards popped in and out, making busy noises. Presently, Jurnet knew, the Superintendent would arrive to be put in the picture, and later still, after elevenses, the Chief himself might descend from the heights for a moment of admonition or exhortation before, like Elijah—only in a lift, not a chariot of fire—ascending once more to that station in life to which Divine Providence and the Police Authority had seen fit to call him.

What a lot of little busy bees they were, to be sure! Jurnet got up without drama, laid the newsagent's list in his Pending tray, and made a discreet sign to Ellers. The two detectives took their coats from the bentwood stand near the door, and thankfully took their way towards the Cathedral Close. As always in the freshness of the morning, the city looked innocent and purposeful. Somebody had scrawled a swastika on the boarded-up front of the Weisingers' patisserie, but it did not look dangerous.

26

The cathedral was having a busy day. At the book-stall, Miss Hanks's hair-do was already showing signs of stress. The vergers had all they could cope with. In the distance Jurnet saw Harbridge, surrounded by visitors seeking information.

At Little St Ulf's tomb they were busy too, clearing up. The drugget was rolled up, bowls and sieves and trowels were piled into cardboard cartons ready for removal. The table, its flaps down, its legs folded, rested precariously against the hoarding. The two detectives found Professor Pargeter and Mosh Epperstein discussing the infilling of the excavation with a narrow-chested young man from the Cathedral Architect's office.

The Professor greeted their arrival with exaggerated delight.

"In the nick of time!" he exclaimed. "Let us hope the strong arm of the law may prevail where the sweet voice of reason entreats in vain! This gentleman—" with a ferocious glare at the young man, who reddened and looked down at his shoes—"proposes, in the name of something he chooses, God save us, to call safe pedestrianization, to seal up this spyhole on a significant moment in the history of Western man with enough slag, scoria, and sullage to make a medium-size supermarket. How, in heaven's name, does he think we're ever going to be able to come back to it, once the tumult and the shouting have died, if we have to blast through a veritable pyramid of Cheops to get there?"

Jurnet said, "The amount of trouble this particular

spyhole's caused East Anglian man, never mind the Western variety, I can only hope the gentleman—" with a courteous inclination of the head to which the young man responded with grateful surprise—"will see his way to using reinforced concrete, unless he can think of something harder."

"Sod you," remarked the Professor, without animus. "And what the hell are you here for, anyway?"

"To see you, for one thing." Jurnet felt in his pocket and brought out the small, semi-transparent envelope the Professor had given him when he had visited his home. For a moment he stood looking down at it, flat on his palm. Then he raised his head and looked at the man directly. "I wanted to know why you told me a lie."

Professor Pargeter did not answer. He looked older. He even shrank: not as much as Joe Fisher, but suddenly there was less man.

Jurnet turned to Mosh Epperstein, who stood moistening his lips with a thin tongue.

"You, of course, have known all along."

"I don't know what you're talking about." The statement, apparently, sounded so unconvincing to the archaeology student himself that he began again. "If you're talking about Stan Brent—"

"I wasn't, actually, but I don't mind if we do."

"He's up in the triforium, helping Liz pack up."

"Oh ah. Pack up what?"

"Her cameras and stuff, of course."

"Ah. Her stuff. Now, that *does* interest me. Think we'll take a little climb up there, and have a word."

Mosh Epperstein cried out, "You know what Stan Brent's like!"

"Yes." Jurnet nodded slowly. "I think I do. A bad 'un. You can smell them a mile off. But you know—" the detective's voice took on the tone of an adult explaining to a child—"it's a funny thing, badness. I often think it's a talent, really, like being able to draw, or play the violin. Something that operates within very narrow limits. Just because you're a ruddy marvel at blowing safes, it doesn't follow you've a bent, or should I say a brent, for pushing drugs. So what's Stan Brent's specialty?"

Professor Pargeter proffered, "There are some all-rounders."

"Certainly." But Jurnet shook his head nevertheless. "Have you noticed how Stan Brent moves? At the risk of sounding a queer myself, I'll tell you. He carries his body as if he was a king carrying his crown and sceptre. Maybe he realizes it's all he's got to be proud of, I wouldn't know, but proud of it he is. And the way I read him, he wouldn't want to risk spoiling it with dope. He once told me what he thought of filling your body with dirt like it was a dustbin. I think he meant it."

Epperstein burst out with, "What's his bloody, beautiful body got to do with it? He doesn't have to be on the stuff to push it."

"He doesn't have to," Jurnet conceded. "Though, speaking personally, I've never yet met a pusher who didn't take a trip him- or *her*self."

"Liz doesn't—" The archaeology student stopped short, aghast at what he had almost said.

"Oh yes, she does," returned Jurnet, understanding perfectly, and noting in passing that even the most appalling sexual humiliation did not necessarily kill love. "Only she, if you'll excuse the vulgarity, takes hers by ejaculation."

They tried the door up to the triforium and found it locked.

Jurnet said, "No sweat. I know from Epperstein there's a couple of doors somewhere with only bolts to undo."

"Shall I look while you wait here? Those two might tip her the wink."

Jurnet shook his head.

"I don't think so. Pargeter knows there isn't a hope in hell for that girl unless we do pick her up. Half a mo." The detective had caught sight of Harbridge hurrying along the aisle, burdened with bucket and mop. Jurnet had to quicken his pace to overtake the man, and the man was not pleased to be overtaken.

"Shan't keep you. Just show me the nearest way up to the galleries."

"The galleries?" The verger's frown deepened. "Keys are in the vestry an' I haven't the time—" He broke off and resumed on a different tack. "Dean won't be happy, I can tell you that. All those police up there before, some of the trippers got the idea it was open to all an' sundry. Could have been some nasty accidents."

"This time it's only Sergeant Ellers and myself. We'll be very careful." Jurnet finished, "And if it's all that dangerous up aloft, maybe you should get the Dean to do something about those doors that only have a couple of bolts on—on this side."

The verger threw the detective a fretful glance, and muttered, "Next one along. Back o' the old stove." He had picked up his bucket and mop afresh when Mr Quest, the head verger, came hurrying, full of the importance of office.

"What's this, Mr Harbridge? I thought you were to be in the Treasury."

"Kid's sicked himself back of the Bishop's throne."

"I'll find somebody to take care of it. You get over to the Treasury." As Harbridge moved away, still carrying his implements, the head verger called out sharply, "Leave'em, man! I told you, I'll have it seen to." When the verger had at last departed, it seemed to Jurnet with bad grace, Mr Quest had time for lesser things. "Anything I can do for you, Inspector?"

"I don't think so, ta. You're busy this morning."

"It's the spring weather." And with a ponderous nod the head verger removed himself before the detective could ask a favour, if such indeed were in his mind.

The stove was easily found, and the door behind it. Jurnet drew the bolts, and the two detectives stepped from the aisle on to a stair that wound narrowly upward between the two layers of the cathedral wall. It was, as Jack Ellers pronounced cheerfully, enough to give you the willies.

To be projected out of that living entombment into the airiness of a gallery full of arches shaped liked hands joined in prayer was a resurrection to be relished. As Jurnet and Ellers took their first steps along the triforium, keeping prudently away from the low parapet overlooking the body of the cathedral, sweet music began to infuse the air about them; a lovely confidence trick that brought to Jurnet's mind—he could not think what.

Exasperated, he leaned out of an arch through which he could see down the length of the presbytery into the choir. The choristers were at practice, their voices bright with youth, their red cassocks aglow against the dark panelling. Up in the organ loft, Mr Amos's head, visible above the console, nodded in time with the music.

The detectives walked along the gallery in silence, until Jurnet stopped and exclaimed, "This must be where Joe collected his pot!"

The two hung over the edge and peered directly down on to the dig, where the impassioned discussion about the infilling appeared to be continuing.

"See what I mean? Everything he described fits exactly, if you're looking down at it from here. The table would have been set up then, he could have seen the broom—everything. Except something I never noticed till this minute. The tomb, the hole in the floor, the most important thing—Joe never even mentioned it. Because, d'you see, he never saw it. That pillar cuts it off completely."

"Does that mean we have to let him go? The stuff *was* found on his premises, even if he didn't do Arthur in."

"We'll think about Joe later. Let's get this over with."

"Look who's here!" Liz Aste exclaimed, down on her knees packing cups and plates into a wicker basket. "The sheriff and his posse!"

Stan Brent, propped against a tea chest, held out the remains of his sandwich and called invitingly, "Here, posse, posse!"

"I'm afraid you're too late," the girl said. "We've eaten up all the food."

Slender throat upstretched to display the white silk shirt open between the breasts, she looked up at Jurnet, perhaps with intent, probably because that was the only way she knew of looking at a man. The detective could see that her heart wasn't in it. Her lips had a bitter twist to them. The blue eyes were dull and wary.

"On the contrary," Jurnet contradicted her. "We're not too late at all, since we've caught you."

"Oh dear! That sounds ominous. What on earth can I have done? Or is it Stan you've got the warrant for?"

"I haven't got any warrant. Just asking a few questions."

"Such as?"

"Such as, did you kill Arthur Cossey?"

She got up then, leaving her packing and moving so close to Jurnet that he could smell her scent. Nothing out of a bottle: the clean, sharp odour of a hunted animal, awaking in the detective all the lusts of the chase.

"You're joking, of course?"

"No joking matter, murder."

Liz Aste asked scornfully, "If I *had* killed that boy, d'you suppose I'd say so, just like that? As it happens, so far as I know, I never even set eyes on him. Where you ever got the idea I can't think—"

"That's easily explained," Jurnet replied patiently. "And please, Miss Aste, in your own interest, don't tell me any more lies—not even little ones, because then, don't you see, I shan't be able to believe a single word you say. You see, I know that Arthur Cossey was your delivery boy. I know all about his paper round and the drugs delivered along with the papers to half the junkies in town."

"If you know all about it," she rounded on the detective, with a spirit he had to admire in spite of himself, "I can't see how it matters whether I tell lies or not. If you've proof, you can always prove me wrong.

If you've proof. Actually, I think you're simply trying to trick me."

"Not trick. Let's say, just trying it on for size."

"But that's disgusting! If the whole thing weren't so utterly absurd I'd get my father, Lord Sydringham, to take it up with the Chief Constable."

"You do that, by all means. Meantime, if, for any reason, you don't feel able to give us a free hand to go through this stuff you have here, I'll have Sergeant Ellers here nip back to Headquarters to pick up that warrant you were talking about. It's up to you."

Jurnet saw the girl's eyes flicker; but she stayed cool and mocking.

"It's too ridiculous! If Arthur Cossey really had been working for me, the way you say, I'd be needing him, wouldn't I? I hardly suppose they'd take a small ad at the *Argus:* 'Wanted, bright boy to deliver hash and the hard stuff to selected customers. Only applicants with first-class references need apply.' So why on earth should I want to do him in?"

"I was hoping *you'd* tell *me.* Mind you, I do have a kind of inkling. Arthur was an enterprising lad. Any little peccadillo of his friends and acquaintances, he was on to it like a shot. And you, Miss Aste, in your line of business, and with your family connections, would be more vulnerable than most."

"There you go again! I'm sure it's dreadfully unethical, trying to trip an innocent person up." Her eyes narrowed. "Of course, I can't say what Stan may have been up to."

Stan Brent settled his red head in a fresh position against the tea chest, and observed lovingly, "Bitch!"

Jurnet said, "Oh, I don't doubt but that Mr Brent's been up to plenty. After all, he's been on your payroll too, hasn't he?—taking delivery from your suppliers, and stockpiling the goods in that hut down by the river. Go down with one knapsack, come back with another identical. So long, that is, as there aren't any fuzz hanging about on the staithe. Or unless the consignment wasn't just the good old pot which never did anyone any harm, but acid and heroin as well, which—and I quote your own words, Stan—was like filling your body full of dirt like it was a dustbin." The detective shook his head in a parody of concern. "Oh, what rows you two lovebirds had because Stan wouldn't have anything to do with shifting the hard! Down at the marina, you made such a racket we could hear it all the way to the nick." Enjoying the startled dismay the girl was unable to conceal, he finished, with mock condolence, "Quite understand how it must have knocked you all of a heap. Stan Brent with qualms! What *was* the world coming to?" Jurnet turned his attention to the young man. "That nifty cabin cruiser with the old folks at home. That was how it was done, wasn't it?"

Stan Brent said, "Very respectable people. OAPs trying to pick up a bit extra. Who can blame them, the stinking pension. You'll never guess what their name is. Potter!" He frowned at Jurnet and explained painstakingly, "Pot. Potter. Joke, son."

"Ho, ho." Jurnet looked at the young man curiously. As the detective watched, a bright flush spread upward over the freckled skin from neck to forehead, and as quickly subsided. The eyes blinked, a muscle in the cheek began to twitch uncontrollably. Stan Brent sprang suddenly to his feet and stood swaying. He brandished the remains of his sandwich in the girl's face, and screamed, "You lousy scrubber!"

The Honourable Liz Aste turned to Jurnet sadly. "Funny. I thought you knew he was into acid."

Stan Brent threw back his head and ululated. The sweet sounds of children and organ encased the dreadful noise, but could not contain it. Below, in the nave, startled people looked up, ready to duck. The young man's body trembled violently, as though it were itself an instrument, twanged by a pitiless hand. His fingers splayed, groping. The scrap of sandwich dropped to the floor.

The sweat of a mighty effort glistened on Brent's face; but a fiercer power consumed him. The drug would not be denied. A tic contorted the strained features. Saliva leaked from the corners of his mouth,

down chin and neck to the welted neckline of his white
T-shirt.

Jack Ellers moved forwards and pinned the man by
the arms, only to be flung back with a force that sent
him reeling. Jurnet, hesitating over a flying tackle that
might bring Brent's head crashing down on the stone
floor, waited a second too long. In that second, Stan
Brent jumped on to the low parapet, and stood there
balancing on the narrow strip of stonework above the
thirty-foot drop to the nave floor.

Liz Aste screamed, "Stan! I didn't mean it! Stan!"
She tried to reach the swaying figure, only to be
grabbed and dragged back by Ellers. The organ had
fallen silent. The children's voices soared towards the
climax, unaccompanied.

Stan Brent spread his arms downwards and behind
him, a diver readying for the plunge. His eyes closed,
his face pale and peaceful beneath the bright red hair,
he shouted joyfully, "I fly! I fly!"

In the instant before he could launch himself like a
bird on to the cathedral air, Jurnet flung himself forward with all his strength and clasped the teetering
figure above the knees.

Not another murder in the cathedral!

The iron band across the detective's ribs burst with
an explosion of pain that projected him into a night-
mare kaleidoscope of pulsing lights and shapes that
expanded and contracted with each excruciating
breath. But he clung on, as if it was his life, and not
Stan Brent's, that depended on it. For what seemed
an eternity the two hung over the abyss which opened
invitingly below them. To fall was so much easier, so
temptingly conclusive, that there was a residual regret
in the exhilaration that surged through Jurnet's ex-
hausted body as the realization came to him that he
had won; that he and Brent, the young man whim-
pering now like a child thwarted of its desire, were
rolling on the stone floor of the gallery, safe.

The Honourable Liz Aste did not look at all pleased.

27

Batterby, who, of them all, had had most to do with drugs in the city, said: "£125,000, £150,000, even, at street prices."

The Superintendent, nevertheless, did not spare a glance for the packages strewn on the table in front of him. He did not look at the detectives either, sitting round the table as if waiting for the cards to be dealt. His gaze fixed upon some remote vista, not pleasing to the eye, he announced, "The truth is, we haven't a single bit of solid evidence to connect the girl with the death of Arthur Cossey. The most we can do is place her on our little list along with the others."

Jurnet who, with his ribs re-strapped, was feeling fragile and unequal to the fray, ventured, "She says she needed him alive. There's something in that."

"Unless he was threatening to give her away. And as to that—" and now it was at Jurnet, and at Sergeant Ellers beside him, that the Superintendent's hostility was nakedly directed—"our likeliest source of information, to wit Mr Stan Brent, refuses to say a word—except possibly, as I understand it, to complain to the European Court of Human Rights. In some way beyond my comprehension he seems to regard an intervention which undoubtedly saved his life as an unwarranted interference with his personal liberty."

"Shock," Jurnet interposed, his voice stronger with the certainty of what he was saying. "He feels violated. A psychological rape."

"Rape?" The Superintendent did not sound notably receptive to the thesis, or at least, not from the source from which it came. "Then he'll get over it. They always do, sooner or later." Jurnet, thinking of Millie Fisher, as the Superintendent, in his present mood, doubtless intended he should, said nothing. The other continued coldly, "Whilst in no way denigrating your personal courage, Ben, I can't say I'm best pleased when a suspect all but falls to his death with two police officers standing gawping within a couple of feet of him."

Jurnet said, "We're not exactly proud of it ourselves, sir. Not that Jack could have done anything. He had his hands full with the girl. Seeing she'd just fed Brent an LSD sandwich unbeknown to him, it seemed a fair guess that what she had in mind was to give him a final push before he could start talking in earnest. But I should've moved faster. In the condition he was in I should never have let him get near the edge, and that's a fact."

"Nearly went over with him, that's all!" Jack Ellers came stoutly to his comrade's aid. He looked at the Superintendent and decided to take a chance. "Maybe he should 'a done, at that. It would at least have shown willing?"

Wonder of wonders, the Superintendent's finely sculptured mouth twitched at the corners. The men round the table looked at the little Welshman with awed admiration. A communal sigh of relief hung in the air as the Superintendent addressed Jurnet in tones very different from what had gone before. "If you'd done any such thing, Ben, before we get this case tied up, I'd have had you on the carpet, if I'd had to scrape you off the nave floor to get you there!" A pause, and then: "*After* is another matter!"

The Honourable Liz, at first, had been quite specific. She knew nothing about the drugs found among her photographic equipment. She could only think that Stan Brent had secreted them there. She had been completely unaware of his activities as a drug pusher, the knowledge of which had come as a dreadful shock. Had she known, it hardly needed saying, she could never have contemplated any kind of relationship.

She had not known Arthur Cossey by name, though

she supposed she might well have seen the child in the cathedral at some time or other without knowing it, since she understood he was in the choir. She had, alas, known of Brent's addiction to drugs, and had constantly pleaded with him to kick the habit. It had been her hope that the love of a good woman—

Yes, she had actually used those exact words, her eyes, lately so dull, bright with excitement. Poor, foolish Stan Brent, to imagine he could escape his ever-loving Liz!

That had been before the arrival of Professor Pargeter.

"Pargy!" She had thrown her arms round him and kissed him full on the lips before he could pull himself away with what seemed to Jurnet, watching, a kind of angry disgust; though whether with the girl or himself the detective had been unable to determine. "Darling Pargy! You've come to get me out of this horrible place!"

"I've come to do what I can to help, anyway. I've spoken to a solicitor—"

"Then you can bloody well speak to him again!" Liz Aste's welcome went into instant reverse. "I've already been offered scores of those. If *that's* the best you can do—"

"Now you're talking like a child."

"Am I? Whose?"

"Liz—" The Professor faltered for a moment, not at all in character. Then, "Do you want me to telephone your mother?"

The girl shrugged her shoulders.

"Suit yourself."

"Liz, you've got to take this seriously—"

"Are you quite sure that's what you want me to do?"

"Liz!"

"OK. Don't say I didn't warn you." The girl had looked up mockingly into the Professor's blue eyes, so like her own. She spoke over her shoulder. "Inspector! Could you get that dishy constable with the notebook back in here again? I've one or two revisions to make."

•   •   •

She certainly had.

Yes, she had pushed drugs, and it had been great fun. She wouldn't have missed it for worlds. There was this man called Cesario whom she had met in a London club and who, would you believe it, was the spitting image of Inspector Jurnet; and when, in the course of conversation, she had wished aloud she could think of some way to make a lot of money quickly, he had said he knew just the thing.

At first, what he had meant by that, it turned out, was getting her on the game. But when she had explained that she couldn't, as a matter or principle, bring herself to charge for what she had always given freely for the sheer joy of screwing, he had introduced her to some people who had set up the whole drugs operation for her, asking in return only a very reasonable percentage of the takings.

In the early days she had traded in pot only, and Stan Brent had been a big help; but then London sent down the names of people in Angleby who were in the market for the hard stuff, and he began to get very grotty. Seemed he had conscientious objections, which was a big laugh, coming from Stan Brent. Still, he had fixed her up with Arthur, who was a kid in a million, and everything had gone like a house on fire until the silly little muggins had got himself murdered, and Stan had refused categorically to have anything more to do with the heroin and the LSD.

Well, yes, as a matter of fact she *had* put a couple of domes into Stan's sandwich. She had only meant it as a lesson, a joke really. It had really been his own fault for thinking he could walk out of an understanding just like that, without giving notice or anything. If he had fallen over the parapet and got killed he'd have had only himself to blame. It wasn't as if she could take him before the Industrial Tribunal, or whatever it was.

All this the girl had related with relish, holding the Professor's hand the while, and watching with tumescent glee the Professor's progressive shrivelling as the narrative unfolded itself. She cheerfully volunteered enough names to make her the pin-up of the year of the drug squads of London and East Anglia. Only when asked why she had wanted a lot of money quickly, did she become coy.

At last she murmured, reddening like a schoolgirl, "You know, Pargy—the roof!" And when the Professor had stared at her in haggard incomprehension she had repeated impatiently, "The roof! The roof at Sydringham!"

For Jurnet's benefit she had gone on to explain that the roof at Sydringham, for years a martyr to damp rot, dry rot, and death-watch beetle, had lately entered a terminal phase; and all the Government had come up with was a measly £2,000. Two thousand pounds for the most perfect Palladian house in England!

"It isn't as if we're National Trust. The rain was coming in in buckets. Darling Siddy was at his wits' end."

In other circumstances, the thought of one of England's stately homes saved from ruin by the profits of a drug-pushing operation might have brought a smile to Jurnet's face. As it was, there was too much ugliness, too much grief, too much death, between him and a smile; and he inquired merely, "Who's Siddy?"

It was the moment the Honourable Liz had been waiting for. She smiled tenderly at the Professor as she answered, "Lord Sydringham, of course. My father."

"I take it," said the Superintendent, as he and his underlings sat round the table, the girl's statement in front of them, "that Pargeter, and not the beetle in the roof, is the real key. Getting her own back on Daddy—the real, as against the official one."

Jurnet nodded.

"Getting back at him, and at every man, I reckon. Drugs must have seemed just the job—not only encourage the bastards to destroy themselves, but make them pay for the privilege."

"Sweet girl! But what about Arthur Cossey? Would she be capable of such a direct and brutal killing?"

"Oh, we're all of us capable," Sid Hale put in unexpectedly, a note of reproof in his voice. "We're all of us capable."

"Quite right, Sid." Jurnet noticed without animosity how readily the Superintendent accepted from others what he would never countenance from Detective-Inspector Benjamin Jurnet. "I stand corrected. Let's stick to what matters, then—namely, opportunity and motive. As to the first, we know Elizabeth Aste was in the cathedral: she actually slept there on the Saturday night. As to the second—"

Jurnet said, "She told me she actually liked Arthur. Except for the newsagent, no one else, of all the people we've spoken to, has said that, not even his mum. Liz Aste said he was the only person she'd ever known with whom she had something in common."

"And what was that?"

"That neither of them needed anyone else."

To Jurnet's relief, the subject was not pursued, Dave Batterby launching into an elaborate analysis aimed, if not at clearing up the mystery, at least at impressing upon the Superintendent that Ben Jurnet was not the only bright hope of the Angleby CID.

Neither of us needed anyone else, Liz Aste had declared, as if it were something to boast about; and Jurnet, pierced through with a sudden yearning for Miriam, had returned sharply, "Everybody needs somebody!"

"I don't," the girl had insisted, before beginning to cry in a clumsy, unpractised way.

The attendant WPC waited a little, then got up from her chair and asked, "Like a cup of tea, love?"

Jurnet had said, "Make it two."

He returned his attention to the meeting to find Batterby leaning back in his chair with an expression of becoming modesty on his face, and, on the Superintendent's a glow of approval in which it took a Jurnet to detect the underlying irony.

"That's a very valuable contribution—" The Superintendent had begun, when the telephone rang: an interruption so well-timed that Jurnet, whose admiration for his superior's powers was boundless, could easily have imagined it pre-arranged, if, after an instant's listening, the latter had not pushed the instrument along the table with an annoyance which seemed unrehearsed. "Seems you're wanted outside, Ben."

Jurnet took the telephone, listened to what the sergeant at the desk had to say, and answered briefly. He got up. Then, cutting into the conversation without excuse, "I think we're all needed, sir. They can't find young Christopher Drue."

28

The woman waiting at the reception desk was distraught but not dishevelled. The elegance was bone-deep, not to be dispelled even by the terror which so clearly possessed her. Only her voice had lost its cool self-possession.

Mrs Drue said, "I waited as long as I dared—longer than I should have, only I didn't want to shame him by phoning round asking if he was there. I had to give up calling for him: he was so afraid the other boys would call him a baby." She moved her hands in a gesture of helplessness.

Jurnet did not insult her with facile reassurances.

"You've spoken to the School, of course?"

"Once I'd decided I couldn't wait any longer, I phoned everybody I could think of, however absurd it was to think he could possibly be there." She managed what was almost a smile at her own foolishness. "I even started to put through a call to my husband— he's in Hong Kong on business—only, thank goodness, I had the sense to put the receiver back. No point in both of us going through this, unnecessarily." She ended, with tremendous effort, "If it *is* unnecessary."

The Superintendent said consolingly, "Let us hope that it is so. Above all, let us hope."

Jurnet demanded, "What did the School say?"

"I phoned the headmaster at his home, and he said he would go over there and make such inquiries as he could, at that time of the day. But I couldn't just sit there, doing nothing, so I rang Mr Amos, and he said Christopher hadn't been at morning choir practice, and when he'd asked the other boys if they knew where he was, they'd said he wasn't in school, so he'd assumed he was under the weather or something. I rang the Deanery too, and spoke to the Dean's chaplain. He said he would go over to the cathedral and take a look round. The boys play marbles in the cloister, you know, and I thought—though I knew it was out of the question, really. The vergers would have thrown them out hours ago." Again that helpless, hopeless gesture. "Then the headmaster phoned back to say he had checked the form register, and Christopher had been marked absent. Only he must have come to school because his bicycle was in the rack."

Sergeant Ellers drove Jurnet and the Superintendent to the Close. The Superintendent, in the front passenger seat, spoke without turning round.

"You realize what this could mean, Ben?"

"Yes, sir. Back to Square One."

"Back to Square Minus One! All our painful delvings into motive go by the board. If there are two dead children instead of one, we're dealing with a maniac."

"Unless—" Jurnet swallowed: it was not easy to speak so of the curly-haired imp with the taking ways—"unless young Christopher turns up minus his genitals, and with a Star of David cut into his chest."

"And that's not mad?"

"Mad, yes. But maybe political."

"Mad!" the Superintendent declared roundly, and spoke no further.

Dr Carver awaited them at the West Door. The Dean looked care-worn but not defeated. He and the Superintendent shook hands with a calm certainty which Jurnet, looking on, recognized for the first time as common to both men. Law and Divine Order against all the odds: a shared faith in the ultimate triumph of right.

"We weren't sure how you thought we best could help you. The staff have gone home, of course, and I thought it best not to recall them, for the time being. But I had Charles, my chaplain, fetch Mr Quest, our head verger. The headmaster, our Vice Organist, and Mr Hewitt, Christopher's form master, are holding themselves ready in the Song School, should you wish to speak with them."

The Superintendent responded, "That *is* helpful." And Jurnet said, "According to Mrs Drue, none of them saw Christopher today. They all assumed he was absent from school." The Dean nodded, and Jurnet went on, "At the moment, and until we turn up somebody who actually saw the lad, apart from the fact that his bicycle has been found in the school rack we have no certain knowledge that he was ever on the premises today at all. And even the bike could have been placed there with intention to mislead."

The Dean's eyes brightened behind their gold-rimmed spectacles.

"You mean, it may be nothing to do with us, after all?"

"I didn't say that. Just pointing out the possibilities."

"Of course." The Dean, whose face had become rather red, went on quickly, "One thing you'll be glad to hear is that there's nothing at all at Little St Ulf's tomb. When we heard about Christopher we hurried there first thing, as you can well understand." Dr Carver produced a handkerchief from his full-skirted coat, its whiteness startling against the dark cloth. He mopped his brow. "God be praised, at least His house has been spared a repetition of that particular infamy."

It was not exactly the way the detective would have phrased it.

"Better not count your chickens," he warned, with a bluntness that, despite the occasion, awakened a discreet twinkle in the Superintendent's eye. "A cathedral's a big place to hide a little boy in."

The Dean's chaplain and Mr Quest had already made a hasty perambulation of the great building. They had found nothing.

"The light's so poor this time of day." The young chaplain was breathing hard. Jurnet guessed, not without sympathy, that he was relieved not to have found the boy—not to have found him, that is, as dreadfully dead as Arthur Cossey. "The side chapels are gloomy enough, but up in the tower it's incredible. Only a couple of sixty-watt bulbs, would you believe it? Just the same, I'd swear there's no one there."

Mr Quest did not take this too well; perhaps because the sixty-watt bulbs were part of his responsibility; perhaps because, like all the cathedral people, he loved the great stone pile with a passion that could not bear to hear a word spoken of it, unless it were in praise.

"No call for anything else!" he asserted, ignoring the upstart youth and addressing himself to the detectives. "Architect's lot, termite men, electricians, never up there but in daylight, *and* bring their own lights along. Reckon you'd better come back in the morning, if you want to take a proper look round."

It was good advice, but they did not take it. The thought of Mrs Drue, waiting for news of her son, made it unthinkable that they should go home tamely to their beds without making an effort, however profitless. For the same reason, outside in the Close police-constables were flashing their torches in back gardens, falling over rockeries in the dark, clattering dustbin lids and frightening the lives out of ecclesiastical cats bound for a genteel evening on the tiles.

They did not find Christopher. They did not really expect to; but at least it enabled Jurnet to go back to his mother, waiting at home, and say truthfully that they had tried.

When, in company with Jack Ellers, he reported that there was nothing to report, Mrs Drue took the news with admirable calm; asked him to convey to all the police officers involved in the search her gratitude, and her apologies for putting them to so much trouble. Her self-possession was far more distressing than tears: a dry despair from which hope had already evaporated.

She proffered sherry, which the two detectives accepted in the hope it would encourage her to keep them company: if anyone needed the help of alcohol it was she. But she poured a bitter lemon for herself and sipped it desultorily as she sat with them in front of the television set, watching the Chief Constable as, grim-faced, he appeared on the News appealing for anyone with information to come forward, anyone who had seen, or thought he might have seen, the child at any time since his departure from home at 7.40 that morning.

A snapshot of Christopher in chorister's dress, with which she had provided the police, was shown on the screen; and even this did not break her. She merely remarked, carefully, as though words were a quagmire which might easily swallow her up if she put a foot wrong, "It should have been one in his school uniform, ideally. Only this was so clear, so like him—" The curly-haired child looked out from the box, acting angelic in his scarlet cassock with the white ruff at the throat, a demureness through which the latent, joyous mischief of the boy could be seen rising like bubbles to the surface of a glass of champagne.

The television announcer went on to the next item, but in the quiet, pleasant room—or so it seemed to Jurnet—the image persisted, imprinted on the air, and an echo of impish laughter was all but audible.

The thought of that lovely child as one more victim of the madness which had gripped the city was intol-

erable. What was it he, the Great Detective, had
missed? Jurnet strained every fibre and again, for a
split second, his mind seemed to encompass something
important and relevant, only to let it go. A mind, he
thought disgustedly, like one of those slot machines
you put your money into and a metal claw moves tan-
talisingly among prizes worth having, but in the event
never retrieves anything but some of those revolting
sweets at the bottom of the case.

He couldn't even win those!

Before the two of them left, Mrs Drue took them
upstairs to see Christopher's room, a charming place
that was playroom, study, and bedroom in one:
shelves where the stuffed animals of babyhood con-
sorted unself-consciously with the Scrabble and aeroplane models of maturity. The bed had a patchwork
quilt, scarlet and white like a chorister's get-up. On
the desk under the window, among a mess of crayons
and magic tricks and plastic soldiers out of breakfast
cereals, a small hoard of glass marbles, contained in
a wooden bowl, caught reflections of the electric light.

Mrs Drue looked at the marbles and said, with the
same brittle attention to every word, "As soon as I saw
he hadn't taken them I knew he couldn't be in the
cloister, not really. Except that, when he leaves home
so early, as he did today, it's always because there's a
game before school. I can't think why he should have
left so early, if he wasn't going to play." She turned
her face towards Jurnet, who did not meet her eyes.
"It *is* a mystery, isn't it?"

29

Outside Headquarters, as was to be expected following the Chief's appearance on TV, the press was waiting: reporters and photographers, and the television

men armed with their macho microphones which they thrust at their quarry like extensions of their own tight jeaned pudenda. Theoretically, Jurnet would have been the first to uphold the media's right to inquire, the public's right to know. Confronted with the nation's fact-finders, his feelings were more equivocal. He detested their assumption of divine mission, their prurient curiosity, their intrusion into private griefs.

"Bring on the hyenas!" he muttered to Sergeant Ellers, as the latter brought the car to a standstill at the kerb: emerging nevertheless to greet several of the hyenas by name, and to regret, with a convincing approximation of sincerity, that at the moment he had nothing to add to the Chief Constable's statement, but be assured, as soon as there were any developments, etc, etc, . . .

He came into the Incident Room feeling soiled by the encounter, and wondering why he had not gone straight home, if that was what you could call it, and to bed, such as it was without Miriam.

The search had been called off until daylight.

Jack Ellers said, "You look all in. I'll drop you off home."

"I think I'll have a cot put up here, thanks all the same. Something might come in. You never know."

Sensing the other's depression, the little Welshman offered, "What's the betting the little perisher's scarpered on his own, just to get Mummy in a tizzy? These cherished cherubs have to break out once in a while, to stop'em going round the bend."

"Yes, Jack. Good night, Jack."

Ellers persisted, "No need to take on before time. We don't know that the kid's dead."

"Want to bet on it?"

"One thing I do know, boyo. I'm not going to bury the little bugger till I'm dead sure he's stopped breathing."

When the Sergeant had gone, Jurnet roused himself and went along the corridor to the closet where the camp-beds were kept, and the pillows and blankets against any emergency. The polite young police-constable manning the duty desk, regretting his inability to leave his post, offered to summon up help at the double, but the detective said no; finding some obscure animal satisfaction in the labour of preparing his own holt or sett, or whatever was the correct word for a detective-inspector gone to earth in Police Headquarters. He thought vaguely of going down to the canteen for a bite, but decided against it, even though he could not remember when he had last eaten. He always had the habit, when absorbed in a case, of forgetting about food altogether; and then, the problem solved, of discovering himself hugely famished.

The problem was not solved.

He lay back on the bed, one hand behind his head, shoes and jacket off but otherwise clothed, lying carefully still so that, when morning came and it was time to give orders to the police officers who would take up the search for Christopher Drue, he would look a colourable facsimile of a leader of men, not a slob in baggy pants. There was a spare electric shaver in his desk drawer, so that was all right.

In the morning, with luck, people would be coming forward who had seen the boy. That vivid, laughing face was one you remembered; not like Arthur Cossey, whom no one noticed because he, poor little tyke, had had the kind of face the eyes slid off, unregistering. Jurnet reckoned that, leaving the house at twenty to 8, the child must have got to the cathedral by ten past the latest: too late, probably, to run into any of the people there for 8 o'clock Communion. If you took your religion seriously enough to get yourself to church at that ungodly hour, you probably took care to arrive at the Lord's table at the time stated on the invitation. Still, by that time one might expect other people to be about in the Close—the milkman, jogging canons, deaconesses walking their dogs. The cathedral cleaners, the vergers.

Assuming he had gone to the cathedral in the first place.

Ought he to give orders for the river to be dragged, the stretch by the cathedral staithe?

It would be too much to say that Jurnet, staring up vacantly at the polystyrene tiles on the Incident Room ceiling, actually thought any of those thoughts: rather that they seeped into his mind unbidden, leakage from a tap that needed washering. Beneath, like the pulse of the double-bass in a symphony orchestra, guilt thrummed its insistent message. *If I'd caught Arthur Cossey's killer, no other child would now be in danger.* After a time, his tired brain began to play tricks with the order of the words. *If I'd caught Arthur Cossey, the killer would*—and *If I'd caught the child*—

Bloody hell!

The double-bass thrummed him to sleep.

Half Angleby had seen Christopher Drue, to say nothing of half Birmingham, Penzance, Aberystwyth, Berwick-on-Tweed, and almost any other town in the British Isles you cared to mention. The crisp white blouses of the WPCs manning the telephones wilted under the pressure of concerned citizens determined to be helpful.

By contrast, the Close had never seemed more delightful: blossom and green, the stillness of stone. The golden weathercock shone on top of the spire, girded, as usual, with its ring of circling pigeons.

"Silly buggers," observed Sergeant Ellers, squinting into the morning sun. Turning his attention to the spire itself, "What's it all *for*? Must be an easier way of finding out how the wind's blowing."

Jurnet, who had slept badly on his makeshift bed, screwed up his eyes in the strong light. "Harbridge is the one to speak to about that. He told me once the spire was a holy of holies. Something to do with parallel lines meeting—I forget how it went." He finished, "Not all we need to speak to Mr Harbridge about. Let's get on with it, shall we?"

The Dean and the head verger were waiting for them just inside the West Door. They looked depressed. Not surprising, Jurnet conceded. The cathedral might be God's house, it was also theirs; and no house owner is keen to have strangers poking about the place, opening cupboards, running their fingers along the picture rails for signs of dust.

Or looking for mislaid children in dark corners.

The Dean, at least, cheered up when he saw that there were only the two of them. It seemed he had expected whole battalions of bobbies, spreading through the building like a blue blight.

"There'll be a couple of cars along any minute," Jurnet explained. "Plain-clothes officers. Their orders are to wait inconspicuously just inside the doors in case we find we need them. I take it, sir, you've told Mr Quest about the keys?"

"He has them here, as you requested." The head verger handed over the laden ring with the air of the commander of a besieged garrison surrendering to a hated conqueror. The keys, each with its own neatly printed label, were few and of modern cut. "As I believe I've already told you, apart from the Treasury, where the insurers leave us no choice, we don't do a great deal of locking up here."

Jurnet took the keys; found the ones marked *Treasury*, detached them from the ring, and handed them back.

"I think you'd better hang on to these. Bad enough you have to let us in, let alone give us the run of the family silver."

The head verger's large face reddened, but there was no disguising the relief that emanated from his portly frame.

"Mr Quest," the Dean said, with affection in his voice, "like all of us who serve this temple of the Holy Spirit, tends to lose his sense of proportion when he fears its peace threatened, in however worthy a cause." He half turned, his spectacles flashing, skirts twirling about his black trousered legs. "I mustn't keep you any longer from your work, your most necessary work, except to state my conviction—and we, after all, are the people who know the cathedral best—that the boy is not here."

When he had left them, Jurnet turned to the head verger.

"We'll start on the chapels, if that's OK with you, and work our way round."

"Whatever you say, sir. Shall I tell off one of our men to accompany you?"

"I don't think we need trouble you," Jurnet said easily. "Just one small point. Communion service yesterday—in St Lieven's chapel as usual, was it?"

"No, sir. That's to say, there isn't any usual. We use all the chapels in turn. Yesterday was St Ethelburga's—south side of the ambulatory."

"I see." Jurnet scanned the wide expanse of the nave. "Mr Harbridge off today? We'll be wanting a word with the vergers."

"He's in, as usual." Mr Quest swivelled his magisterial gaze around, as if to conjure up the absent verger by act of will. His glance fell on the central altar, which was looking rather bare. "Ah! He'll be in the cavea, doing the vases."

"The—?"

"Cavea. Latin for birdcage, so the Dean says. It's a joke for the cubbyhole next to the vestry where the Ladies' Guild do the flowers. They always do them fresh for Sundays. Harbridge'll be giving the vases a polish-up. The ladies, bless 'em, are willing enough, but they haven't the elbow grease."

Jurnet commented, with professional sympathy, "All go, isn't it, being a verger? Spit and polish, answer questions, clean up the kid's messes—"

"That was a funny thing yesterday," Mr Quest said.

"Oh ah?"

"What you just said brought it to mind. After I told Harbridge to get on over to the Treasury—remember?—I sent one of the other vergers to clean up the sick behind the Bishop's throne. And you know what? There wasn't any!"

"You don't say!" Jurnet thought about this for a moment, and then inquired, "Did you take it up with Mr Harbridge?"

"He said some woman with a little boy with her had come up to him and told him the kid had done it." The head verger smiled indulgently. "Funny lot they are, some of the people you get here."

First the detectives looked into St Lieven's chapel, where a glance through the wrought-iron railings was enough to make it plain there was no place to hide a child, or where a child might hide. A square of stone lighter than the surrounding area was the only reminder that here, only a little time before, the name of God had been taken in vain and aerosol. On the altar, St Lieven, mouth wide, proffered his bloody tongue with undiminished enthusiasm.

Jurnet, knowing what to expect, kept his eyes averted. Jack Ellers exclaimed, "Looks like we go to the same dentist!"

In the FitzAlain chapel, the plastered wall had been painted afresh. The place had the look of quarters taken out of circulation, the rush chairs removed from their neat rows and piled, rather precariously, against the wall.

Again, there was no possible place for a child, unless it were the basement of Bishop FitzAlain's tomb, where Arthur Cossey's murderer had hidden his victim's clothes, and where that child of long ago, imprisoned overnight, had emerged raving. It was unthinkable that the cathedral people had not already examined such a notorious hiding place; but, just to make it official, Jurnet bent over and levered out the metal grille.

The two detectives, squatting on their haunches, peered into the dusty cavity where the stone skeleton of the richly bedecked gent upstairs lay grinning at a joke which had not lost its point in 400 years.

This time the little Welshman's comment was a heartfelt, "Hope we don't go to the same doctor!"

The Sergeant took the grille and fitted it back in its sockets. Jurnet straightened up, steadying himself against the tomb where the good Bishop slumbered with his accustomed tranquility. Yet—perhaps it was the sharp morning light, perhaps the unusual angle of the detective's vision—there *was* something different about the reverend gentleman; a suggestion of raffishness Jurnet did not recall from his earlier visits to the chapel.

Puzzled, he peered closer at the alabaster face beneath the painted mitre, and discovered that somebody had given the Bishop a Che Guevara moustache. An apparent attempt to remove the appendage from the porous stone had not been notably successful.

Moved by a sudden inspiration, Jurnet strode across the chapel floor.

"Give me a hand with these, Jack."

The two detectives just had time to move the piles of chairs from against the chapel wall when, behind them, the voice of Harbridge demanded harshly, "What do you think you're doing?"

Jurnet turned round and looked, not at the man standing there, but at the brush and the bucket of whitewash he held in his hands. Then, without speaking, the detective turned back to that portion of wall which had been hidden behind the chairs.

An uneven patch showed where the wall had been recently washed: scrubbed, rather, to judge from the vicious striations across the plaster. It was clear that someone had gone at the job with vigour and without concern for the old surface.

But not vigorously enough to obliterate the words deeply incised there—words Jurnet had seen before, only done then with a niceness of calligraphy which made the present straggling inscription doubly offensive SOD GOD.

When the detective turned back to the verger, the brush and the bucket of whitewash were on the stone floor. The man had gone.

30

While Ellers spoke urgently to the men on the doors to make sure no verger left the building, nor—supposing the man to have divested himself of his tell-tale garb—anyone answering to Harbridge's description, Jurnet ran from the FitzAlain chapel, scarcely knowing which way to go, and choosing one direction rather than another simply because to stay still and wait upon events was not to be thought of.

He ran through the presbytery and the choir, and veered into the north aisle under the organ loft, pushing aside sightseers without apology. His heart pounded, not with effort, but fear. One Little St Ulf was more than enough; two an obscenity, and three—For the first time, in that great stone ship, Jurnet prayed: if not to God, to Something, Someone.

To notice within seconds of that appeal something which in his haste he might easily have missed, was a matter he set aside for later consideration. The door hidden in the shadows behind the old stove was an inch or two ajar.

Jurnet launched himself at the narrow stair, ramming his body unmercifully round its unyielding spirals. On the first floor the parade of arches stretched away on either side, untenanted. The detective leaned over the parapet that gave on to the nave, and having, with his customary resistance to gadgets, providing himself with no other means of communication, shouted, "Jack! Up here!" on the chance that the little Welshman would hear him. Some trick of acoustics transformed his words into a roar that filled the enormous space like a warning of Doom.

Whether Ellers got the message, Jurnet did not wait to discover.

The way, he knew in his bones, though he still could not remember how he knew, had to be upward. He found another door, and a stair that took him into the tower, and there he found no fewer than three more passages, layered one upon the other in the thickness of the wall. He climbed until he seemed no longer to be part of the cathedral, but a disembodied being looking down from some distant star on a toy world below.

At the very top of the tower, past the belfry and the silent bells, and when it seemed that, short of taking wing, there was no possible way of going further, Jurnet found yet another spiral tucked into the northeast angle of the mighty edifice; and pushing open yet another little door, he was out on the tower roof, under a spring sky, the flowery Close below him, the silver river threading the water meadows, and the distant pulse of city traffic filling the air.

Disturbed by the detective's arrival, half a dozen pigeons rose up from the roof and rejoined their comrades round the spire; and Jurnet knew for certain he was on the right track. On the sun-warmed leads, pigeon-pecked but unmistakably fresh, lay some bits of bread and green stuff that once had been part of a sandwich. The detective's heart leaped with thankfulness at the sight.

Ahead of him, filling in the view in a way that, at ground level, he could never have visualized, the spire receded out of sight above his head as if it went on for ever. A door in its base, like the door in the north aisle, stood a little ajar. Could it be that the man wanted to be found in his Holy of Holies?

Jurnet went through the door into the spire and into another world. The shaft of daylight to which, leaving the door wide open, he had given entry only rendered more explicit the dusty darkness within. The very air seemed mummified, air that the spire's builders had captured and enclosed back in the fifteenth century, and never allowed to escape. Overhead, at diminishing intervals, pencillings of grey outlined the meagre light let in by the tiers of louvred windows.

The detective found himself standing among towering, rough-hewn timbers, a dead forest whose tops were out of sight. He brought out his torch and shone it upward, revealing a complicated framework of struts and platforms which only later he was to learn constituted the framework round which the original stone shell had been erected. For a disorientating moment he saw that medieval jungle gym alive with stocky men in brown hoods and tunics and queer pointed shoes, each one of whom turned upon him a glance of amused comprehension out of eyes, one brown, one of bright blue glass, before resuming his interrupted labours. Jurnet blinked, and the vision vanished. Some metal ties which caught the beam of his torch had a reassuringly modern look. At least someone else beside himself and a possible murderer had been up here in 400 years. Best of all, and most to Jurnet's purpose, were the iron ladders which zigzagged from level to level as far up as the light reached; though the thought of a child, captive on one of those wooden shelves, unrailed and accessible only by a ladder that a murderous hand or foot could only too easily dislodge, made Jurnet's blood run cold.

He shouted up into the darkness, "Christopher! Christopher, are you there?"

The voice of the verger came back.

"Go away."

31

It was a beautiful night, if you were dressed for it; spiked with the sweet treachery of spring. The little group of men on top of the cathedral tower looked pinched in the glare of the arc-lamps that, in summer, were used for the *son et lumière* performances which brought tourists by the coachload to the Cathedral Close. Below, by the West Door, the reporters and the television crews waited, fortified for their vigil with sheepskins and hip flasks. Beyond the FitzAlain Gate the crowds, allowed to come no nearer, stood silent, eyes on the spire, until the cold drove them home to watch the next act on telly, so much cosier than real life.

Up on the roof, the men shivered with cold and the suppressed anger that was part of knowing a child at risk and nothing to be done about it. Every now and again, Sergeant Ellers, seemingly unaware of what he was saying, muttered through clenched teeth, "The bastard!" The cathedral contingent, standing a little apart, consisted of the Dean, the head verger, and the young man from the Cathedral Architect's office whom Jurnet had last seen at the Little St Ulf excavation deep in conversation with Professor Pargeter. He had, presumably, been brought along to answer any question which might relate to the structure of the spire. The young man stood drawing nervously on a cigarette. Silently, without making a production of it, the Dean appeared to be praying.

Jurnet exclaimed, for the umpteenth time, "I don't understand it!"

"So much we've already gathered!" The Superintendent's voice was chillier than the night. Immaculate in wool and cashmere, he nevertheless, to Jurnet's way of thinking, looked, for the first time in their long acquaintance, untidy if not actually unkempt. The disorder, it dawned on his subordinate, was in his mind, not his dress. Just like the rest of them, the Superintendent hadn't a clue what to do.

Now he snapped, "Having advertised it so often, Inspector, perhaps you'd share your ignorance with the rest of us?"

"What I can't understand," Jurnet said, not afraid to sound simple-minded, "is why he brought the child up here in the first place."

"Do you know of a better place to conceal a body? The surveyor says that in the usual way they only go into the spire once in five years—and Harbridge would know very well there's another three years to go before the next time."

"That's to assume the boy's dead. We haven't any proof of that."

"We haven't any proof he's alive either. Until we can figure out some way of getting up high enough for a proper look—"

Jurnet shook his head. "We know Harbridge brought some food with him. Why should he come up here at all, and risk being followed, if the boy was dead all the time?"

The Superintendent thought this over, and then capitulated, with the grace that, as ever, put all to rights between the two of them.

"I pray you're right, Ben. Only, if murder's not in the man's mind this time, like it was the last, why doesn't he let us at least get a glimpse of the boy—let him say a word or two, so we'll know?" The Superintendent finished, "Though why one should expect reasonable behaviour from a maniac heaven knows."

"He once told me that the spire was the holiest place in the cathedral. Something about parallel lines converging, and the point where they met was God." Jurnet paused, considering what he had just said. "Odd thing. It sounded OK at the time. Churchy, but not mad."

"Not mad now, either." The Superintendent brightened up. "A very powerful metaphor—and, perhaps, an insight into the medieval mind that has never occurred to our students of ecclesiastical architecture. Our murderous verger is a bit of a mystic, it seems."

"That's why I don't understand—" Jurnet pulled himself up. "Sorry! What I mean is, if the spire is Harbridge's Holy of Holies you wouldn't think he'd want to profane it with murder. Unless—" casting about for the truth like one who knows where the river is, but not the pool where the trout lurk—"he caught the kid painting a moustache on the Bishop and writing 'Sod God' on the wall, and brought him up here to punish him. Or, maybe, to make him ask God for forgiveness in the holiest place in the whole cathedral."

"More than he did for Arthur Cossey! Let's hope he doesn't see a Holy of Holies as the right place for a blood sacrifice." The Superintendent beckoned to Sergeant Ellers, hovering at a respectful distance. "Get on to Inspector Batterby. He's parked in the Deanery Yard with Mrs Drue. I've lost count of how long she's been sitting there, poor woman, while I've been deluding myself we don't have to subject her to this ordeal." With a sigh, "I was mistaken. Sergeant, let Mrs Drue know that we need her up here."

Mrs Drue came into the spire with an eager step, her eyes bright with hope and desperation. Where Jurnet, earlier, had been overwhelmed by the darkness within, she now flinched in the glare. Powerful lamps, their reflectors tilted, had been deployed round the octagonal floor. Others had been balanced on horizontal beams, and upon several of the lower platforms, loops of flex festooning the ladders that led up to them. Above a certain level, about half-way to the top of the spire, at a point where the eye was more conscious of the walls leaning towards each other than of the space between them, there were no more lamps. Everything above was Harbridge the verger's territory. On the platform where he kept guard nothing could be seen by the watchers below but the profile of his stocky frame, and just occasionally, when he moved forward to peer over the edge, a glimpse behind him of what might, or might not, be the body of the missing boy.

All colours were bleached out by the merciless light. There was only white and black—white walls punctuated by the black louvred window recesses, black shadows thrown by the angular framework, black-painted ladders angled alternately to right and left, to left and right, as if across some vast three-dimensional board game from which someone had removed the snakes. The woman confronted by the surreal scene shuddered momentarily; then braced her shoulders and, pushing aside the loud-hailer proffered by an anxious young police-constable, called out in a sweet, clear voice that seemed to soar straight towards the apex, "Christopher darling, can you hear me?"

There was no answer, and after a moment she called again, no less clear, but with a kind of agonized pity replacing the sweetness, "Mr Harbridge—this is Mrs Drue. What have you done with my son?"

There was a silence in which those below waited with indrawn breath. Then, far above, a head appeared over the edge of the platform, and the verger called back sulkily, as if resenting the imputation, "I haven't done nothing with him. What he's done, he's done of himself."

"He's all right, then!" the woman positively sang. "Oh, thank you! Thank you!" Tears ran down her cheeks, but her voice remained steady. "God bless you, Mr Harbridge! Knowing you, I was sure you could do Christopher no harm. But why are you keeping him up there? Why won't you let him come down?"

The head withdrew from sight, leaving the question unanswered. Jurnet came close, and spoke urgently. "Tell him you're very sorry for what Christopher did, and you'll make sure he never does it again."

Even in her extremity she stared at him angrily.

"And what is Christopher supposed to have done?"

"We think he wrote 'Sod God' on the wall of the FitzAlain chapel," the detective explained apologetically, as if the fault were as much his as the child's, for even mentioning it.

"Christopher!" The disbelief in her voice was like a knife.

"For Christ's sake!" Under the silently approving eye of the Superintendent, Jurnet lost his patience and his temper, not entirely without guile. The world being what it was, there was always the occasion when principle had to give way to expediency. "What the hell does it matter what you say, so long as you get the boy back in one piece?"

Mrs Drue capitulated instantly; but her voice, when she cried out again to the unseen presence high in the spire, was pierced through with shame for her betrayal of her child's trust.

She called, parrot-fashion, "Mr Harbridge—I'm very sorry for what Christopher did. I'll make sure he never does it again."

The response from above took the waiting listeners by surprise. Something between a bray and a jangle of keys assaulted their ears. It took a full minute for Jurnet to realize that the verger was laughing.

"You'll see he doesn't do it again! That's a good one! And if he does, what'll you do, eh? Send him to bed without his supper?"

Lost once she had been untrue to herself, the woman looked to Jurnet for instruction. Dr Carver moved forward and whispered to the Superintendent, who nodded assent.

"Harbridge!" called the Dean, his splendid voice, well-used to directing petitions towards heaven, rolling upward without effort. "You are a servant in this House of God, even as I am myself. For many years we have worked here together, joyfully serving the risen Lord. How, after all your time in the cathedral, can you, in Christian conscience, so disturb its holy peace?"

"Beggin' your pardon, Dean—" the words, so normal, so respectful, were all the more shocking— " 'tain't me that's doing the disturbing."

"The Lord knows the hearts of all men," the Dean reminded his unseen listener. "Only think, man—what must our gentle Saviour, He who suffered little children to come unto Him and forbade them not, think of a man who seizes by force one of His precious lambs and holds it prisoner against its will and the will of its parents?"

The answer came back robustly, "Jesus knows what I'm doing, never fear." There was a pause, and then, "I'm that sorry for his Ma, I am, really."

Mrs Drue, come to the end of her tether, screamed, "Let him go, then! Let Christopher go!"

"I'm really sorry," the verger repeated, ignoring the

interruption. "You're a very nice lady, Mrs Drue. Beautiful way you do the flowers. Beats the other ladies into a cocked hat. Why, only this morning, in the cavea, I give the big brass vase—the one you had the lilies in, an' the flowering currant—a special go-over. Mrs Drue'll be wanting that one, I said to myself—"

Mrs Drue whispered, "Please!"

Jurnet took the tall, trembling figure by the arm and put her gently aside. It was not the moment to explain that enlightenment had suddenly flooded in upon him like the morning sun shafting gloriously through the crimsons, blues and golds of the cathedral's East Window. Unbidden, unanswerable, everything fell into place, came together like the walls of the spire at its apex. Complete. Remembering what he had thought forgotten, making sense of what he knew, the detective had a momentary fantasy of himself suddenly transported outside the gigantic cone, perched on top of the golden weathercock, crowing triumphantly to the stars.

His elation was succeeded by a great sadness.

He called, "Mr Harbridge! If you don't let Christopher speak, how can he say what you want him to?"

The answer came back angrily, "Don't accuse me of putting words into his mouth! All I want is for him to say the truth."

"He can't say either truth or lies with a gag in his mouth."

"No answer."

Jurnet said placatingly, "Sooner or later you'll have to come down from there, even if the boy hasn't said a word."

"Oh, he'll say more'n that, all right! If he don't, I'll push him over the edge."

Behind the detective, Mrs Drue moaned. Someone was importuning the Superintendent, "Let me have a go, sir!"

Jurnet made a gesture for quiet. He shouted through the megaphone, "Can Christopher hear me?"

"Little nippers have big ears."

"Then, Christopher—listen to me! This is Inspector

Jurnet. You know me—we've spoken together. I and my friends are trying to help you, but we can only do that if you help us too. You know what you have to do, don't you? Tell the truth when Mr Harbridge takes your gag off, and he'll let you come down safe and sound. Otherwise he's going to kill you, do you understand? And there's nothing we can do to stop him."

"Hold on!" the verger shouted down. "I weren't born yesterday! He's as artful as a cartload of monkeys, you know that! You tip him the wink, he'll say anything to save his skin!"

"Just as you will to save your soul." There was no reply to this and Jurnet hammered the point home. "Does there really have to be one more child murdered in the cathedral before justice can be said to be done?"

There seemed to be some movement up on the platform; exactly what, those waiting below could not be sure. At his back, as the seconds ticked away, the detective could sense fear mounting, hope draining away. Possessed himself of a calm certainty, his voice rang out, "Mr Harbridge! How can you call yourself a Christian and have no faith in God?"

There was a long silence, and then Christopher Drue's childish treble wavered down the air.

"It was me killed Arthur Cossey."

32

After Jurnet had exchanged a few words with him, brief but to the point, and received into his hand that which the man now proffered willingly enough, Hale and Batterby took the verger away, less gently than Jurnet could have wished. Constables and electricians and the men called in from the Fire Brigade were immediately busy clearing up the mess. One by one the big lamps were disconnected, until only enough remained to light the octagonal floor of the spire. The upper reaches returned to their original mystery; a structure without a purpose, to be accepted on faith. Which perhaps, in the context, was purpose enough.

In the Close below, an ambulance waited to take Christopher Drue to hospital.

Sergeant Ellers, his face unusually pale, murmured in Jurnet's ear, "Looks like his mum needs it more than he does."

Mrs Drue did indeed look ill. Her eyes, which she seemed unable to take off her son, were sunk deep in her waxen face. The boy, by contrast, was amazing; unless, thought Jurnet, suddenly feeling his age, the resilience of youth was something he had underestimated. His clothes filthy, his face streaked with dirt, the tumbling curls grey with dust, the terrified child who had needed to be carried down the iron ladders to safety was, with safety achieved, transformed almost instantly; shrugging off the blanket in which a solicitous police officer had enfolded him, jumping up and down with excitement, overflowing with high spirits and a naive pride in his own cleverness.

"He's mad, isn't he? Batty, wacky, off his rocker! I knew he was the minute he made me go up into the spire. He said he'd kill me if I cried out, so of course I didn't dare, in case he meant it. And then, what do you think, he tied me up and said he wouldn't untie me till I said I'd killed Arthur. Well, I couldn't say that, could I, it would have been a lie, so every time he said it I just shook my head to mean no, because by then he'd tied a hankie over my mouth and I couldn't speak." The young eyes opened with remembered fright. "It was horrible! I could hardly breathe, and he only took it off to let me eat—"

"Hush, my darling—" The child's mother, emotionally drained, could hardly speak. "There'll be plenty of time to talk later."

Surprisingly, the Superintendent, who had been standing in quiet conversation with the Dean, heard her. He looked up, and said, "Yes. Later."

The boy looked round at them all, with his bright, mischievous smile wonderfully attractive. He burst into a peal of laughter.

"Did you think, just for a moment, when I said that, up there, that I really *had* killed Arthur, instead of just saying it? As if children killed people! Did *you* think that?" The child wheeled round to face Jurnet directly. "Wasn't I good to cotton on so quickly? I knew I *had* to say it. Anything to get away—"

"Except—" said Jurnet, finding it difficult to speak, now that the time had come at last. He opened his hand, and disclosed what Harbridge the verger had consigned to his keeping. "Except that it's true."

The child looked at the glass eye nestled in the detective's palm. The eye seemed to be looking back at him.

He said shrilly, "That's my eye! Did Harby give it to you?" He held out his hand. "I'd like it back, please."

"It was Arthur Cossey's." Jurnet made no move to hand the object over. "It belonged to his father. Mr Harbridge told me he found it, when he made you turn out your pockets in the FitzAlain chapel."

Christopher pouted. "Silly old fool. All I did was crayon a moustache on the Bish."

"You also wrote some words up on the wall."

The boy tilted his head and looked up fetchingly through thick lashes. "It *was* naughty," he admitted. Raising his head in charming defiance, "I still don't think silly old Harbridge should have carried on like I'd committed the sin against the Holy Ghost."

Mrs Drue opened her pale lips to speak, then closed them as if the effort was too much for her.

"Maybe not," said Jurnet, "except that it wasn't the first time, was it, he'd had to put up with your artwork in the wrong place. I expect he thought enough was enough. Even so, being the kind of man he is, he didn't want to accuse you unjustly. That's why he made you empty your pockets out—to see if there were any crayons or coloured pens. That's when he found Arthur's glass eye."

"*My* glass eye!" the boy insisted. "Arthur gave it to me ages ago!"

"Mr Harbridge says Arthur had a very special feeling about that eye. Said it had magic powers and one day it was going to make his fortune. It was the one thing he'd never, by any stretch of the imagination, give away."

"Well, he gave it to *me*!" The boy broke into laughter again. "Is *that* why you think I killed Arthur? Because I've got his silly old glass eye?"

"That's why Mr Harbridge thought so."

"Potty old Harbridge! Still, *he* doesn't know what a tremendous crush Arthur had on me—"

"But potty old me does?"

"I didn't mean that!" Christopher blushed, glanced fleetingly at his mother, and back to the detective. "You know what I told you," he whispered.

"About you and Arthur and the dog dirt?"

The boy nodded, head down so that the curls flopped forward, hiding his face.

"I shall want to talk to you about that presently," said Jurnet. "I shall want to talk to you about a lot of things." The detective turned away, looking for someone in the little group behind him. He spied the head verger, standing disconsolate. "Thank you, Mr Quest."

The man looked up, startled.

"Sir?"

"You and Harbridge between you, really. But it was you who told me that the ladies always did the flowers fresh for Sundays."

"So they do." Uneasy at being singled out for attention, "But I don't see—"

"Fresh for Sunday, like the choristers' ruffs." Jurnet turned towards Christopher's mother, his voice warm with pity. "You weren't much of a one for starch, were you, Mrs Drue? Too floppy one week, too stiff the next. Not like Mrs Cossey, who always got Arthur's just right. And that was why—" the eyes of everyone left in the spire were fixed on the detective; including the eyes of the boy, bright with amusement and a certain detached admiration—"Christopher here borrowed it the morning Arthur was killed. He was one of the earliest in the cloakroom—he told me so himself—so how could he be so sure Arthur wouldn't be coming along needing the ruff himself, unless he knew he was dead already?"

"I *told* you," the child said. "He was always early. I knew if he wasn't there by then, he wouldn't be coming."

The detective shook his head.

"He wasn't, you know. Early. The newsagent he worked for says he was always the last back from his round. He had to be, he had so far to go. He couldn't do that round and be early into the cathedral." He waited a little. Then, "Except the day he was killed, when he never delivered the papers at all."

Christopher Drue tilted his head to one side like a bird, and demanded, "Wasn't it clever of me, the way I turned him into Little St Ulf?"

33

"I'm glad I killed Arthur Cossey. Mummy says it's a terrible sin to kill somebody and I ought to be sorry and pray to God to forgive me, but I honestly don't think killing Arthur is a sin, and as she says I have to tell absolutely the whole truth I have to say what I think, haven't I? And I feel pretty sure God will forgive me without any more praying than I do usually, because I don't honestly think He thinks it is a sin either. I think Arthur was a kind of mistake, like King Herod or Jack the Ripper, that even God makes once in a while, and I shouldn't be surprised if He's really quite glad I have wiped Arthur off the face of the earth.

"Actually it was an accident so it isn't murder, and I hope you police will take notice of that because it is very important. But if it hadn't happened then I am pretty sure it would have happened sooner or later, because if you had known Arthur you would have known he was someone who ought to be dead because he was so horrible. Of course God could have arranged to have him run over by a bus but for some reason best known to Himself He didn't.

"Everyone at school thought he had a crush on me and at first I thought so myself because of the way he used to follow me about and buy me sweets and marbles, etc. It is very hard to explain exactly how things happened the way they did because I always thought he was a drip and when I was there with my friends we always took the mickey out of him and he would just stand there with a silly grin on his face, but when there were only the two of us he was quite different, still a drip but very bossy and powerful.

"It is something that is hard to put into words. I mean, for instance, when you have a crush on someone usually, you want to do whatever they want, because you want them to like you, but Arthur never did what I wanted, but only what he wanted. You won't believe this but even when I was taking the mickey out of him when my friends were there I was only doing it because Arthur wanted me to. Anyone at school will tell you I am not really the type who takes the mickey out of people. I do not think it is very nice. I know it is hard to believe that anyone would actually want to have the mickey taken out of him but that only goes to show how awful Arthur was and how different from anybody else.

"The funny thing is that with all the other boys I'm always the one who says what you do and what you don't do. When we're picking sides to play a game, it is always me who gets picked first. I once heard Mr Hewitt say to the headmaster, 'He is a born leader,' meaning me, and I can't tell you how horrible it is to have a drip like Arthur make you do something when you really want to do quite the opposite.

"I never wanted all those sweets Arthur gave me either. My mother will tell you I actually have a savoury tooth not a sweet one and at home I hardly ever eat sweets at all except just sometimes a liquorice all-sort if I am constipated, and only then because Mummy tells me to. Sweets are bad for the teeth and I don't want to have false ones when I grow up and have to take them out at night and put them in a glass of water. Just the same, when Arthur gave me fruit bonbons and coconut-ice and some awful gooey toffees they sell on the Market Place, I always ate them even though I felt like being sick sometimes, they were so horribly sweet. Arthur would say 'Have another' and something about the way he stood there holding out the bag—I would have to take one. I *had* to, I don't know why.

"I wasn't afraid of him. It was more like a spell. He had this glass eye which he said his dad had left to him in his will and endowed it with supernatural powers so that he could make anybody do anything he wanted them to. I thought, if only I can get hold of it I will go down to the river and chuck it in and that will be the end of it, only I never got the chance, worse luck.

"Another thing Arthur Cossey made me do was deliver papers and magazines for him. It wasn't as bad as some of the other things except that I had to get up early when I didn't want to because some of the places I had to go to were quite a long way away. Inside the papers were little packets which I had to be careful didn't fall out. Sometimes I had to go back to the same places and collect some envelopes which had money in them. I know because one of the envelopes came unstuck once and there were a lot of pound notes inside.

"I can tell from some of the questions Mummy and the policeman have asked me that they think Arthur and I must have done things together, I don't like to mention what things but you know the kind of things I mean. I suppose the reason is that I cut off Arthur's diddle, which I shall explain in a little while and which has nothing at all to do with anything like that. As a matter of fact, there are several boys in the school who do those things quite a lot, only don't ask me to say who they are because that would be telling tales. All I will say is that Arthur wasn't one of them, quite the opposite. He never touched anybody and he couldn't stand being touched himself. In PE, if we had to form a circle and hold hands, or something like that, he used to pretend his shoelace had come undone or that he had pins and needles suddenly, anything to get out of touching.

"The day I killed Arthur I got to the cathedral early because Arthur had told me to be there. I said what about your paper round, and he said bugger the paper round and he was going to put the papers in a black plastic bag so they looked like rubbish and leave them out for the dustman to take away.

"I said what will Mr Doland say and he said bugger Mr Doland and he was thinking of turning in the paper round anyway. He said he had other plans but he did not say what they were.

"He said I was to meet him in the cathedral where they were digging up Little St Ulf and when I asked why there he said it was to get some buried treasure. He said that when he had been going past those boards they have up all round it he had heard some people talking inside, and he heard that big man with the moustache who is sometimes there say that in the old days people used to bring offerings of gold and silver to Little St Ulf's tomb and there was some evidence that the offerings had actually been buried in the tomb along with Little St Ulf's body. Somebody else said, 'There's been blow-all so far,' and then the man with the moustache, the one with the very loud voice, said he reckoned a couple of days more and they'd be down to the pay-dirt. Pay-dirt in case you don't know is a word gold-miners use, meaning gold.

"Arthur said that the people who did the digging never came there on Sundays so if we went there on a Sunday and found the silver and gold and took it away they would simply think it had never been there in the first place and we would be millionaires for the rest of our lives.

"I wasn't keen because it was stealing, and stealing from a saint which was even worse, especially in a cathedral with God looking down all the time, but Arthur only laughed and took out his glass eye and said it was more powerful than God and Little St Ulf put together.

"At first I wasn't going to go, and then I decided I would, partly because I always seemed to do what Arthur told me and partly because I knew that Little St Ulf had worked a lot of miracles in the past and I thought that perhaps if he looked down from Heaven and saw what Arthur was doing at his tomb he would be so angry he would turn him into a pig, or into a slug which would be even better. I thought once a saint always a saint, and I didn't see why all the miracles had to happen in the Middle Ages. Anyway it was worth trying.

"Nobody saw me coming into the cathedral, I am sure about that. Although it seems so open it is very easy, if you are a chorister and know the place the way we do, to go about like the invisible man. There are pillars and monuments of all kinds to dodge behind and all those passages in the walls for getting from one side to the other side without ever once stepping foot on the floor of the nave or the choir or the sanctuary or anywhere. It is a marvellous place really and very good fun besides being so holy.

"That morning I could hear the Communion service going on in the St Lieven chapel. Otherwise it was very quiet. One of the vergers was messing about in the south aisle but I made sure he didn't see me. I opened the door in the boards round the tomb and went inside. It said private but I didn't take any notice, I'm sorry to say. Inside it was awfully dusty and there wasn't anything much to see except a table and a big hole in the floor. Arthur hadn't arrived and I was glad because it gave me time to say a prayer to Little St Ulf about working a miracle for me. There was some matting on the floor and I knelt down on it because I wanted Little St Ulf to know I was serious, not just bowing my head the way you do sometimes because everybody else is doing it, and I was still down on my knees when Arthur came in.

"When I saw him I was going to get up but Arthur pressed his hand on my shoulder and told me to stay where I was. He said he was going to get down into the hole to look for the gold and the silver and if I stayed down on my knees he would be able to hand it up to me once he had found it. When he took a look over the edge and saw how dusty it was down there he took off his blazer and his trousers and put them on the table. He didn't have any vest or underpants on which I don't think was very nice, do you, just his shirt and school tie.

"There wasn't any ladder but the hole wasn't all that deep, so Arthur took a three-legged stool that was there and put that in the hole and used that. I handed him down a trowel and he started scrabbling about but he couldn't find any gold or silver just a lot of dust. All the time he was down there, though I didn't say anything out loud, inside me I was praying hard to Little St Ulf to do what I asked.

"After a long time Arthur gave up the search for the gold and the silver. He was in a very bad temper for having wasted his time on a wild-goose chase. He got up on the stool to get out of the hole but it was easier getting down than getting up and even though, as I told you, he hated to be touched, he told me to reach down and pull him up, which I did. Unfortunately, the bottom of the hole was very uneven and the stool, having only three legs, was very rickety. Just as I was about to take hold of Arthur it started to sway. Arthur was holding on to me so tightly I was afraid he was going to pull me into the hole as well, so to stop myself falling I grabbed at the nearest thing which was handy which just happened to be Arthur's tie. It may have been the way he had tied the knot but personally I think it was Little St Ulf working a miracle, because what happened was that as I pulled it, the tie tightened round Arthur's neck and his face went awful. He tried to say something but only a choky sound came out. His eyes went sort of fishy and round, like peppermint humbugs only not striped.

"I honestly did not realize Arthur was getting killed. All I was thinking of was how to stop myself from falling into the hole. When he gave a kind of gurgle and his head fell to one side I was really surprised. He became very heavy and didn't seem able to hold himself up any more, so all that was holding him up was me holding on to his tie.

"I felt frightened then and let the tie go, and Arthur fell back on to the floor of the hole with an awful thump only of course, being dead, it didn't hurt him. That was something at any rate. Fortunately too he had fallen on to the shallow part of the hole. I couldn't pull him quite out of it but I pulled him most of the way.

"At first I was going to run and fetch a verger, only I felt shy about saying what we had come to Little St Ulf's tomb to do. I was afraid people might think it was my idea and not Arthur's, and then where would I be? Once I mentioned the gold and the silver the verger would probably think I was a thief and call the police, even though I was innocent. I knew Mummy would be very upset. I thought at least I had better put Arthur's trousers back on before I told anyone because otherwise, on top of everything else, they would probably think we had been doing things to each other when we hadn't at all. So I went back to the table to fetch them, and that was when I saw the knife.

"All the time inside of me I did not stop praying to Little St Ulf and I really believe it was him put the knife there just when I needed it. Arthur was lying half in, half out of the hole where Little St Ulf's tomb was supposed to be and there suddenly came into my mind, I don't know why, the way Little St Ulf had been found with his diddle cut off and a Jewish star cut into his body. So I thought, if I do that to Arthur people will think it was the Jews, not me, which will serve them right for killing Jesus and all that.

"The knife was nice and sharp and I was very careful not to get any blood on me, and I knew from detective stories about wiping the knife so there weren't any fingerprints.

"At first I was going to leave Arthur's blazer and trousers where they were and take away just the diddle and flush it down the lav or something, but then I thought it would make it more mysterious if I took the clothes and hid them with the diddle in Bishop FitzAlain's tomb. I thought even if somebody finds them there, the more mysterious the better.

"So I took the glass eye out of Arthur's blazer pocket and put it in mine, and then I took off his shoes and socks as well because he looked awfully silly with no trousers and his shoes and socks on. I bundled the clothes up, putting the diddle inside one of the shoes.

"I put the stool back where it came from. There was a broom on the table and before I went I leaned over and swept the bottom of the hole so there would be no footprints and I swept it over the matting and dragged it along behind me so all the footprints there were rubbed out too. I held the broom with one of Arthur's socks because of fingerprints, and I left it just inside the door. I really think I thought of everything.

"Nobody saw me. I went by the triforium mostly, then down by a little stair which comes out almost at the side of the FitzAlain chapel. After I hid the clothes I went back up the stair, only this time by the passage into the north transept, so that when I came down, in case anybody was about, it would look as if I had just that moment come in by the Bishop's Postern.

"The whole thing didn't take long at all and when I got into the cloakroom at the Song School I was still one of the earliest. We have a clothes brush there hanging on a nail and I gave myself a good brushing, I can tell you, because it is very dusty in Little St Ulf's tomb and I hope the people who dig there wear masks because dust like that is very unhealthy and can make you ill.

"Arthur's peg and locker were the ones next along to mine, and when I saw his ruff hanging there all lovely and stiff and white I didn't see why I shouldn't wear it because he wouldn't be needing it any more, ever.

"I am sorry now that I took it because that was what gave me away, wasn't it? Otherwise you might have blamed the Jews like I hoped you would. When Mr Harbridge found the glass eye in my pocket he thought *that* had given me away but he couldn't really have proved, could he, not to a judge I mean, that Arthur hadn't given it to me as a present like I said. If he had tried to prove it, I would have told the judge that Mr Harbridge had it in for me. I do not think he likes children. He made me miss a whole games period not long ago just for colouring a broken-down old tomb nobody ever looks at anyway. I promised to wash it off before school next day but he said, 'Oh no you don't my lad, you do it this minute,' which I think was very nasty of him, don't you? That was the reason why I didn't just give the Bishop a moustache but wrote 'Sod God' on the wall as well, the way Arthur did, just to teach him, although I'm sorry to say that not being an artist like Arthur I couldn't print it nicely the way he did.

"I am also sorry I didn't leave Arthur's glass eye in his blazer pocket after all, because if it is magic it doesn't seem to work for me, perhaps because Arthur's father did not leave it to me in his will, and if Mr Harbridge hadn't found it in my pocket he would not have kidnapped me and made me go up into the spire which was very frightening. Anyway I think now that Little St Ulf is better than a glass eye any day, because more than once I thought Mr Harbridge was going to chuck me over the edge of that platform and in the end he didn't, and I hope Little St Ulf will always protect me as long as I live.

"I am glad that you know everything now, because now you know how hateful Arthur was and how it was all an accident anyway.

"Being dead Arthur couldn't sing the solo part at the morning service and Mr Amos chose me to sing it instead. I want to say that I enjoyed singing it very much and afterwards several people came up and said

I sang like an angel, so I am pretty sure that God does not mind about Arthur because otherwise He would have made me sing flat or forget the words or something.

"I think that is all except what I told you about the dog do and Arthur eating it to show what a crush he had on me. I am being honest now about everything and I am sorry to say I told you a fib about that. Actually it wasn't Arthur who ate the dog do. It was me and Arthur made me do it. I didn't want to, I can tell you, which is another example of how horrible he was."

34

"I knew all along there was something that didn't fit. I just couldn't put my finger on it." Affronted by his own stupidity, Jurnet jumped up from his seat and strode heavily about the room. The gilt chair on which he had been sitting—itself a token of his state of mind in that he had been so unthinking as to entrust himself to it in the first place—teetered on its inadequate legs. Taleh, whose nose had been resting on the detective's knees, sat up and watched his coming and going with anxious eyes.

"What gets me is, if only the blasted penny had dropped when it ought to, none of the rest need have happened."

Rabbi Schnellman joined his hands over his paunch and inquired comfortably, "Since when did the truth ever stop those who live by lies from going on lying? Calm down. It would have happened. It will go on happening." He spoke without regret or self-pity. "You have nothing to reproach yourself for. You couldn't be expected to think the unthinkable."

"I could, you know! Ask the Super. He'll tell you

it's all part of the job." Jurnet came to a halt, and stood looking down at the fat man slouched in the absurd chair. "D'you want to know the truth? What really riles me isn't so much that I missed a tiny but vital bit of evidence until it was almost too late. I shouldn't have; but that's water under the bridge. It's *why* I missed it that gets me all churned up inside."

"You mean, it never occurred to you to suspect a child?"

"Do me a favour, will you! I'm a copper, not trailing-clouds-of-glory Willie Wordsworth. I've known kids the very thought of whom sends cold shivers up my spine. Arthur Cossey was a kid too, wasn't he? That didn't stop me from accepting that he was also a blackmailer and a drug-pusher. But after all my years on the Force, to be so taken in by a mop of curls and a winsome smile—!"

"Oh, I see!" Leo Schnellman exclaimed. "It's not the case we're discussing, then, but your offended vanity?"

For a moment Jurnet stared in anger, then burst out laughing. Taleh, relieved that the problem, whatever it was, had resolved itself, sprang to the detective's side and nuzzled him enthusiastically.

The Rabbi continued, "When all's said and done, was your estimate of this Christopher of yours so far off the mark? Admittedly, there's a certain discomforting adroitness about the measures he chose to cover up his tracks. But selfpreservation is a very powerful instinct, and Arthur Cossey's death, after all, *was* accidental."

"But was it? That's the whole point." No laughter now. "Christopher writes us out a confession which we swallow whole, partly because we're beguiled by the sheer charm of it, partly because, when you come down to it, we've no other choice. It accounts for Arthur Cossey's death satisfactorily, so fine! Close the file and go on to the next thing. But how can we be sure we haven't all been led by the nose? Can we really be certain, as Christopher repeatedly assures us, that there was no explicit sexual element in the two boys' relationship? *Was* Arthur the evil little manipulator Christopher makes him out to be, or was it in fact Christopher who made the running? In Arthur's drawer we found a drawing of Little St Ulf with the title crossed out and 'Little St Arthur' substituted for it. We now know that the writing is Christopher Drue's. So is it possible that he had it all planned long before it happened, and was only waiting for his opportunity? When that kid comes to court, you'll see, he'll dazzle everyone in sight, just like he's done the Angleby CID. They'll dish out some token punishment that won't mean a bloody thing—and who's to say we won't have loosed on the world some heartless little monster who hugs to himself the knowledge that if you're as clever and fascinating as he is you can get away with anything, even murder."

"Mm." The Rabbi pondered. "You'll have to keep a continuing eye on that young man."

"And how are we to do that?"

"Have you spoken with his mother? Has she glimpsed the possibilities?"

Into Jurnet's mind came an image of Mrs Drue's face as he had last seen it, hag-ridden by fears she would never be able to put into words.

"Oh, I'm pretty sure she's glimpsed them all right, but I certainly haven't discussed them with her. One can hardly, without a tittle of proof, go to a mum and say you think her kid may be a cold-blooded assassin."

"*May be.* That's the crux. And maybe not. Personally, I'm still inclined to think you should have a chat with Mrs Drue. She might find it an inestimable relief to discover she doesn't have to bear alone the guilt of suspecting her own child of an abominable crime."

Jurnet shook his head decisively.

"Not on. After a bit, when all this has died down, she'll think she was imagining things. After all, she loves the boy."

"Ah!" said the Rabbi. "Love!"

"And what's that supposed to mean?"

"What indeed?" echoed the Rabbi, settling his *yar-*

mulke more firmly on his head. "Incidentally, I have some good news for you. I was at the hospital this morning. They're flying Mort home today."

Filled with a great thankfulness, Jurnet did not feel called upon to explain that, in the interests of self-preservation, he had stopped inquiring after the young American. "Is he OK, then?"

"Far from it. But there's hope. He opens his eyes and he recognizes his wife."

The golden princess in the English mackintosh. There is hope, thought Jurnet.

"That's not all." The Rabbi went on, as if what he had to say further was of some slight interest. "Miriam's back. She says, don't phone her, she'll be in touch. As a matter of fact, she's been back in Angleby a couple of days."

"Miriam!" cried Jurnet. "Why didn't you tell me? Why the hell didn't *she* tell me?"

"Ah, love!" said the Rabbi, for the second time.

From the synagogue, Jurnet had told the Rabbi, his next stop was the Close: a valedictory visit, though this he did not say. It sounded foolish, since Angleby was his home and he had no plans to leave. Instead, once in the car, he drove yet further into the suburbs, to the shabby Victorian house embedded in laurels which was Willie Fisher's new address. On the way he passed without stopping at the psychiatric unit where Millie Fisher cultivated oblivion. One could not visit all one's family graves at one go.

Mrs Longley, the house mother, greeted Jurnet with that special brand of institutional cheerfulness which he always found utterly dismaying. Still, inside, the house was better than one could have guessed from without: sparkling with colour, warm and homelike.

Except to Willie Fisher, to whom home was a scrapyard, and a trailer coated with grease.

Beginning to wish he had not come, the detective followed Mrs Longley into a room where several children were busy spreading finger-paints on paper and themselves. The conversation was loud and animated.

Jurnet's heart sank when he saw Willie, apart, a small lonely figure burrowed deep into an armchair as into a makeshift womb. The detective approached and stood quietly, waiting. The child had a book in his hands, and presently Jurnet moved, so that his shadow fell across the open page.

At that Willie Fisher looked up, and immediately down again.

"Jim and Jane are in the field," he read aloud, in a voice that trembled with pride immeasurable. *"There is grass in the field. There is a cow in the field. The cow eats the grass. 'Look!' says Jane, 'The cow is eating the grass.'"* Willie looked up again, and his peaked little face blossomed like the rose. "Mr Ben! I can read! I can read!"

The Close was unchanged. More tourists than usual, that was all, milling about between the generals, seeking a better viewpoint from which to photograph the spire where the wicked verger had held that poor little boy hostage.

The warm weather seemed to have brought spring and summer simultaneously. There were flowers everywhere. As if the earthen beds could not contain them, they flamed along the tops of the old walls, or discovered rootholds in crannies where a flint had fallen away, or whence tits or house-martins had nibbled the mortar.

What was it the doctor, Haim HaLevi, had said, so long ago, dying upside down on a cross? "Water my plants."

On the top of the cathedral spire, at the point where parallel lines met as in infinity, the golden weathercock swung gently against the sky.

Jurnet hesitated: then moved briskly towards the West Door and so into the nave, the great stone ship anchored in the Angleby water meadows where time flowed past, an unending sea. He waited impatiently for a Women's Institute outing to pass through the small door in the north-west corner so that he could read once more what was carved there in the shadows.

At last they were gone and he could look his fill, unimpeded, at the words incised with such simple eloquence into the ancient stone.

Miriam my wyf,
Joy of my lyf—

Someone behind him was repeating the epitaph aloud. Jurnet wheeled round, and there she was, smiling.

ABOUT THE AUTHOR

S. T. Haymon was born in Norwich, England, and presently lives in London. Other novels that feature Detective-Inspector Ben Jurnet include: *Death and the Pregnant Virgin*, *Death of a God*, and *A Very Particular Murder*.

"Charming...Ms. Brown writes with wise, disarming wit." --
The New York Times Book Review

WISH YOU WERE HERE

A Mrs. Murphy Mystery by Rita Mae Brown and Sneaky Pie Brown

Small towns are like families: Everyone lives very close together ...and everyone keeps secrets. Crozet, Virginia is a typical small town -- until its secrets explode into murder.

Crozet's thirty-something postmistress, Mary Minor "Harry" Haristeen, has a tiger cat (Mrs. Murphy) and a Welsh corgi (Tee Tucker), a pending divorce, and a bad habit of reading postcards not addressed to her. When Crozet's citizens start turning up murdered, Harry remembers that each received a card with a tombstone on the front and the message "Wish you were here" on the back.

Intent on protecting their human friend, Mrs. Murphy and Tucker begin to scent out clues. Meanwhile, Harry is conducting her own investigation, unaware her pets are one step ahead of her. If only Mrs. Murphy could alert her somehow, Harry could uncover the culprit before another murder occurs -- and before Harry finds herself on the killer's mailing list.

On sale soon wherever Bantam Crime Line Books are sold.

AN345 -- 10/91

TO SPEAK FOR THE DEAD
by Paul Levine
author of *Night Vision*

Miami trial lawyer Jake Lassiter "ex-football player, ex-public defender, ex-a-lot-of-things," is defending Dr. Roger Salisbury, a surgeon and womanizer charged with malpractice in the death of wealthy Philip Corrigan. But the dead man's daughter insists that the doctor and his sexy stepmother conspired to kill her father -- and wants Lassiter to prove it.

Can Lassiter really defend his client for malpractice and build a case against him for murder? Turning for help to the wisdom of his old friend, retired county coroner Charlie Riggs, Lassiter hopes to get the evidence he needs from the dead man himself. But outside the courtroom, he soon finds more trouble than he ever imagined possible -- murder, missing persons, grave robbery, kinky sex, and deadly drugs -- as he searches Florida's steamy streets and tropical swamps for a cold-blooded killer.

"Move over, Scott Turow...*To Speak for the Dead* is courtroom drama at its best." -- Larry King

TO SPEAK FOR THE DEAD
by Scott Turow
Available wherever Bantam Crime Line Books are sold.